NINIAN'S I

Other titles by Freda Davies

Published by Caeriw, Pembroke
THE TANNER'S WIFE   (2004)

Published by Allison and Busby, London
LET HEAVEN FALL   (1995)

Published by Constable and Robinson, London,
and by Carroll and Graf, New York.
A FINE AND PRIVATE PLACE   (2001)
BOUND IN SHALLOWS   (2003)
FLAWED SCALES   (2005)

NINIAN'S DAUGHTER

A PEMBROKE STORY

Freda Davies

Published by
CAERIW PUBLISHING Ltd

Caeriw Publishing Ltd
Glanafan, Hundleton, Pembroke SA71 5RD, UK

A catalogue reference for this book is available from
the British Library.

ISBN 0–9546676–1-1

Typeset by Photoprint, Torquay, Devon

Printed by Antony Rowe Ltd, Chippenham, Wiltshire

For Eleanor

Chapter One

Journeys had begun before the first fingers of light stroked in the dawn and glistened a heavy dew.

It was market day and from all corners of land south of the River Cleddau there was a sense of urgency, of haste, as men, women, children, followed the tracks and rutted roads towards Pembroke. Any goods which could be sold that morning were carried, sledged, carted and there was hope filling all the travellers for a profitable exchange, pouches of copper and even silver the aim of every trader.

From farms large and small they came, from wind-whipped gwennies and even from under sheltering bushes, each one anxious to be amongst the first to reach the township below the castle high on Pembroke's ridge of rock.

Under a clear sky, more than a few bodies shivered in the cool air as they waited for the sun to rise in the east and shed warmth on them. The roadway from that direction had a steady stream of people but they were scattered to the safety of the hedgerows at the sound of a galloping horse. A huge animal and its rider swept past, raising a great cloud of dust. There were mutters amongst those on foot.

"What can be amiss?" a frightened woman asked her man as she rested.

"Sir Odo riding from Manorbier at this time of day? No man with him, so it is not war, woman!" he shouted at her and raised his hand until she picked up the rope of her sledge of firewood.

Cheese, butter, eggs were arriving in the town and fights over stalls were soon settled, the foodstuff spread for sale. Cabbages, ageing onions, cuts of meat and fish fresh from yesterday's sea joined the piles displayed in the open space at the east end of Pembroke where houses were few and many of those little more than ramshackle gwennies.

Sir Odo de Barri steadied his mount to a gentle canter, there being too many people in the narrow way between the houses below the castle. He had time to look around and see sleepy journeymen taking down the shutters of shops, small boys and girls sweeping dirt and dust into the roadway while their masters counted the goods for sale. Tavern keepers booted out last night's drunkards and only the baker's shop seemed alive and fresh with smells.

"Cynfan!" Sir Odo bellowed as he reined in his mount, and the baker appeared, a basket of small loaves at the ready. The knight picked out a handful of hot breads, tossed a coin to the baker who caught it and grinned.

"Thank you, Sir Odo. God be with you this day, sir," he called after the moving figure but received no answer. Cynfan watched the grizzled man ride on, knowing keen eyes at that height would miss nothing of early morning Pembroke. "I wonder what bug bit him in the night to put him in such foul humour?" the baker muttered to himself as he returned to his oven.

Folk already weary trudged up from the stream which kept fresh the mud to the west of Pembroke. Coracles had carried them over the water and the climb up the hill alongside the palisade around the outer bailey of the castle was making breaths hard to come by. They approached the gatehouse set high over the palisade at the same time as did

Sir Odo but their thoughts were of relief while his were only of fury.

"May God and all the saints give me strength!"

Sir Odo de Barri was a formidable figure when on foot. In the saddle of his favourite destrier, protected by a strengthened leather tunic and fully armed, he terrified the lone guard. The poor man did not understand Sir Odo's Frankish words but the knight's obvious temper sent the wretch scurrying to open the massive gates of Pembroke Castle.

"Shire reeve?" Sir Odo demanded as he reined in a horse anxious for water.

"Breaking his fast, sir." The guard leaned against a wooden upright for a moment as he struggled to catch his breath.

"Fetch him!" came the order in good Welsh. "I will keep the gate until you return."

Still in the saddle, Sir Odo turned his mount, the better to watch the town beyond the high wooden palisades go about its business. He had time to see much activity, recognising few of the people but noting from which directions they came and to which they went.

"Sir Odo! Good day to you, sir."

Stiffening himself to look down at the unpleasantness which was the shire reeve, the older man did not return the greeting. An over-stuffed green tunic shiny with silk and spattered with grease did nothing to enhance the looks of Roger fitzHugh. He was short and plump, with limp dark hair, and his smug face with its red-rimmed pimples told of youth and indulgence. Sir Odo silently cursed the lad's absent and important mother who should have allowed her precious son to be fostered and trained to a worthy manhood. In a well-run household he could have learned the skills of living and survival which would have stood him in good stead when faced with the hardships of frontier life. At least Roger's kinsman, the Bishop of London who ruled in lieu of the crown in King Henry's absence, had had the sense to exile the boy to Pembroke and the tough existence all Franks faced in this far corner of Wales.

Dismounting in a smooth movement which belied his age, Sir Odo handed the reins to the guard and ordered him to water and walk his horse. Only after the underling's ears were beyond his reach did he turn to the castle's keeper. The older man's features were grim: the broad nose and strong chin below keen dark eyes like those of an eagle did not reassure the shire reeve.

"You have news of Sir Gerald?" Roger fitzHugh asked.

"The Constable still searches for his wife and his son and he has not ceased to be an angry man," Sir Odo replied in French, "but his choler will be as nothing when he reaches Pembroke and sees for himself what you have caused here. You still feeding your face when you should have been about your business? Only one man on the gate, his clothing and arms a disgrace!" He pointed to the soldiers moving slowly inside the castle's walls. "Every man's pike should be sharp, gleaming – and what do I see? Useless lumps of metal which could have been stirring privy pits for a week! As for the sword of your one and only guard – I would hazard a guess it is rusted in its scabbard!"

"There has been a sickness among the men –"

"You are surprised?" the knight asked, sweeping his arm towards a rotting corpse dangling from the castle's gate-house. "How long has that been there now? I swear I saw it on my last visit."

Roger fitzHugh was annoyed but was at last learning to be careful. "The body remains as a warning to the towns-people. Iolo was a murderer," the shire reeve pompously reminded Sir Odo.

"And will continue to kill if you let him. Get him cut down – and make sure the men who deal with him cover their faces and wash themselves well after they have buried him deep. His murdering humours could be what is causing the present sickness." It satisfied the older man to see the shire reeve blanch with fear. "When you have personally seen that accomplished, get two sharp-eyed men who can be trusted on watch up there," he said, pointing upwards to the housing above the gates. "This castle must ever be ready for an attack from raiders. It was always Sir Gerald's command and has saved Pembroke many a time."

"Sir Gerald," the young Roger said softly, his lips curling in a sneer, "who was unable to save his own estate. It must have caused him great distress to crawl to freedom through the ordure of his burning castle in Emlyn. I was told he could hear his wife screaming in agony as she was raped, his children sobbing as they were carried away – the prisoners of his enemy."

Sir Odo forced himself to calm his breathing as he tried to decide which caused the greater offence, the words of a young hound not yet blooded by battle or the demeanour of a shire reeve entrenched in a false assumption of rank. "I am surprised," the knight admitted at last.

"Surprised, sir?" Roger's tone was barely civil as he tapped his foot, impatient to be gone.

"Yes. You have spent too much time cosseted in the swirl of schemers at the king's court in London yet you are so ignorant. It is a wonder to me you have survived so long. Be sure while you are in Pembroke you learn the ways of your enemies as speedily as your half-witted mind allows." He flung an outstretched hand towards the town, its inhabitants intent on their daily lives. "You see them clothed in what you would consider rags and think of them as poor peasants. You hear them talking to each other in words you barely understand and are too slow to learn, thinking the noises they make the grunting of boars wild in the forests."

The shire reeve's neck was held in a firm grasp and he was made to face the town below them.

"Look again, reeve," Sir Odo ordered. "Look at your enemy and come to understand him, be alert to the workings of his mind – as did the Constable while you were waking sodden in your cradle. You see a conquered people?" The older man shook his head and threw the youth from him. "No, it is a mighty force biding its time, with warriors as wily and cruel as the worst of our own. Sir Gerald knew them well and many a time saved Pembroke and its people. It was his courage and his daring which outwitted the hordes at these very gates. Do you truly believe he was afraid to die fighting for his home and his family?"

Roger fitzHugh shrugged his shoulders and raised his eyebrows. "He lives."

The easy words enraged Sir Odo who raised his fist and would have quelled the youth's arrogance. Instead, he lowered his arm and pushed his face close to that of the shire reeve. "And had the Constable been slain that night, what then? His wife has the blood of generations of Welsh kings in her veins. As a widow she could have been wedded to Owain ap Cadwgan. Through her, that hellhound could have laid claim to her father's kingdom and roused every man in Wales to follow him. Not one of our castles would have been safe, not one of our homes, our families. The fat in your body would have burned well amongst the ashes of Pembroke – after Owain's men had had sport with you."

It pleased Sir Odo to see the shire reeve's unhealthy skin pallid, his breaths short and shallow with fear.

"The Lady Nest understood, just as she knew her children – Sir Gerald's children – would be the first to die, ensuring there was no Frankish blood left to challenge Owain's claims. Oh, yes," he said softly, "the Constable was persuaded to crawl from his burning home but he has barely slept since in his attempts to free his family. Three of his children are already safe home and he will not cease until Nest and his eldest son return."

Sir Odo tried hard to rein in the disgust aroused in him

by the young Frank who had at last begun to realise the danger in which he stood.

"Know thine enemy, boy, and do not be deceived as easily as you were by those who wanted the tanner's wife dead. They played you like a fish, those who envied her and would have laid claim to her land and her children. I am concerned you are so easily fooled." Once more Sir Odo gestured towards Pembroke town. "A child waking out there today could dance round you with ease. What chance have you against a spy or a real warrior? Believe me, they can be out there now, prepared to take and hold this fortress as soon as darkness falls. Anyone with a grain of sense would be able to spot harmless-looking men walking amongst the farmers come to market or journeymen taking a look at what is on offer in Pembroke."

Roger fitzHugh's flushed cheeks lost colour as he glanced nervously at what could be seen of the township from where he stood. To him it seemed peaceful.

The older man's lips thinned with displeasure. "You think men from the north or the Irish from across the sea would be out there shouting their intent? No, reeve, they will choose a time when they think this castle's defences are weak and will wait calmly for darkness to fall."

"Sir! There is the couvre feu at night!"

Sir Odo's laugh splintered the air with its bitterness as he thought of the law which decreed Pembroke's people must be within the walls of their homes by nightfall and all fires covered. "For townsmen who wish to wake here tomorrow it is enough – but for an armed raider on silent feet? The weakness you allow here is a godsend to them." The knight straightened his armoured jerkin. "I will return in an hour. By then I want every man in the castle at his post and ready for inspection – and that includes the wounded men sent here by ship to be medicined by Mistress Mabli."

Indignantly, Roger fitzHugh stood as tall as he could. "Sir! You forget my rank!"

13

"Rank? You?" Sir Odo's patience was almost at an end. "There were others before you who had rank – and to spare. Fine knights they were and thought to help a young castellan defend Pembroke's castle against the wild ones from the hills who were nothing more than dirty, useless peasants. Then came Cadwgan, father of the Owain who robbed Sir Gerald of his kin, with his warriors. They struck and the very important young knights feared to lose too much of their precious blood. Cowards all, they would have taken ship from here before the siege worsened and they could not flee, but Sir Gerald stood between them and the gate to the river. Sword in hand, he vowed to strip every one of their holdings and their titles and give all to their squires – the lesser men prepared to fight. Rank? In a battle, shire reeve, you stand alone. Neither your rank nor your family can help you then."

Reeve Roger seemed to have shrunk inside his garish tunic. "The knights? Did they get away?" he asked, finding it hard to keep his voice steady.

"They believed Gerald spoke the truth," Sir Odo said softly, as he remembered. "Not one sailed that day. All stood their ground and fought like men. The siege was lifted – Pembroke's castle and its people were freed from attack. Now, after you have carried out my orders in every detail, I will see for myself the state of the kitchens as well as the armoury and the stables. If they are not as the Constable would commend, be sure your ears and your backside will be red hot before you reach the saddle of that unfortunate animal you call your horse and ride east – back to your uncle!"

Not another moment was wasted on the shire reeve, who had paled at the consequence of failing to fulfil the orders given him. Sir Odo had already turned and was marching towards the homes which had been built nearest to the palisades and the gatehouse. Their owners were the wealthy men of Pembroke town, with goods and animals ready to flood into the safety of the fortress should there be an attack. These houses had the look of prosperity and were larger than the dwellings which straggled either side of the roadway furthest from the castle.

He stopped in front of the most imposing. It had been simply built of wood, was of sound construction and had weathered well. Two doors faced him, the main one carved in the Welsh way but studded with iron for added strength. The smaller one at its side was also reinforced and led into the workshops of Ninian, the silversmith. Sir Odo knocked on the entrance to the man's dwelling. He did not have long to wait, the mass of timber moving easily on well-greased hinges.

"Sir Odo! Come in, come in. You have news?"

Luned, Ninian's daughter and his only child, beckoned him to enter and hurried to shut the door behind him. A tall, comely woman, she had always appeared composed, her beauty of serenity rather than mere countenance. She had aged little over the years, but he could not know that her skin was smooth only because of a fierce determination to keep always a pleasant countenance for family. In the past no one had been allowed to guess the anger and hurt she kept hidden. Today her cheeks were hollowed, her clear skin whitened and under the feather strokes of her brows her lustrous eyes were dark with fear. "Please, tell me – my son. Is he still alive?"

"My dear," he said, taking and holding firmly the hands she held towards him, "the best I can tell you is there is no news of your William – or of the Lady Nest. The hunt continues for their abductor and I have my doubts Owain will be running hither and yon with a furious woman and a helpless boy in his train. Rest assured they will be safe somewhere and when that accursed son of Cadwgan is dealt with, Nest and the boy will return."

He watched the fervid hope he had seen in her die. For a long moment she despaired, then her graceful hands smoothed the blue linen of her tunic. As she lifted her head, the soft cloth of her kerchief framed the strength of her will.

"Father Prior wishes a new chalice for the altar of the priory as well as a paten and candlesticks," she told him. "My father is gone to see him and has promised to pray for William in that holy place. It is all we can do, he and I, pray – but Sir Odo, William is so young! He is but a child. How can he survive and come home?"

Sir Odo reached again for her hands and comforted the distraught mother. It disturbed him to see the control he had always admired disintegrating after months of worry. "Never forget Gerald is even now struggling with all his might to return to you the son you bore him."

Anger flared, fed by her misery, and she tore her hands free to beat at him. "Is he seeking William? Or is he only anxious to get back the woman who holds the strings of a fat purse from King Henry?"

Odo held Luned as she sobbed against him. He had been her friend when Gerald de Windsor was the castellan of Pembroke Castle, holding it for Arnulf, the young brother of the Earl of Montgomery. Gerald had been with Arnulf, one of the great de Bellême family in France, when he had ridden south and west from Shrewsbury that fateful spring of 1093. King Rhys ap Tewder had died and his kingdom was sliced apart by the iron teeth of hungry men.

In the still, quiet room furnished with the best work of Pembroke's carvers, the knight waited as the sobs lessened. He remembered Luned as he had first seen her in the early months of her womanhood. She was not beautiful as are some whose prettiness coarsens with time but he had watched as Gerald caught sight of the silversmith's daughter, blood flaming in the younger man until it could be quenched only in her bed.

When Owain had attacked Gerald's new castle in Emlyn, he had raped Nest, Gerald's wife and the daughter of King

16

Rhys. Then he had taken her against her will to Ceredigion, together with all four of the children found in the burning castle. The eldest, William, was the first of the children sired by Gerald and born to Luned.

"Come now, cariad, you are too harsh on Nest. She is but a woman like yourself and parted from her children. I know her. She will care for your boy and see he comes home to you."

She was too angry to cry. "How can you be so certain?"

"I have it from the nursemaid who was taken by Owain that dreadful night. Her mistress pleaded and bargained for the children's lives – all Gerald's children, yours as well as Nest's."

Her small fists beat at him. "The ones Gerald sired on her are safe in Carew!"

The strong lines of Sir Odo's face softened. "Remember, Luned, there is the son Nest bore the king. Have you forgotten? When his queen demanded King Henry's favourite be exiled back to Wales, the king insisted the boy stay at court and be fostered there by a family of substance. Nest came back home with empty arms –"

"Soon filled by a legitimate fitzGerald. Was that why Owain still holds my William prisoner? Was he less than her babies because he is a bastard – as you Franks would have him named?"

"No, Luned, never! Owain is cunning. He kept one child as a hostage, to ensure Nest was tame in his bed. William was but the eldest of the four he snatched from Gerald's castle as it burned and, as Gerald's first-born, the closest to his father's heart."

Silent, she leaned against him, drawing strength from his certainty. He heard the pattering of a dog and heavier footsteps.

"Is all well, Mistress Luned? Tegan was anxious."

The man who disturbed them wore the clothes of a silversmith's journeyman in the midst of his work but his

17

height, wide-set green eyes and trimmed reddish beard were allied to a casual arrogance. The intruder's careful speech hinted at gentle breeding. Even the man's Welsh was not of the fields and workshops.

Luned was once more erect, controlled. "Thank you, Sulien. There is no need for your concern."

Ninian's assistant bent his head a little in acknowledgement and moved close to Luned before turning to face the knight. "You have news of William, Sir Odo?"

Tegan was a massive hound, nuzzling its mistress's hand as she soothed the animal, grateful for its solace as it sensed an awkwardness in the air. "I have learned all there is to know, Sulien," she told the man, an unaccustomed firmness in her voice. "You may return to your work."

The man stood his ground as would a member of the family. "Of course, mistress." He turned to Sir Odo. "You must understand, sir, with the silversmith from home, I felt I must ensure all was well." He used French to inform the knight, surprising the older man with his smooth words.

"That is something you may safely leave to me," Sir Odo said with equally grave courtesy. His solid, Frankish features gave no hint of his thoughts but Sulien was astute enough to sense the annoyance he had caused Sir Odo and, with a gracious bow to Luned and then her companion, he withdrew.

"Who is that fellow?" the Frank asked when the passageway no longer echoed.

"A man of skill, my father tells me."

"I thought Ninian was satisfied with his man – what is his name?"

"Margan. He was as my father's right hand but now is unwell and slow to recover. Sulien was in Pembroke and used to visiting our workshop – from interest, he said. He had learned skills with silver from a master in Cardiff and began to be of use. Margan does not get better and Sulien stays."

18

"You do not like him?"

Luned sighed. "He is always courteous and attentive so there is nothing to dislike," she said as she pulled gently at the dog's ears, "but Tegan is uneasy with him."

As the day became weary, farmers and their wives had begun to pack up their stalls in the market at the far end of town. Barrows were loaded with goods unsold which could be brought back another day, while foodstuffs which could not be used were begged by those too poor to pay or barter. Brothers from the priory at Monkstown carried huge panniers as though they were donkeys, crying loudly for remnants of meats and vegetables which could be turned into a nourishing broth for the sick in their infirmary. Scraps were few but the monks persisted. As they walked back towards the castle, they continued their pleading from shopkeepers still to be seen, the baker, Cynfan, the most generous with broken loaves.

After they had gone, Cynfan stood at the door of his shop. He watched barely laden and rickety barrows pushed past him. A farmer reeling from strong drink leaned on his staff while the man's wife struggled behind with an unwieldy pack of goods strapped to her back.

The steady beat of hooves on the roadway caught Cynfan's attention and he turned towards the sound, seeing a very tall rider leading two more horses.

"Good day to you, Ugo!" Cynfan called. "Is all well?"

"Thank you, it is," the man replied in a strange Welsh. He slid from the saddle and urged the horses to follow him as he approached the bakeshop. "Any news since I have been away?"

They were an odd pair, the short, stout, red-faced baker and the very tall, big-boned rider in worn leathers, his long narrow face tanned by sun and wind. Both men had the look of those who had risen early that morning and toiled hard, Cynfan still thoroughly speckled with the dark brown

19

flour which, as bread, was the main fare of the folk of Pembroke and its castle.

"Let me think, now," Cynfan said and pulled at his beard. "The shire reeve eats well and I must save all my good white flour for him – so he says. Few troopers leave the castle these days and our sleep at night is undisturbed by them enforcing their damned curfew – and Iolo's body has been buried at last!"

"God rest his soul," Ugo added quietly.

"God? Maybe – or maybe it will be Satan himself doing the honours. At least it will be easier for Mistress Manon now Iolo's bones no longer can be seen."

"She is well?" Ugo asked, unaware a sudden sharpness in his stance and expression revealed his secret.

Cynfan nodded. "Aye, Ugo. She begins to bloom again," he said softly. "Mistress Mabli is content enough to be back in Carew now all is well with Gerwyn's widow."

"So that is why . . ."

Cynfan guessed there was gossip in the air. "Why?"

"I encountered a man I know on the road beyond Lamphey. He said five wounded men in a boat had not been allowed to land at Pembroke, they had been sent on to Carew."

"The shire reeve's work?"

"It must be him who gave the order." Ugo shook his head. "That youngling will not sleep easy when the Constable returns – or even Sir Odo, should he come from Manorbier."

Cynfan's laugh was hearty, ribald, the air speckled with his humour and a sifting of flour. "The very man! Sir Odo rode past the shop this morning on his way to the castle. Who else do you think brought about Iolo's disappearance from our sight? I heard he stood at the gatehouse and shouted at the shire reeve before going off to see the silversmith's daughter."

Ugo frowned as he tried to remember the lady, his puzzlement easing as he recalled a tall, slender figure, the few times he had seen her in the town. Always her face had been obscured by a veil and only her eyes revealed her beauty and her sadness.

"I have rarely seen her in town – is she the woman who was Sir Gerald's bedfellow before he wed the princess?"

"Aye, Luned. Perhaps there was news of her son, the other William."

"With God's grace, there is," Ugo said quietly. He had been a father until his children drowned with his wife when the sea engulfed their Flemish home. "I have heard the king is still in France but has letters each day, carried to him by the fastest horse as well as ships whose rowers must stand and pull hard at the oars even if they have a good wind behind them. He will have the Princess Nest, as well as Sir Gerald's son, freed as soon as God wills."

The two men began to talk of a tavern closed as its owner lay in an apoplectic stupor but they were interrupted by the sound of a large horse at the gallop from the castle. Tired townsfolk and market people scattered from the roadway, out of reach of flying hooves. The knight in the saddle was massive and what could be seen of his face was dark red with fury.

"Sir Odo has learned of the wounded at Carew," the baker decided.

"Aye, Cynfan, and he is too angered to sit patiently in a boat and be rowed upriver. His horse must bear its master's fury as well as his weight." Ugo spent his time finding and caring for the best horseflesh to be found for miles around, keeping the Constable, his friends and their men well mounted. It irked him a good animal must strain to the limit because of the shire reeve's stupidity. "Roger fitzHugh may consider himself of great importance but I am glad not to be in his boots this day."

"Agreed, Ugo, even if they are the most costly boots ever to be seen in Pembroke."

With Sir Odo gone from sight there were only weary travellers trudging home.

Ugo stirred in his saddle and shook the reins. "Gerwyn lives on after his burial – Sir Odo's boots are made from Gerwyn's leather. They will be sound in all weathers and today may have helped the noble lord from Manorbier deal out justice on a fat backside before he rode to Carew."

"Father, you are tired? I will bring wine."

It was almost time for couvre feu and Luned was anxious, but Ninian smiled at her and waved away her offer. She was so like her mother, he thought, feeling refreshed at the sight of her.

"The children are well?"

"Aye, and busy. Meleri is shaping barley cakes for your supper and Walter helps in the smithy."

"The heat and the dust! His cough –"

"Does not trouble him, Father. I have a syrup of honey and hyssop ready should he need it. Come, sit by the fire and tell me of your meeting with the prior. Has he agreed the work to be done?"

Ninian hesitated. He was a tall, thin man, the bones of his face proud under stretched skin. Age showed in whitened hair, short about his ears, while the snow of his beard was sprinkled with burned spots from the sparks of his trade. "A strange man, the prior," he said at last. "For one who is so holy and excluded from the world, he has the tightest grip of business I have ever known – but I have the order. A chalice and paten as well as a pair of candlesticks to bear the largest candles which dress the altar and two more pairs which will help furnish the holy table of the cross."

"Father! The whole church will be as day!"

"Yes, Luned, Father Prior would have us all realise the light which warms us comes from God."

"As indeed it is," she agreed. "The prior was fair with the price of your work?"

The silversmith's smile was gentle. "Eventually. At first

he would have me provide all the silver and copper as well as the workmanship as a measure of my fidelity to Mother Church."

Luned was shocked. "He would pay you nothing?"

"That was his intention. He wanted me to understand I should consider myself fortunate to have done so well out of the Constable's ambitious furnishing of his new castle, as well as from the contributions Sir Gerald makes to the upkeep of my home."

Luned's veil slipped from its anchorage, swinging free of her neck and exposing the paleness of her skin. She stared at her father, her eyes huge with surprise. "He would have you give him everything! How could he?"

"It is but part of the haggling which any trader must endure – even from the most unlikely quarter. No matter, my child. I was little older than your William when I first entered the service of my master, Magnus, in Edinburgh and I learned well from him. I swept his floors as does young Gwri for me and I listened and watched. Many would have cheated Magnus but he was wily, biding his time, never agreeing until the trade would profit him."

"And Father Prior?"

"Was determined to get his chalice for free."

"Did he?"

Luned saw in her father's manner and in the mischief of his smile a little of what had enchanted her mother.

"Not quite. He is content to pay me nothing for the chalice and I am content he pays me more for the candle-sticks and paten than he would like. We are both easy with the situation. When the work is delivered he will find fault and try to reduce the price – but that is another day. Now, supper. I confess to being hungry."

"I am glad. Deris found some lamb at market this morning and has had it roasting in Cynfan's oven. She will call us when it is on the table." Luned rose from her stool.

"Wait."

23

Something in her father's voice frightened her. "What is it?" she asked, even as she feared the answer.

"The prior, he has long ears. Monks, pilgrims, travellers, they all bring tidings."

"William?" was the faintest of questions but Ninian shook his head.

"No, all the talk is of Owain –"

"Who should be damned to hell!" Luned's fury soared at the mention of the man.

"If it is God's will, my child, one day he will be. No, do you remember Richard, the Bishop of London, who made a pact with Owain's kinsmen Madog and Ithel for his capture or death?"

She frowned. "What of it?"

"They were to join with another who had reason to hate that son of Cadwgan and all three, with their armed men, were to meet where Owain had been sighted. Madog and Ithel were ready to ride on but this third man persuaded them to wait overnight, talking always of the importance of Owain and his blood. They waited until morning."

"And Owain had gone?" Luned asked bitterly.

"Aye, to Ireland." Ninian shook his head. "Always he has friends who help him escape what is due to him for his actions."

"These men, these great men, did they have any concern for William?"

"There was no mention of the boy – or of Princess Nest. I believe Owain is frantic to save his own skin. Will he be burdened by a woman and a child? They are no help to speed his escape."

"Sweet Jesus! Then where are they?" burst from Luned in her anguish.

"Somewhere – and alive."

"How can you be so sure?"

"As the prior said, we would have heard all too quickly of their deaths."

Luned shuddered at her father's words but she realised he spoke only the truth. Silently, she bowed her head and misery engulfed her. "Father," she said through her tears, "William is alone amongst strangers and must be so afraid."

Ninian caught her hands and held her, preventing Luned from slipping to her knees in despair. "He is with the Princess Nest, remember that."

The name of a woman she hated roused Luned to fury. "How can I forget? It is because of her all this has occurred! The witch took Gerald from me and from his children to give her safe passage back to Wales and now, because of the spell she casts over men, William is in the greatest of danger. I should never have agreed to his going north with his father and that woman." Luned stood and paced the floor of the small room. "Why could she not have stayed in Westminster! If the queen was jealous there are surely enough Franks in England for the Lady Nest! Instead she must come back here and live in grace in a castle at Carew. It is her husband, the man she stole from me, who must be Constable of Pembroke to give her importance and her money which helps him build his castle."

"Aye, my little one, a castle on the estate which will one day belong to William. Gerald has worked for this for years. Our William is the Constable's first-born, yet the boy can never have Carew, it must go to Nest's first-born and not Gerald's. Because of King Henry's dowry of silver to the Lady Nest your Willliam can have his birthright – as is the way of your mother's people."

Luned listened to the reasoning and stilled. She lay against the one man she knew she could trust and sobbed herself into a hiccuping peace. Ninian was gentle with her as though she were the same age as her little Meleri, busy in the kitchen. He held his palm against her cheek, cooling her fever.

"Trust the princess, I beg you. Remember, I have seen her with William and she is kind to him. When he comes home again he will tell you himself that the lady did all she could to ensure his safety and his health."

"Return? When?"

"Hush, cariad," Ninian soothed her. "It is not just the king and Gerald who are urgent for the sight of Nest and your boy. From here to all the borders Wales has with its neighbours, men – aye, and women – are watching for them, determined to see they come back to those who love them. Only then will there be peace," he added quietly.

Chapter Two

At that time of day the rutted track from Pembroke towards
Carew was quiet. He had left behind the foul smells and
raucous sounds of the town and breathed air which had the
sweetness of greenery tossed by breezes. Nudd stopped to
listen to a bird singing from the shelter of a bush and sat on
grass shadowed from the sun by branches, closing his eyes
as the lilt of the tiny feathered creature delighted his day.
There was no need for him to see the bird to recognise it,
although he did not bother with a name. Alone, he had
grown from a tiny child in the freedom of the woods so each
bird and its song was as familiar to him as his own fingers,
knobbled as they were with growths such as were on his
face and which horrified men and women. Strangely, children did not see them so clearly.

With a final trill the bird ceased its singing and Nudd
could imagine it sitting on a twig, head cocked to one side
as it waited for a response from its mate. There it was, faint
but clear, and the songster was gone.

Refreshed, Nudd stood and turned towards the castle
dreaming at the edge of the river. From nearby gwennies
smoke idled, seeming unwilling to leave the fires from
which it came and scenting the air as he walked towards
the palisade and the men guarding the gatehouse. He
sniffed. Someone had killed a pig, he could smell it roasting

on a spit in the open. It would be well cooked by supper time,

Inside the palisade Nudd could see the roofs of the sturdy wooden buildings, which had weathered well. Erected where once an old fort had stood, the new estate spoke to him of wealth, with no sign of waste anywhere.

It was a place of strength and peace, he thought. The lines of the fortified great hall were long and low, as were those of the stables and workshops huddling in safety behind the wooden stakes and logs which could be easily defended from earthworks within and by a surrounding outer ditch. Franks built well, Nudd decided as he neared the gate and heard fishermen shouting at each other on the river. They convinced him they were stupid and must be Frankish soldiers. Did they not know fish could hear?

The guard on the gate was as dull as his friends, shouting at Nudd and thrusting his spear in a way which threatened Nudd's manhood at the very least. The youth persisted, tossing aside dusty, straw-coloured hair as he repeated again and again, "Mistress Mabli." The soldier took no notice so Nudd reached into his pouch and pulled out a handful of narrow green leaves. "Mistress Mabli," he said once more as he offered the plants. Another man, entertained by the disturbance at the gate, persuaded the guard to open it wide enough for a hand to come through and grab the stalks. Nudd smiled and settled himself cross-legged on the ground to wait, pleased it was a good day and he could enjoy such warmth from the sun.

He was not left there for long. A stern order from a deep-voiced woman reached Nudd and he stood, beating dust from his clothes and smoothing coarse hair roughened by the wind. The gate creaked open and he was beckoned in, seeing beyond the guards an ample figure in a brown tunic, her hair and throat swathed in clean white linen.

"Mistress Mabli!" Nudd beamed as he hurried towards

her and she smiled, the twisted cheek of her kindly face making it a rictus of pleasure.

"Nudd, my friend! You are a welcome sight, but is something amiss with Manon or her children for you to be here?"

He shook his head, opening his pouch and carefully lifting out the precious plants.

Mabli smiled gently. "The first of the garlic. I knew it could only be you at the gate. Is that why you came?"

"Aye – no. It was a way to make sure you knew it was me."

She nodded, turning her bulk to lead the way to the river. "Let us walk as we talk. Manon? Is she well?"

"Aye, mistress, well enough. She still cries for Gerwyn in the night, Gwen tells us, but by the time she has broken her fast and had her arms round her children, she can smile again."

"The babe she carries?"

"Thrives and kicks lustily. Gwen is careful to see the mistress eats all you directed."

Mabli called to a passing steward and asked for bread, cheese, milk to be brought to the traveller. While they waited, Mabli lowered herself on to a bench facing the river and patted the seat beside her, insisting Nudd sit. "So, they are all well but you are worried – and please do not say you came to bring me garlic. No one knows better than you how much of it grows in the shade around Carew, its children ever anxious to bring me all I can use here."

She gazed at Nudd, seeing a boy who had grown to manhood during the terrible weeks when Gerwyn, the tanner, had been found murdered and Manon, his widow, was named his killer. At that time Nudd's body was bent, his speech barely human, his walk always a crab-like shuffle. It had been Gerwyn who had found him as a discarded waif-child struggling to rear himself in the woods near the tannery beside the river. In the comfort of Gerwyn's home and at work in the leather shop, Nudd had learned to be part of a family. It was when the boy's distress at Manon's treatment by Reeve Roger turned to desperate efforts to help free Gerwyn's widow from the threat of death that Nudd had straightened and gradually begun to walk and speak like the man he now was.

"You are very worried, Nudd, and I know you well. It is with good cause. Tell me," she added gently.

The steward was approaching. He placed the food within Nudd's reach and handed him a foaming cup of milk. Mabli thanked the man and let him go again about his business.

"Well?" she asked after Nudd had drunk deeply, wiping froth from his mouth with a gesture more careful than it would once have been.

"Margan," Nudd said and saw his listener had no idea of the name. "The main man in Ninian's workshop,"

"Ninian, the silversmith?"

Nudd nodded and tore off a crust of bread, nibbling at it as he arranged his thoughts. "Gwri, the sweeping boy at the silversmith's, likes to come with me when I go to the woods for fresh plants. He is becoming very good at recognising the ones which can heal – and the ones which can kill. He is sure Margan is being poisoned."

"Surely not!" Mistress Mabli exclaimed and gazed at Nudd. She saw the youth had spoken with great care. "Who on earth would want to harm this Margan?"

He did not answer and the woman was puzzled by Nudd's face. His lips were closed tightly and he frowned.

"Ah, you have an idea but you do not wish to name the culprit in case you condemn the wrong man. If that is so, Nudd, I am proud of you – as would have been Gerwyn."

Nudd was suddenly shy, hiding his pleasure at her words.

Mistress Mabli, who had been trained by her father, king's mediciner and twelfth in importance at court, was intrigued by the mystery. "When is Margan receiving the poison?"

30

"Gwri says it can only be with his supper. Every other meal Gwri carries to him."

"Another sometimes carries the food in the evening?"

Nudd nodded slowly, carefully. "Gwri has seen it is only after they have taken the food bowl to him that Margan becomes worse."

"Hmm," Mabli mused. "What I really need is the scrapings of the bowl to see if I can taste what is being administered."

As she was speaking, Nudd's hand went once more to his pouch and the woman saw she was being handed a stoppered vial, such as she remembered taking to the leather shop with a tincture for Manon. Mabli smiled broadly at her companion.

"You think as do I, Nudd, and I am pleased. Few men and even fewer women do so."

Nudd watched as Mabli carefully removed the stopper, pouring a few drops of its contents on to the palm of her hand. With the smallest of her fingers she conveyed some of the brown mess to the tip of her tongue.

"A good stew," she decided. "Old lamb, I think, onions, but little else and no hint of any kind of herb." She saw Nudd nodding agreement. "You knew that already. If the poison had come from a plant you could have helped this poor sufferer yourself."

As he grew Nudd had learned which herbs brought health and which caused cramping pains and distress by watching the other animals in the woods. They had considered him one of themselves and did not hurry away, unwittingly sharing with him the knowledge of their lives as well as the world of plants.

"Finish your food, Nudd, and we will go to the workplace where I keep my herbs. Perhaps there we can understand more of this problem."

He needed no more urging. Bread, cheese, milk disappeared in haste and he was still munching as Mabli led the way to a wooden structure beyond the stables. Nudd had been there before but he still marvelled at the variety of plants hanging to dry, while others grew in earthenware pots, their leaves fresh, green, ready to heal. Shelves held stoppered vials of every size and all were out of the reach of children. He sniffed, loving the mixed smells of the woods and the wine shops.

Mabli wasted no time. What Nudd had brought her was emptied into a small copper bowl, anything left in the vial washed out with clean water. She stirred the resulting liquid with a small horn spoon and then watched it closely as the heavier parts settled. When all was still she carefully poured off the water and all that floated into a second bowl but scrutinised carefully what was left. Again, water was added, she stirred, but now she stretched a square of old linen across a clean bowl and emptied her washings on to it. Nudd peered at it with her until they could see what the linen held and revealed. Caught in the fabric were dark grains. Almost like sand, few were large, most very small.

"There," Mabli said quietly, "you can see Margan's enemy."

Nudd stared at the scattered grains. "What are they?"

"Silversmithing, Nudd. Do you know anything of it?"

"Nothing, mistress."

"There is a source of silver, a rock which can sometimes be broken and crumbled by the hand. It leaves grains like that," she said softly. "I have seen it before when my father was trying to help men who dragged such rocks from below the earth. Too many died young, my father told me, and once the poison from the rock was in their bodies, there was no cure for what ailed them."

Mistress Mabli's father had been physician to King Rhys and in good standing at the court of a man sliced from his kingdom by the swords of Franks and their allies sixteen years before. His daughter busied herself collecting more

32

squares of linen, stoppered vials, two small copper bowls and a horn spoon.

"Put all this in your pouch, Nudd. You know now what you must do. To be sure, you must also study the remains of food Gwri has carried."

"And keep the linen from those meals separate?"

She nodded and would have said more but there was noise in the bailey. A man was shouting, others running and Mabli was suddenly anxious.

"Dear God be merciful and let it be news of my sweet lady," she said and was gone as fast as her stiff limbs could carry her.

Nudd followed when he had sealed all in the leather bag at his waist, and outside the shed he saw the commotion surrounded a very angry horseman, his mount exhausted and ready to collapse. He recognised Sir Odo de Barri, the Constable's friend from Manorbier Castle.

"The wounded men, you fools! Where are they?" the rider was demanding of the men at the gate until he saw Mabli approaching. At the sight of her he dismounted and handed his reins to a soldier with orders to see to the mare.

"Well, ma dame, where are the men you were wrongly sent?"

"Beyond the great hall, Sir Odo, in God's good air. I have tended their wounds which were dire but they are young men and with time and patience should recover."

"Fit to be moved?" he demanded to know.

She was not disturbed by his manner. "In a few days," she told him calmly.

"Today, Mistress Mabli," he insisted. "They should never have been delivered to you. That strutting young cock in Pembroke takes too much upon himself and must be taught a lesson. The men will return to his care as the tide turns."

The castle at Carew had been built at the highest point on that arm of the River Cleddau which the tide reached.

"Then I doubt for the faculties of the wounded, Sir Odo," Mabli said, annoying him with her serenity. She had been used to dealing with the king of all these Franks and no lesser man made her tremble.

Sir Odo pulled at his chin, the redness of his skin causing Mabli some concern. It would not be good for him to die here, in Carew, of an apoplexy, she decided but said nothing, leaving the Frank to spill out his anger.When he finished speaking she bent her head in agreement.

"The matter must be put right, there is no doubt of that," Sir Odo said more quietly. "If he knew what has happened, the Constable would be furious beyond reason with the shire reeve. In his present state my friend could issue orders and take actions which might harm his own interests with the king. For Sir Gerald's sake, the men must go back to Pembroke."

"And I with them – but in the morning, Sir Odo?"

"Now!"

"Very well, but the risk to their lives is yours, sir," Mabli said quietly. "Come, Nudd, I need your help. If these men are to travel and be kept healthy, one pair of hands is not enough." She ignored Sir Odo, leaving him to curse the inactivity of being rowed back to Pembroke and shouting for a fresh horse.

With Nudd's help the mediciner gathered the ointments, lotions and infusions she needed and packed them with a mass of clean linen for bandages. Nudd carried it all to the ship at the quay, its deck cleared for the litters which would hold the men while the rowers stood waiting at their oars.

Food came from the kitchens. There was all the red meat Mabli could find as well as the freshest of vegetables, in plenty at this time of year. After that the fitzGerald children came running, and Mabli hugged each of them, instructing them as to their duties. William, Maurice, Angharad, were three forlorn little people standing on the quay as Mabli climbed on to the ship, waving to them as well as the nursemaid holding the baby, David, in her arms.

Slowly, the wounded men were carried aboard and stowed as Mabli decided, the captain waiting for the tide to turn. As it did he gave the order for the ropes to be released and Mabli waved again to the children.

When the ship turned the first bend in the river Mabli gave a great sigh, sat on a net of onions and closed her eyes in agony. "See to the men, Nudd. I can do nothing for them at sea."

He hid a smile, the narrow river as nothing to the sea which pounded the coast not so far away. Crouching beside the stricken woman he gently held her wrists, alternately rubbing and pressing the inside of each until Mabli stirred and opened surprised eyes.

"When did you learn that?" she asked.

Nudd did not answer immediately then, "I saw people vomit, then rub there when they were still held by their sickness."

She was startled by Nudd, as had happened often in the past. "My father would have made good use of you as he trained you," Mabli said softly. "When we tie up at Pembroke you must get home to Manon and the leather shop. Make sure you sleep well because you know what you must do tomorrow. First, ask Gwri if there is anything in the silversmith's workshop which matches the grains. After that it is a matter of washing and straining until you have the proof. When you are sure, tell me who would kill a man slowly and with such great pain."

It was nearing the time for couvre feu. The roadway from the castle was quiet, a few men and women hurrying, rascally children being chased by their mothers, the odd customer at a shop or stall still open for business.

From the far end of the town came a group of men, hauling between them a woman who screamed abuse at

35

them and struggled mightily, the men suffering great discomfort. The woman they dragged was as tall as most of them, raw-boned and broad. As she fought her captors the skirts of her old green tunic flew high, revealing sturdy legs ending in a man's old boots. A linen kerchief which had been knotted around her head had come loose and hung from one shoulder, dangling there amongst hair of a fiery red.

After the heaving mass draggled three or four shouting, sobbing women, angry as they called on Satan to stop his men and release the woman they were treating so harshly. One called loudly on "Sweet Jesus and all the Saints!" to protect their sister in distress.

Nothing stopped the furious progress towards the castle and as the horde swept past the baker's shop, his remaining customer turned to gawp and shudder.

"Cynfan, what was that for?" asked Gwen. She had come to collect meat roasting in the baker's oven, needing it for supper in the kitchen behind the leather shop. Like all good men of his trade he encouraged the women to bring him their meat to cook as the oven cooled after a day's baking.

"The reeve's men," Cynfan told her, his normally jovial red face dark and grim.

"They had Sennen."

"Aye, Sennen," Cynfan said and sighed. "She has been protecting women of the town – the ones who lie with men unsatisfied by a wife. It earns such women a crust and the occasional coin but the reeve's man, Brede, would take the copper from them. Only if they pay him will he allow them to stay in the town. Sennen has been defying Brede openly and you have seen what happens."

"That Brede is the worst of the reeve's bullies."

"It is said he is trying to break the strongest of the women. If he succeeds, which of them will be daring enough to say him nay? No, Sennen will stay rotting in the castle until the man has her money in his pouch."

"The shire reeve allows it?" Gwen asked, guessing the answer.

"I doubt he even knows but Brede will convince the fool he is working hard to keep the town peaceful."

"Peaceful? A town filled with screaming women?" Gwen asked. She lifted her basket and carried with her an aroma tempting a stray dog and two hungry little boys to follow her. The dog she ignored, the boys she gave part of a loaf to tear between them, then made her way thoughtfully the short distance to the leather shop, banging her basket on to the table in the kitchen.

Manon could see something had upset the normally cheerful girl. "What is it?" she asked and was horrified by Gwen's account of what had been seen of Sennen's removal to the castle.

Together, the two women covered the large, scrubbed table with fresh bread, pitchers of goat's milk and beer, bowls of raw onion sliced with fresh garlic and other herbs which Nudd had grown for them in his little garden.

"Can we do anything to help Sennen?" Manon wanted to know. She still had about her an air of grieving but these days it was tempered by the contentment she felt as the babe she carried kicked and punched at her. Her recent hardships had fined flesh from her face and body, revealing an even greater beauty in the creamy skin and large eyes, her dark hair curling again where it was free of her kerchief.

Gwen did not answer quickly. She was smaller than Manon, her hair straight, fair, and she was more rounded of arms and face. Like her mistress she was clean and neat, plain features coming alive when playing with the children or when Kamal, the leather worker, appeared in the kitchen. "Brede is the worst of the shire reeve's men. He is the one who smiles and is pleasant but when he is determined on profit, he uses cruelty well."

Manon sliced a loaf apart to relieve her feelings. "Trying to get money from those poor women! They barely live as it is," she protested. "Sennen was a good friend when I was in need of one. There must be something I can do?"

"Not tonight, mistress, it is time for the Franks' curfew," Gwen said, not managing the French words very well. "In the morning, perhaps you could visit Mistress Mabli?"

"But she is in Carew."

Gwen shook her head. "That was something else Cynfan told me. Sir Odo rode there today determined the injured men the reeve would not house were returned instantly to Pembroke, Mistress Mabli with them to tend their needs. Sir Odo came back himself and would have whipped the reeve for his selfishness – had a whip been to hand. He used his boot," she said with smug delight, "and had the reeve dancing merrily to avoid it."

Manon chuckled as she imagined the reeve's punishment. "I heard Sir Odo was in a fury and riding horses into the ground," Manon said slowly.

Gwen hid a smile. Where horses were concerned, the handsome Fleming Ugo was the expert and visited her mistress whenever he could. "Did you also hear Nudd was with Mistress Mabli? If he does not return in time for his supper he will be staying tonight at the castle to help her with the wounds."

Manon was startled, holding her knife in the air as she turned to Gwen. "Our Nudd?"

"Aye. When he went off this morning it was to Carew. He walked there to see Mistress Mabli and came back in the ship which carried the soldiers."

Gwen's news startled Manon. "Nudd? What was so important he must walk to Carew to see Mistress Mabli?"

Above the houses, shops, taverns, smoke lessened as fires were kicked apart or watered. Couvre feu at this time of year was no real hardship for the people of Pembroke's town, the days so long it was a relief to sleep and be ready for the first light of the next day, even if the air then was chill. The roadway to the castle and all the alleys leading from it slumbered in the quiet night air, peace disturbed only when the shire reeve's men clattered their way around as they searched for those breaking the rule from the castle.

In the night that followed the start of couvre feu, men and women sighed when they were woken, remembering a time when the Constable was in his bed beyond the gatehouse. Under his stern eye soldiers walked softly and anyone found breaking the order to stay indoors spent the night caged inside the castle, with usually only a sore head next morning and a kick on the backside to send them home when the huge gates opened. Geoffrey, the last shire reeve and a good man, had gone to better himself and these days Sir Gerald spent every possible hour searching unending greenness in Ceredigion and elsewhere to find his wife and son.

Pembroke was left with Roger fitzHugh as the shire reeve and many cursed him as they turned on their wool-stuffed pallets or loosely packed bracken. No one was safe, an open door enough to permit entry for the reeve's rabble of troopers. Townsfolk they encountered were beaten, the men robbed and the women raped.

Because Reeve Roger's man, Brede, had his way at the end of that day, nothing moved in Pembroke through the darkness, not that could be detected. For the more ingenious of Pembroke's inhabitants there were ways around the town.

In the kitchen next to the silversmith's workshop, Ninian, his family and workers gathered for supper. They were near enough to have heard some of the rumpus going on across the roadway as Sennen was dragged through the castle gates but Deris clattered bowls as she apportioned the meat for each person according to their size and their attention returned to the smell of hot food. Ninian had a goodly helping and let it cool as he waited for Walter and Meleri to receive their share. The children were silent, watching Deris make sure their mother ate well. Luned's long, shapely fingers sliced bread for each of them and Gwri came to the table with Margan's bowl, holding it tightly so no one could take it from him.

After Ninian asked for the Lord's blessing on their food and good fortune, it was a quiet meal. As they ate, the family heard Sulien call 'God be with you all,' before the side door to the roadway banged shut. Deris hurried to bolt the wood in place, saw Gwri start to eat and carried the basket of barley bread to any needing more to satisfy hunger after a long day.

Not even Gwri seemed very hungry and the servant girl was not surprised. It had been this way since word had come their William was a prisoner of the hated Owain, son of Cadwgan. Deris saw her mistress pick at her food, passing scraps of meat to Gwri when Walter shook his head, and all were relieved when Ninian smiled at his grandchildren and waved them away to their beds.

"Can we pray for William, mother?" Walter asked.

Sudden tears filled Luned's eyes. "Yes, cariad. We may do so here, where he will sit with us when he returns."

No one needed urging and all were sitting straight on their stools with heads bent and eyes closed over clasped hands. Ninian began the litany, each of them making their own plea for William's safe return, little Meleri adding a whispered prayer that her brother did not go hungry to his bed that night.

When Deris had eaten her supper and Gwri had collected and dealt with Margan's bowl, they settled themselves in their sleeping places, Deris in the warmth of the scullery alongside the kitchen and Gwri wrapping himself in an old cloak in the corner of the woodstore outside the kitchen.

Luned was the last to close her eyes in sleep, staring into the darkness until her eyes dried as she longed for her son.

40

Tears ran at last and brought a release, almost a sense of peace to the unhappy woman. There was nothing she could do except pray and this she did, whispering into the air until she stilled and the house was silent.

Fitfully, Margan woke, his emaciated body shivering with imagined coldness, occasionally vomiting into an old bowl Gwri had left by his head. The young man was feverish and his mind wandered. How would his mother and sisters survive without the wages and food he earned from his toil in the silversmith's shop? Tears of weakness and fatigue ran from him and he wiped them away with a limp hand. He must get better. He must.

Further away from the castle, Manon was restless, angry. She had been appeased when Nudd was home in time for supper, even though all he would say of his visit to Carew was that he had to take Mistress Mabli some leaves. With Rhodri's distant gentle snores keeping her awake and the baby growing inside her kicking and stretching furiously, she had time to think again of Brother Paulinus. That day the fat, smug little monk had rested his basket of broken food along with his backside on one of the trestles in the shop as Gwen swept and Kamal waited to raise the shutters, locking the unsold leather goods into safety.

"I am glad to see you restored to health and good fortune, mistress," Brother Paulinus had said in his strange Welsh from the north.

She knew he was only catching his breath before going down to the quay and a coracle which would ferry him across the mouth of the stream leading into the river. From the other side of the muddy water it was a steep walk to the priory and the kitchens. The scraps he had collected would be added to the soup for the poor.

Manon did not speak to him, remembering too clearly his vicious words helping Father Prior in the attempt to take everything she held dear because, holy men or no, they coveted her land and her children, her death the way to their success. Father Prior had been thwarted but here was Brother Paulinus being pleasant. She waited to learn his purpose.

"It would be charitable of you, Mistress Manon, to make an offering to the church in gratitude for your relief. Surely, the gift of your tannery land to the Benedictine order would be a simple way to ease the burden of your wealth on such young shoulders."

Manon was speechless at the man's daring. The tannery had been Gerwyn's and she had determined, as was Gerwyn's wish, it should be passed in good time to his first-born son, Meurig. Biting out the words she stated her intent, then turned away and went into her kitchen so she could pound the solid table there until her fists hurt.

Gwen had heard the exchanges and came running, the girl almost as indignant as her mistress when she learned the reason for the inflicted pain. It took much persuasion and a soothing draught of medicine which had come from Mistress Mabli to persuade Manon to calmness. Only when supper was being eaten did she feel easier. She could see Meurig, marked with his father's dark, good looks as were her own Rhodri and her lovely little Heledd. All were enjoying their food, while in a small chair by the fire Dybion, looking so like his father, was banging away with a horn spoon his mother had given him as it made less noise than his favourite wooden one. Kamal, another of Gerwyn's foundlings, and Old Twm were in place and Nudd, returned from his visit to Carew, ate without speaking, his thoughts elsewhere.

Manon was hurried to bed, "Now the children are settled," Gwen explained, but her mistress knew it was so Gwen and Kamal could sit in the light of a flickering candle as it smoked to the roof. What they talked about she did not know, but she guessed and smiled. It was good, Manon admitted to herself, to lie in her bedspace and let the day's worries drift away. Meurig was promised the tannery and he would have it, whatever it cost her.

"Are you there, Gerwyn?" she called softly as she stared up through the darkness to the roof. Did she imagine it, that she heard the answering soft 'caw' of a raven? "As long as you are with me – and with your children – we are well."

The new baby stretched slowly, curled up and gave her space to breathe, then sleep.

With the stench of stale beer rising in his nostrils, the man huddled in the cleanest corner of the roof space built a man's height above the tavern floor. Stinking women had been growled away and he lay with his back to the wall, his knife ready in his hand, his pouch beneath his body. He did not bother with prayer to ease his mind, instead he counted those who had offended him, wondering what misery he could cause them. First to suffer must be the dog, Tegan. That day the huge hound would have had a hefty kick where most damage could be done but the brute was wary, dodging out of the way of retribution as Sulien's boot met the cur's water bowl instead, a tall, sturdy hollow of clay, and water spread across the kitchen.

In the darkness the throbbing of a sore toe kept Sulien awake long into the night, but by morning his plans were made.

Chapter Three

In Pembroke town Cynfan was the first man at work next morning. Roger fitzHugh liked his morning rolls still warm when he woke and an order from the shire reeve gave the baker leave to start the fire for his oven before the first light appeared in the east.

They were very special rolls, tiny loaves of the finest wheat flour sifted by a miller through increasingly fine linen until the white powder falling on to clean sacking could be blown to the winds by a single sneeze. The miller charged well for his labour and Cynfan added to the price of Reeve Roger breaking his fast, explaining with an innocent air all the special care needed in handling such a wilful ingredient.

A servant girl from the castle was already in the bakeshop with her basket and clean linen when Gwen came from the leather shop and Deris from the silversmith's. While Roger fitzHugh's bread cooked, the girl who must carry it was full of news and she wasted no time passing on what she had seen and heard. A thin, tired woman from one of the taverns came in as did a child from the butcher's family, creeping into the morning warmth. Cynfan, too, liked to keep abreast of events and he listened as he waited for the different kinds of dough to rise, set, brown and become crisp.

They all heard of Sir Odo arriving in the castle in a bad mood but determined his horse should be well tended after the fast ride back to Pembroke. It was getting late and he was irritated by a rumpus inside the gates as Sennen was dragged into captivity, demanding to learn the cause of the disturbance. Reeve Roger had tried to explain but Sir Odo still had no patience with the man and immediately insisted on hearing the other side of the story.

The girl from the castle licked her lips with glee when she told how Sennen had thrown off the men who were holding her, trying to keep their great hands across her mouth. Triumphantly, and in language suitable for the understanding of soldiers, she had told Sir Odo of Brede's scheme to fill his own pouch.

A practical man, Sir Odo understood her Welsh words, although a few escaped him. They were of the old Welsh and spat in Brede's direction, allowing the knight to guess their meaning. The seasoned campaigner did not take long to make up his mind. A garrison town needed women like Sennen if the good matrons and their daughters were to be left unharmed. It was time to overturn Brede's so-called attempt at controlling whores, to recognise it for what it was.

The Constable's friend shouted at Roger fitzHugh, blaming him for his men's activities, their zeal ready to set the town afire against the castle. Like so many other workers inside the palisades, the servant girl had huddled in a corner, delighted to hear a man she hated being called to question for his behaviour and his lack of control of the bullies he used to enforce his will. She saw it as her duty to be first through the gates next morning, making sure everyone she met heard of the shire reeve's discomfiture and that a source of money for Brede's evil had been eliminated.

By the time Pembroke town was awake and stirring, hardly a household did not know Sennen had not been thrown into confinement but had been freed to go home to her own bed and Sir Odo had slept in the reeve's bedspace, forcing the unpleasant young man to lie in the great hall with the rest of the castle underlings.

When the gates were at last shut firmly behind Sir Odo that day, Roger fitzHugh allowed his anger at the man to be seen.

"Now I will have my way!" he declared, then caught sight of an ungainly figure trudging across the bailey. "That idiot! Why is he here?" he asked a grubby soldier of Nudd.

The guard muttered something in Welsh but all the reeve could understand was 'Mistress Mabli'.

Reeve Roger's choler grew in an instant when he heard the name. "The mediciner? Bring her here – and that witless wretch!"

Nudd was held by two of the guards while Roger fitzHugh paced a dry patch of grass in the bailey, glaring at sheep with their lambs in a nearby pen.

"You! Mediciner!" he shouted at the stout-bodied woman approaching him, a twist of her cheek emphasising her own annoyance.

"Are you ill?" she demanded to know.

"Moi? Non, mais tu es dérangée – deranged." The reeve was annoyed he must speak in Welsh to be understood. "You know I will not have that excuse for a man about me. Why have you disobeyed my order?"

"Your order, reeve? Of greater importance is the word of Sir Odo because he speaks for the Constable. My orders from him are to tend the wounded you forced into extra travel and discomfort. One of those men is sickening and like to die, perhaps because of you. I will fight death in him as I would in anyone but I need God's help as well as the skill of this poor boy you scorn so."

"If you are the force you claim to be, surely your own skill is enough?"

The tilt of his chin and the sneer she must endure made

Mabli's palms itch to smack him like a badly behaved child but she clenched her fists in her skirts and stared at him.

"The sick man has an impostume above a joint. I can prepare plasters but they will take time to work in him. First, I must have fresh mugwort to bruise with egg yolks. This will take the worst of the heat and only then can I use rue, water pimpernel, snails, all to boil with pig fat. I rely on Nudd to bring me what I need."

Reeve Roger was puzzled. "This – impostume?" he asked, struggling with the word.

A light danced in Mabli's eyes for a moment, then she became serious. "A spreading inflammation of the skin, reeve, a livid colouring and a burning pain at the bone. Untreated, the tendons would slough away with the disease and the only help then would be to cut off the limb." With satisfaction she watched his skin turn a yellowish green.

"You can cure the man?" Roger asked at last after he had choked back nausea.

"With God's help – and Nudd's. Who knows, reeve? One day we may be able to save even you."

Breathing heavily, he turned from her, gesturing his men to release Nudd before walking away with unsteady steps. Mabli watched him go, a smile flickering in twitching lips.

"Come, Nudd. You have the mugwort?"

He nodded and patted the satchel he carried. "Water pimpernel, too. Snails you have here. I have seen them."

"Aye, lad." She nodded towards Roger fitzHugh's back. "And toads."

Beyond the palisades Pembroke town went about its business. It was not a full market day but Pembroke women liked their food fresh and there were always farmers ready to supply them. They and their wives had trudged through heavy rain before dawn to carry, cart or drag on sledges their foodstuffs to the market space. As the tide turned on the beaches a strong breeze had come, increased, then

47

steadied, blowing away clouds and darkness until Pembroke glistened in early summer sun. There was a freshness in the air and the ordure along the roadway had been washed, releasing its smells anew. Few noticed, most intent on setting up their stalls or heaps of cabbages and onions.

As the sun rose higher servant girls carried baskets filled with the best of the food back to their mistresses, careful wives picked over what was left and bargained for a cheaper price. Small boys darted amongst the legs and stole what they could, the slower caught and beaten about the head and backside as a warning.

A whisper flew faster than a wind through the crowds. A ship had docked. There was a surge of movement towards the castle and then the slope leading down alongside the palisades to the river and the stout wood of the quay. It was a large vessel, long and low in the water with the weight it carried, its sails dark with wear and ribboned here and there with age and gales.

Excitement grew on shore, it being decided this was a craft from a great distance. The heat of Arabia? The cold of the north? Only when the unloading began could the sailors be seen clearly, their thin clothes and dark skins marking them from the seas of the Romans and the Hellenes. It was the whips and the harsh shouts which told the people of Pembroke the outlanders' crew included slaves.

Slaves or freemen, they struggled up the rise to the castle with great jars potted skilfully and dried in a hot sun. 'Oil,' the knowledgeable said. Huge baskets held strange fruit. Olives, some would have them, while others insisted dates, grapes. There were bright balls of gold Pembroke people had learned to call oranges although only one or two in the crowd could boast of having tasted them. Then came the less perishable goods, cured skins of animals never seen before. Alive, they would have been small, pale-coloured and with slender limbs. With great care was carried armour, lighter than had been seen on the Franks riding through the town; even the swords looked almost dainty but sharp and deadly as the steel shone in the sun.

With everyone intent on the cargo, no one noticed one of the slaves put down his slipping load at the castle gate and dash into the crowd which instinctively parted to let him through. A bellow of rage and the slave master was giving chase, his voice screaming outlandish noise and his whip threatening any in his way. He was hampered by the men and women he encountered and he turned, beckoning castle guards to help his progress. They came shambling from their posts but could not penetrate the constantly moving mass of bodies facing them. Legs and arms got in their way, shoved them, even tripped them up so they clattered to the ground cursing.

The escaping slave ran along the road from the castle, his leanness an advantage as he outdistanced his followers. Luned saw him as she stood at the door of her home and prayed for his safety. Past beer shops he ran, receiving drunken cheers from men who had slept as they sat and were only now able to greet the day itself. Nudd and Manon saw him as he passed the leather shop where they were working at the trestles.

Hearing the shouting, Kamal had hurried from the workshop and quickly understood what was happening as he saw the slim figure race past. It had not been so long since he had taken the same road to freedom, hiding in the woods near the tannery until rescued by its master. "Gerwyn," he said quietly, then prayed to Allah to be with the fleeing slave. "May you find a man as good as Gerwyn to give you a home," he whispered to the man's back.

At the door of the bakeshop Cynfan stood, arms akimbo. He was a shrewd man, quick-thinking, and reached for a loaf in a woman's basket. "You shall have a bigger one, Mistress Moelwen," he assured her as he stepped into the roadway and handed the food to the runner. Cynfan's reward was a radiant smile, then the man was gone, disappearing from view in the crowds at the market too intent on their bartering and haggling to worry about a runaway.

"What about my bread?" the woman demanded to know. Although her dark blue tunic was of good wool and recent make, she was not young, her skin and expression coarsened by age and bad humour. "You play the good Christian but I am the one to pay – you already had my coin for the loaf!"

Cynfan called to his journeyman who pulled open the oven door. With a wooden paddle he hefted one loaf, then another into the shrill woman's basket.

"Satisfied, mistress?" the baker asked.

"Satisfied you are feeding an outlander come to murder us in our beds?"

"No, Mistress Moelwen, only a slave needing food – and his freedom."

"Freedom? Then why here? Too many in this town expect to live off the hard work of others. There is that dreadful woman, Buddyg – taking food from my grandchildren's mouths and clothes from their backs!"

Cynfan was astonished at the outburst. "Mistress Buddyg works all the hours of daylight, sewing to keep her daughters fed and clothed."

"Mistress, you say? Huh! She lies with a man and my daughter's husband must keep her brats alive."

Now the baker understood. "Your daughter is wed to Griffin, a fine man – I knew Idris, his father, well. Aye, Buddyg shared his bed and was his wife but only after Griffin's mother died and the old man was lonely. Their daughters are pretty young maids and would make any father proud to own them his – as did Idris."

"More fool him! He was old and that whore, Buddyg, could have lain with many a man to get with child. Only Idris was stupid enough to believe them of his blood and

50

Griffin as stupid as his father calling them his sisters!" she declared and marched from the shop.

A happy man of good heart, Cynfan was shocked by the viciousness of Mistress Moelwen's attack. He had envied Idris his little family and tried to think of ways to help the young woman and her children.

"What will happen to the slave who ran?" his journeyman asked him, diverting him from the recent unpleasantness.

"Oh, the slave? If he has wits and will work well, he will survive in this shire of Pembroke – wherever he was born," Cynfan assured his workman. "Let him be thankful he did not make a run for it into Gwynedd or Powys. He would be sold to the Danes in Dublin for less than thirty pieces of silver up there amongst the gogledd."

Cynfan's man snorted. "The gogledd know the devil well but even as close as Ceredigion, Owain ap Cadwgan would have him on a slave ship to Ireland soon as look at him."

"Aye," Cynfan said slowly, "Owain. He gets his silver off other men's backs – and women's bodies," he added softly.

As was her custom, Luned stood at the open shutter of the room which looked towards the castle. From there she could not herself be seen but was still able to watch movements in the crowds gathered at the top of the slope down to the ship. Mostly, the colour she could see was brown, the same hue as the soil from which so many earned their daily food, but here and there a brighter note caught her attention. Sennen, the massive woman who serviced men, wore a tunic which was once red but had been washed clean so often it was soft and muted. Her kerchief was tied around her hair but she defied respectability and left her throat free, a strong column of her pride. Green shimmered in the corner of Luned's eye and she turned to see a servant girl from the castle in an old tunic of the shire

51

reeve's, Ninian's daughter guessing how the maid had earned the garment.

Her own sleeve was being tugged urgently and turned to see an anxious Gwri.

"Mistress," he whispered, his face twisted, unhappy.

Luned's attention turned from Pembroke people and dark-skinned men stumbling with their loads, her concern for Gwri instant. "What is it?"

"Margan, mistress, he is very bad. Please come."

As the boy ran through the building to Margan's bed-space, Luned followed, already dreading what she must see. The smell of vomit was stronger than ever it had been as she neared the stricken man and then she saw him. His body was naked, the upper half of him lying out of his covering and on the floor.

Lifting him gently Luned was shocked by how light he was, how thin, and she sent Gwri scuttling to Deris for cloths, water. The girl brought them herself and helped her mistress with Margan, the cool, wet linen soothing as it wiped away sweat and worse.

Margan was past speaking except for one word, "Mam."

Luned reached for a fresh bowl and with a corner of the cleanest linen soaked up water, then twisted the cloth, allowing droplets to reach his parched lips. Swallowing was difficult for him but he struggled to drink until he lay back too exhausted to move.

"How can he suddenly have become so sick?" Ninian asked. He had come so quietly Luned had not known her father watched her.

"Yesterday he seemed to be better and I had hopes he would soon recover but now I am feared for him, Father. Only a mediciner can help him now and there is no such man in the town."

Once more Gwri pulled at her sleeve. "Mistress Mabli is in the castle," he said but Luned shook her head.

"The lady would not come to such as Margan," she said

52

quietly and was surprised by a knowing look from the boy.

"Yes, mistress, she would. Will I fetch her? I can run."

Luned smiled at Gwri and nodded but they were interrupted.

"I should go. I speak a little as do the Franks. They will listen to me and let me pass the castle gates."

Ninian and Luned gazed up at Sulien, surprised by his sudden appearance and the leather apron over his tunic as much as by his offer.

"Mistress Mabli knows of me," Gwri insisted. "She would come at once if I asked her."

"No doubt she would," Sulien said and patted Gwri's shoulder as though he were a very small child, "but if you do not persuade the guards at the gate, what use are you? No, I will go."

Amazed by his sudden authority, Ninian watched as Sulien strode away, following him to the door which opened on to the road and standing there to watch his assistant's progress. With determination the young man thrust his way through the men and women still gawping at cargo being carried into the castle. He kicked small boys out of his way and elbowed aside traders ready to buy goods as he approached one of the shire reeve's men and spoke quickly. The guard was clearly no stranger, listening and nodding at whatever it was his acquaintance had to say before going through the gates and leaving Sulien outside.

Puzzled, Ninian waited in the doorway of his home but not for long. The stout body of Princess Nest's mediciner appeared at the open gate. Sulien approached and spoke to her, being answered only by a stare from the lady before she marched like a stiff-legged soldier through the ranks of the townspeople towards Ninian, Sulien left behind as he thanked the reeve's man.

"Where is Gwri?" Mistress Mabli asked as soon as Ninian had greeted her and brought her into his home.

"Gwri? You know him?" Ninian had thought the boy had been boasting.

"I know of him and would talk to him. Now."

When Gwri came she stood apart with him, the two talking in their quiet Welsh. Mabli appeared to be enquiring much of the boy and he always answered quickly but he did question her once. The only reply she had for him was a gentle hand on his shoulder and a shake of her head. Gwri turned away to hide his sorrow. The dog, Tegan, which had been at Luned's side padded to the boy and leaned close, trying to reach and lick away tears.

"Take me to Margan, Gwri," the listeners heard Mabli say.

He hesitated. "You will do what you can?"

"Yes. With God's help, I will," she promised as Gwri led her deep into the house.

Awkwardly and with difficulty, Mabli knelt by Margan's pallet. Her words were soft and in Welsh familiar to him, easing him. From the satchel she carried Mabli took out a stoppered vial, dripping some of the contents slowly into the side of Margan's mouth. He swallowed thirstily and she poured more.

"Will it heal him, mistress?" Ninian asked.

"No, only comfort him a little and let him sleep."

With gentle fingers she stroked Margan's forehead, his cheek, finding the skin clammy. Against the healthy flush of her fingers the watchers could see the yellowish hue of Margan's waxy skin. Greyness already invaded him and they saw, as Mabli had done, the corpse Margan would soon become.

"Have you encountered this sickness before?" Ninian asked Mabli as he helped her rise.

"Aye, once." She moved away so Margan would not hear their words. "It was a man King Rhys brought to mine gold at Dolaucothi, which was near the court at Dynevor. A very skilled miner he was but already a sick man when he reached the king's service, having learned his trade in the diggings at St Brynnach."

"St Brynnach," Ninian repeated slowly. "I have heard of the place. It is in the north of this shire where it borders with Ceredigion." Ninian frowned. "A silver mine – although there is little silver to be smelted from the rocks."

"And the lead?" Mabli asked softly.

Ninian's eyes widened. "In plenty. The rock is poisonous – and not easy to smelt," he said slowly, "but Margan has never been in a mine in his life, certainly not St Brynnach. How could he be ill in such a way?"

"Only our good Lord can be certain. To me, it would seem the mine is inside him," she said. "Now, however he became so affected, I know he has evil humours against which I have no defence. Had he encountered noxious material from God's own plants, between us, Nudd and I, we would have an answer, but I know from the man in Dolaucothi, there is no cure for what has brought Margan to death's door."

Ninian bowed his head to hide his grief, his fondness for the younger man grown over many working years. Mabli saw his distress and put a firm, warm hand on his shoulder.

"Come, there is much to be done. You can help ease his last days. I have fed Margan enough poppy juice to make him sleep soundly. Gwri tells me the young man calls for his mother. If you can find a farmer with a cart at market who will carry Margan to his home, I suggest you arrange it – and perhaps some silver coin for the family?"

"Of course! I am to blame if Margan has been made ill through his work."

Mistress Mabli shook her head. "No, you may rest easy on that point, Ninian. You are a good man – and a good master. Believe me, it was not through you the lad became sick unto death."

The urgency of her words puzzled the silversmith but they had carried the ring of truth. "Is there nothing more I can do?"

"I will give you poppy juice for the mother to administer. Take Gwri with you. He has been a true friend to Margan and will take his turn by the sickbed."

The silversmith would have hurried away but was stopped by Sulien. "Let me go with Margan," he said, catching hold of Ninian's arm to enforce his demand.

"No!" Mabli's sharp tone had all heads turning her way. "Leave Margan to those who know him well – and know this part of the shire."

"But –"

"You are a stranger, Sulien. We will trust you when we are sure of you."

The man was angry and would have argued but was stopped by Mabli's stare. "Long ago our enemies dressed as Danes and came in their long ships to pluck from us all we had," she said softly. "After them came the Irish and, like the Danes, their boats could be seen landing on our beaches. Worst of all were the men who came lately to destroy us, dressed and armed as are our own men but first they sent in spies to walk among us and seek out the best grain, the fattest cattle – and where so many of our fine young men could be rounded up with swords and whips, ready to be sold to the Irish as slaves. The people of this town of Pembroke have learned bitter lessons and they are wary of strangers who come seeking their fortune."

With fury reddening his skin Sulien took a step towards Mabli, one fisted hand rising to strike her. As he moved, Tegan growled and left Luned's side. The dog bared his teeth, reminding them all of the wolves in his ancestry.

"As you say, mistress," Sulien said, forcing a smile. "It is better I stay here and ensure all is well with the workshop – and with Mistress Luned and the children."

Mabli reached out a hand towards the dog and Tegan

edged close, leaning against Mabli as he would a friend, but the dog's eyes never left Sulien.

The cart moved slowly through the town. Word had spread quickly of its destination and folk leaned in to bid farewell to Margan, each calling on God's blessing for one of their own. Cynfan, ever practical, had a basket ready, laden with bread and roasted meat from his oven. Manon handed a small pouch to Ninian and it clanked gently with coin as he accepted it for a mother soon to see the end of her dreams. Farmers added their share as they bid Margan 'God speed', Buddyg hurrying to the cart with precious whitened linen. It was all she had left of the lengths stitched so recently for Princess Nest's bed in her husband's new castle. It seemed to her Margan's need of it as a winding sheet was urgent. Ceinwen came to the cart to bless the sick man, holding his hand in hers as she prayed. Prince Hywel was beside her, growling helpless enmity in his blindness to any who had speeded Margan on his last journey.

Luned stood at the doorway of her home long after the cart had gone from her sight. As it went from view a thought had wormed into her mind. Was this the way her William would return? Dying or already dead in a cart? It was a constant nightmare and sudden terror had washed through her in huge, unending waves, rising and engulfing her so fast she could not catch her breath as she leaned on the doorpost. Gasping, sweating, she fought her silent enemy until she was able to pull herself upright and lift her head. If it was to be, William's spirit would find her a mother of whom he could be proud.

She realised Tegan stood close, nudging her gently with his huge head until she put down a hand and fondled his ear. His presence helped her breathe steadily and her body cooled from its fervid heat as thoughts became born more of reason than of fear. William would return, she must believe that and she would. For the sake of Walter and Meleri she had to be strong, smile for them, let them be the children they were. As if they understood her, Meleri ran to her mother and pulled her towards the kitchen.

"Deris is making us honey cakes for supper!"

Walter smiled awkwardly at his mother as he hid his own unease and went to shut and bolt the door to the town.

The kitchen was warm and had been tidied of its recent urgencies. Deris had a stewpot bubbling quietly over the fire and wheaten cakes were growing in a pile as she knelt by a hot, flat stone to bake them.

"You and the children come and eat now, mistress," she said as she turned a flushed cheek towards them. "All is ready."

Luned looked at the table. Only three bowls and spoons were laid. "Your place?"

"I will eat later, when I have fed Sulien. It will be good for the three of you to be on your own for once as you thank God for his bounty and hearten yourselves with the stew. It has been a hard day for us all."

Walter lifted Tegan's empty food bowl and ladled stew into it, blowing on the savoury mass to speed its cooling. Luned was proud of the boy. Without being asked he had taken on Ninian's duty, ensuring the helpless animal would not suffer in the silversmith's absence.

It was a good time in the quiet of the kitchen. Luned smiled as the children ate well, Meleri hurrying to move a stool and climb up to a shelf to get the honey for cakes Walter lifted from the fireside. They talked of William, promised what they would do to make ready for his return, reminded each other of times he was with them and laughter had filled the whole house.

"He will come home soon?" Meleri asked her mother.

Luned nodded. "All who know her say your father's wife will take the greatest care of William and will have him back with us before we can turn round." It had been hard to ensure her voice was as certain as her words.

Meleri was smiling happily as she reached for another

58

cake and honey but her hand was frozen in the air as Sulien strode in, his face suffused with anger. "Why was I not told supper was on the table?"

Deris had hurried in behind him. "They were having their meal on their own. You would have been called when the family had finished."

Even Meleri and Walter noticed Deris's tone as she spat the words 'the family' at Sulien.

He turned on the servant. "It is not your place to decide such matters."

"Deris, will you fill a bowl for Sulien and take it, with some bread, to the workshop?" Luned asked. "I am sure he will enjoy his food more pleasantly there – in my father's absence."

"Aye, mistress, in Ninian's absence. Have you forgotten my promise to him to look after his family?"

"No, Sulien, I have not forgotten but such a promise does not make you the head of the household and free to give orders to my servant."

The man had thought Luned quiet and biddable, easily turned his way. She was still softly spoken but the woman at the table with her children had a backbone of steel and hardness in her words to match.

"After all that has happened today I am anxious for your welfare. Because of that I will sleep here tonight, Luned."

He had made free with her name and Luned's eyes narrowed as her lips tightened into a firm line. "You are too kind, sir. I am grateful for the work you do for my father and I hope you find it possible to continue as his assistant until he can find a permanent replacement for Margan. You should know my father likes to keep his work and his family life separate. I think it best you do not sleep here at night. This is a small town avid for gossip and I will not be party to feeding such an appetite. Having said that, Deris has cooked us all a very flavoursome stew. I would wish you to have your fill of it before you leave." Luned gathered errant crumbs into a small pile on the table. "If you intend to continue working in the smithy, we will see you when you arrive in the morning. Walter is in charge of all the locks and bolts and will be awake to admit you."

Sulien fought to control his temper. "Walter is but a child. You are very brave, mistress," he began, emphasising her title, "but what of the children? They are too young to protect you."

Luned's head rose and her back straightened. "Walter and Meleri? Remember who is their father! Only a man as foolish as Owain ap Cadwgan uses the Constable's kin for his own purpose and even Owain must now be regretting his arrogance."

Deris had busied herself at the fireplace and turned to Sulien, a brimming bowl in her hands. "I will leave you to carry your supper, Sulien. Your hands will be steadier than mine with such a burden. Here, I will bring your spoon and the bread." Satisfied by the turn of events, she smiled at him and he had no choice but to turn and leave them. They heard him later, banging about in the workshop to relieve his anger.

"What have we done to make him so cross with us, Mama?" Meleri asked.

"Nothing, cariad. There is a saying in the town, 'I may look like a cabbage but I am not green.'"

Meleri chuckled at her mother's words but Walter was silent as he gazed at her. He had watched Sulien stand close to his mother at every possible opportunity, hovering at her shoulder like a hawk and watching her every move and expression as would such a bird of prey. The boy had begun to understand Sulien's purpose, then he saw Tegan pad his way to the door of the workshop. The massive hound settled there and lay still, his head raised, his eyes alert as he guarded Luned and her children.

Chapter Four

"A beautiful bird, Deris! You were very clever to find one so healthy and clean." Luned bent to the chicken in the basket, lifting it out and examining it further. "Never have I seen such good feathers. Be sure you save all when you pluck. My father's pillow is becoming quite thin and these will plump it up to greater comfort for his sleeping."

"Aye, mistress, I will – after I have spread them for a while so any of God's tiny creatures may wander off in search of fresh blood."

Luned chuckled. "You are very wise, Deris. My father's blood tempts them beyond measure and they leave him swollen and scratching. He said his mother was the same. Now, what will you cook with the chicken meat?"

The two women delved into the basket, spreading onions, a cabbage, herbs, leeks. Walter sat on a stool and watched while Meleri helped arrange the goods into a pattern she found pleasing.

Sounds of shouting outside the house were followed by a tremendous thump on the main door and every head turned in that direction. Tegan growled as he bounded towards the disturbance with Walter not far behind. Luned called to her son to take care as she hurried after him, Deris and Meleri in her wake.

Another thump and Luned nodded at Walter's unspoken question. Holding tightly to the tough leather of Tegan's collar the boy unbolted the door and slowly swung it wide. Almost immediately two women's bodies, writhing and with fingers tight in each other's hair, fell across the doorstep.

Luned pulled her son away and stood over the two aggressors, demanding they cease brawling in her home. She continued to order them to stop but they took no notice, each determined to do as much damage as possible to the other. Deris thought quickly and ran to the workshop, returning with a pail of water which she emptied on both the women. Spluttering and struggling to breathe in the dowsing, they fell apart.

Luned pulled them upright and held them away from each other. "Now, why do you behave at my home as would a couple of witless urchins?" she demanded to know.

The older of the women was the first to reply, a confused mix of old Welsh and new, condemning her opponent for starving her children. The younger one was slower to recover and, with dawning horror, Luned and Deris could see she was heavy with child. In the roadway beyond them stood three children, a boy of six or seven holding a mewling baby while a girl who could only have been four years old clung to her brother's tunic. All were thin and poorly clad, shrivelled by hardship and unending hunger. Nearby stood a skinny man in a stained tunic which had once been green and cut for someone much larger than its present owner. Grey hair straggled either side of a tired, worn face scarred by pox.

"Who are you?" Luned asked but the man stood mute.

"I heard of them in the market this morning," Deris said. "Country wife has come to sort out town wife. That waste of breath standing there laboured for Onfel until a storm smashed a huge branch into him and near broke his back. Onfel, being the meanest thing on two legs, turned the weakling off immediately, and when he could walk again he came to Pembroke to earn what he could."

"Ah! Country wife stayed in the gwennie with her children –"

Deris nodded towards the younger woman. "And she needed a man to keep her fed and warm when it was cold."

"It would seem more than a fire was started in her." Luned turned to her own children. "Go with Deris and bring sops for the children. They should not go hungry because of this fight."

"Shall we take them to the kitchen?" Meleri asked.

"No, cariad. Your grandfather will be home soon and you know he does not endure fleas and lice with any fortitude." She had watched the boy and girl scratch their heads and bodies. "You!" she called to the father. "Take your women away from here and see your children – all your children – live in safety. They will follow you when they have had some food."

For the first time the man showed interest and would have hurried into the silversmith's house.

"No!" Luned's finger pointed along the road into the town. "Go now, your women with you. Were the Constable here he would have you labouring hard to care for your family. Be thankful he is from home and you escape a whipping." She stood immovable and watched as, muttering and discontented, the wretch grabbed each woman by an arm and dragged them away.

Deris had assembled bread and meat on an old platter, milk in cups, but the boy would have nothing until the baby had been fed bread soaked in milk until it was sated. With Luned standing over them, the children finished every scrap and every drop, Meleri running to fetch a pitcher of goat's milk to make sure the baby could take no more.

With a strange courtesy the boy thanked Luned and her helpers, hefting the now sleepy baby to comfort on his shoulder and taking the hand of his sister. A shy smile later he was trudging after his parents.

"That child is more a man than his father can ever be," Luned said quietly and Deris nodded, then scratched.

"Dear God, mistress, they have left us a gift!"

"Patience," Luned counselled. "My father will stay with Margan's family – for a while. We have time to get clean."

"Aye, he is a good man, the master," Deris said as she squirmed and scratched. "He will succour Margan and his family until after the funeral."

"Three days since they left," Luned said as they returned to the house and locked the door behind them. "I would have thought Margan could not have lasted the journey – God rest his soul."

"Amen to that. Perhaps Gwri and the poppy juice stayed his passing, along with the milk Mistress Mabli insisted Margan should have. Nothing but milk."

"She knew she could not save him," Luned reminded the servant.

"Aye, mistress, but poor Margan will have time to be at home and say 'God be with you' to those he loved," Deris said and made the sign of the cross.

Hours passed slowly for Luned, day succeeding day until it was time for another full market when there would be sellers of all kinds as well as farmers. The weather had turned warm, catching everyone unawares with sudden summer. Luned's home was cool, the builders and then her father having made sure that what could be a cosy shell in the winter was easily adapted to having air hurried through it in the summer.

Noise from outside the opened shutters tempted her, having in it a quickening, an excitement that good weather had arrived. Luned thanked God and His Son it should be so, adding a prayer that William's comfort might be increased and his return speeded.

"Deris, I am going to the market," she called and heard the girl drop a bowl.

"Mistress! Is all well?" Deris asked as she came running and wiping her floury hands in her apron. "We have enough fresh food for a day or two."

"So we have – thanks to you," Luned said and her smile pleased the servant. "No, I will leave you a little peace – and Tegan. Meleri may come with me and see what the traders at the east end have to offer."

It was a hot day in Pembroke, air scarcely moving amongst the crowds which seethed this way and that between the houses. Fresh food was long gone from the market stalls and the beer shops were doing a good trade. Even costly wine left over from shipments to the castle and the priory was slipping down thirsty throats.

Luned and her daughter were enjoying the bustle of people and dealing around the stalls and piled handcarts. They were shown wilting vegetables at very good prices but Luned always shook her head as she thanked each trader for their offer. Meleri dawdled by a stall covered with toys of all shapes. Carved from wood or moulded from clay, they had been painted by a careless hand, the colours crude. Her mother wondered why Meleri was so absorbed in the wares for sale. The girl was past the age of many of the playthings and those she kept in her bedspace at home were of far better value.

"Come, cariad," Luned said and would have gently pulled Meleri away but a shrill voice nearby had all heads turning that way.

"– of course you may spend your coin freely, stolen as it is from my grandchildren. Shame on you!"

Like everyone else, Luned was amazed at the woman whose words were so intemperate. She saw someone still healthy but advancing in years and of ample girth. Her tunic was generously cut and flowing in a mass of blue so dark it could be black while the linen of her kerchief was clean but had not been whitened. It was swathed around her throat, leaving her face exposed. A pity, Luned thought, as it showed thickened skin and deep, deep, lines entrenched there by so many years of discontent and disapproval.

What surprised Luned most was the object of the woman's vicious attack. Buddyg, the seamstress, was standing white-faced, too shocked to move.

"You cheated Idris – making an old man believe he could still father healthy children. Twice, you did it! Then what happens? His will says Griffin must feed and clothe them always as his sisters. You deceiver! Griffin is an honest man not able to give to his wife what she should have because of you, while you spend his coin on your bastards!"

"They are not!" Buddyg was stung into shouting a reply. She was slighter in build than her accuser, and her brown hair had begun to escape her kerchief as she twisted this way and that to avoid the woman. Her usual kindly face had lost its pleasant smile and there were tears in her eyes, ready to fall.

"The words of a whore!"

Buddyg stood as tall as she could, struggling to calm herself before she spoke. "My daughters were born of Idris. He knew the truth – as did his son, Griffin. We were all happy while Idris lived – and you are mistaken," she told the virago. "I receive no coin from Griffin. It is my pride I earn that myself –"

"On your back as usual, I have no doubt!"

"No, mistress!" Luned surprised even herself as she stepped between the two women and faced the harridan. "You do not live in the town, as I do, but all here know Mistress Buddyg to be an honest woman who spends long hours working with her needle. Why, the tunic I wear today is her work," Luned added as she lifted blue linen of the skirt of her tunic, "and I defy you to find fault with a single stitch."

66

For a moment the adversary was silent, then she looked up and down the length of Luned before choosing her words. "Trust you to defend her – you are no better than she. All your children were born out of wedlock and you are still kept in comfort by a man stupid enough to have believed your lies."

Around her Luned heard gasps of horror but she sensed that in the crowd would be those who agreed with what had just been said. A big, unkempt woman smelling of a pig sty pulled at her friend who was so consumed by hate. "Moelwen, come away – you have said too much. I have told you before your tongue will be your undoing."

"Leave me alone, Drydwen! I speak only God's truth and if there are those who do not like what I say then it is because they have sinned."

"In that you are mistaken – Mistress Moelwen, is it?" Luned was all that was pleasant but her kerchief had slipped below her chin and everyone saw the strength of her features and her determination to be heard. "God's truth binds and commands us all but you twist it to hurt and to condemn. It is not God's work you do but like the devil himself you get pleasure from seeing others suffer."

A tall, red-headed woman pushed her way towards Luned. "You are right, mistress, and God be thanked for people like you. Moelwen is an old witch and a turn at a burning stake would do her good."

"No!" Luned was horrified her mention of the devil might have earned Moelwen a witch's fate.

"Have no fear," Sennen said and patted Luned's arm as she tipped her head towards Moelwen. "She is not worth the bother. Now, you and Mistress Buddyg, get yourselves away from here and the stench of hellfire Moelwen carries with her. Remember, it is in the way of our people," she said more quietly to Luned, "anything that woman wishes on you or me will come back to bedevil her threefold."

*   *   *

The day was quietening when the sound of hoofbeats stirred the last of the crowds to move aside. The rider had slowed from a canter to a trot and many turned to look up at him on his massive chestnut, the feathered hairs above its hooves flickering. The man was as tall as any in the castle, his beardless face open, honest. The leather jerkin and broad-brimmed hat he wore were familiar wear in Pembroke. Any with the silver could buy the same in the leather shop, but strangers in the town could see this was a Fleming by his boning and by that they knew he was from the castle.

"Ugo! God be with you," Cynfan shouted. The baker had an empty shop and stood in its doorway, seeking any wayward breeze which would cool. He had pulled off his cap whitened with flour and mopped his head and neck with a kerchief sadly in need of a wash.

"And with you, Cynfan. You have the look of a man who has traded well this day."

"Aye, a busy one but I have no angry customers so I may sleep easy."

Ugo's laugh was a warm, deep bellow. "That is more than some of your fellow traders can boast."

Cynfan beamed at his friend, then nodded at the horse. "You have ridden far and he is in need of rest and water."

The Fleming's features had darkened. He slid from the saddle and stroked the horse's face, seeing the whitened sweat marks and wiping them away with his hand. Satisfied, he turned to Cynfan but waited to speak as he gave himself time to choose his words.

"I have been out towards the warren," Ugo said and Cynfan nodded.

All in Pembroke knew of the deep foundation to a wall which surrounded fine green grazing, gaps in it each protected by a wooden door into a small enclosure. Animals like hares but smaller had been brought over alive from France and the Low Countries to live and breed on the enviable green. To catch them a door would be opened. Lush grass beckoned and when enough of the animals had lolloped in to feed, the door would be closed and the animals quickly rounded up. Franks could then have fresh meat all through the winter, meat which a few inhabitants of that part of the shire, expert at private hunting at night, could swear tasted like tender chicken.

"You meant to tire your horse?"

"To stretch his legs for him, aye. He has to be strong to carry Sir Gerald. I came back past the tannery."

Cynfan's eyes narrowed, became shrewd. "All is well there?"

"Flourishing. Gerwyn's son Meurig works hard, the old man told me."

"The old man – Myrddin? With no Gerwyn, he would be a good teacher." The baker sensed Ugo was uneasy. "What was wrong?" he asked softly.

"Myrddin says the work goes well but there have been almost daily visits by two monks from the priory. They spend their time talking to Meurig."

Cynfan swore oaths Ugo had never before heard but they sounded of the old Welsh. "The land! Those bastards want the land."

"More than that, they want Meurig."

The baker was too shocked to speak.

"The boy could not see it, thinking they were doing as they told him, seeking to help him find eternal peace in the priory."

"Yet all the time . . ."

"They knew if Meurig went into the service of the church, the tannery land would go with him and he would finish childless and on his knees."

"Ugo, what can we do? Gerwyn would never wish this for his son. He knew the boy had begun to lust for women and think of children of his own."

"When she has been told what is happening we must talk to Manon. She still holds the deeds for the land."

"Aye, thanks be to the good Lord she does. Will we go now?"

Ugo shook his head. "No. I must get this beast to the stables and we must give Meurig time to tell her. In the morning?"

"You are sure the boy will have told her by then?"

"Certain," Ugo said, his mouth a grim line. "I made him swear to it on his father's grave."

"Good. Manon is a strong woman, she will outwit the prior if she can – mind you, I can understand why he wants the land. It would make a fine mill."

Something in Cynfan's voice intrigued Ugo. He looked hard at the baker, who was looking at a nearby roof.

"Just imagine it, Ugo. With the dung pit cleared away as well as the sluices and the tanning shed with its vats. It would not take skilled men long to build a dam across the stream where it widens and where Gerwyn used to dive after he had cleansed himself with clay. A mill wheel set into the side of the dam could turn huge grindstones – I know just how it should be done."

"And we could all have the best of bread flour?"

"God willing." Cynfan sighed. "The miller who sends me sacks for baking does his best but the flour is already costly enough and the grain should be sifted first to take out the grit."

"You could do better, my friend?"

Cynfan was surprised by the question and he pondered for a while. "Aye, Ugo. I believe, with God's help, I could."

The Fleming continued his ride through Pembroke, easing his horse past the last of the townsfolk abroad before couvre feu. A movement from a house near the castle gates caught his attention. Someone was sneaking from a door at the side of the silversmith's home, the individual short and scabby,

70

looking from side to side to make sure he had not been noticed. Ugo heard the bolts shoot home after the man's departure but he kept his face turned towards the guards at the gate. From the corner of his eye he watched the strange little man scurry away into the increasing shadows of the town.

"Now, why would he be in there, I wonder?" Ugo asked himself. "Ninian is still from home and he is not the sort of servant Mistress Luned would choose to have about her."

Luned knew nothing of the man. As far as she knew, only Sulien worked each day with the bellows and crucibles. She had been into the workshop each evening to make sure all was safe from an uneasy flame and had been impressed how tidy Sulien left the workshop and its storage huts, yet there was no Gwri to sweep clean.

The three days of her father's absence had turned into a week and she longed for his return. Words Deris had spoken lightly kept coming back to haunt her. 'She needed a man to keep her fed and warm in bed.' Luned understood the tavern woman's yearning. Gerald ensured neither she nor any of her children were ever in want but when it was dark she was lonely in her bed.

Seeking cool air, Luned leaned against the upright of an open door and let her thoughts wander. It was Earl Robert of Shrewsbury who had been at fault, setting himself against the new king who had once been his friend. Because of the huge de Bellême estates in France which also were his, the earl believed himself more powerful than King Henry of England. His defiance of royal rule had seen a royal army march against him and Earl Robert become exiled for ever. Submission to the king must be shared by his brother, Arnulf de Montgomery, whose castle of Pembroke had to be passed to King Henry, as well as Cilgerran which had also been built by Arnulf. As for Gerald, he was forced to leave the shire he helped create.

The graceful lines of Luned's face were sad as she remembered the glorious days in Pembroke's castle when Gerald was its castellan. He had been a forceful lover and a proud father, even as his thoughts were with the safety of the castle and its town.

Time and again Cadwgan and his men had sought to destroy Pembroke, the castle and the people of the town. When besieged, the Franks as well as the native men and women who had taken refuge behind the palisades were helpless as Cadwgan's raiders robbed the countryside of anything movable. It was Gerald who had outwitted Cadwgan each time he would add this most important flame to the ring of burning castles.

Now it was Cadwgan's son, Owain, who was Gerald's undoing by coveting his wife. Because of his lust for her the new castle in Emlyn had been destroyed. It had been Gerald's pride and when he lost that, Luned also lost her son to the enemy.

As she sorrowed for her beloved William, anger ate into Luned like one of her father's acids on metal. From a child she had been unused to hatred. When a woman and hurt by life's arrows, her soul became scarred, her peace of mind destroyed. The agony would not let her sleep and her wakeful hours were filled with prayers for William and memories of nights when she felt loved and alive.

Sulien had sensed Luned's moods and had been discreet. He had time on his side and he made her aware of him with a gentle bow, sideways glances and half smiles. This was a proud woman, beautiful, serene, and he would not risk frightening her. Instead, he handled her as carefully as he would a spirited mare he wished to break to his ways.

Deris was a problem to him, the girl always suspicious of what he would do. Sulien had banned her from the workshop, saying he would not risk her getting harmed by molten metal flowing untamed from a tipped crucible. The children too, he preferred they stay far from him as he worked or face his displeasure.

It was a strange house while Ninian and Gwri were at a distance with the dying Margan. Each member of the household went about their daily business, God's hours passing with an inexorable slowness as they all waited for something to happen. When it did, it was as though they had been unlocked from a spell.

Ninian, Gwri behind him, came home.

"Luned!"

She ran to her father and he was puzzled to find her shivering in his embrace.

"What is it, child?"

"You have been gone so long. Margan?"

Ninian bent his head and hid his face in Luned's kerchief. "Two days ago. Gwri administered the poppy juice so the boy slept his way to God. It made it easier for his mother and sisters to bear. We buried him at first light this morning."

Luned whispered a prayer for the soul of the quiet young man who had been a part of their family for so long.

Ninian shook his head. "Even now I have no understanding of why he was so afflicted. One day I must talk to Mistress Mabli. She seemed to know what it was caused his death."

"Then you must hurry, Father. The word is that the mediciner is soon to return to Carew and to the Lady Nest's children."

The old man was anxious. "There has been no news?"

"Of William and the princess? None."

Ninian frowned in thought. "I will go and tell Sulien he can work without me one more day so I might visit and speak with Mistress Mabli. Now you, cariad, how have you fared?"

With a smile, Luned reassured him. "Deris has a potage rich with early vegetables waiting for you and Gwri."

Tegan had been a patient witness to the reunion but, as Ninian moved, the great hound bounded to his master and would not let him walk one pace until their greetings had been exchanged.

"This fierce brute has looked after you well?" her father asked her with a smile. "All of you?"

Luned nodded. "Every one of us, except . . ."

Ninian waited.

"Tegan does not take kindly to Sulien's presence."

The silversmith was not surprised. "Sulien is a new man about the place – has a new smell on him. Tegan will learn acceptance in time."

It was raining when they woke but the morning began with their daily prayers for William. When Ninian had spent time in his workshop ensuring all was well, he made his way the short distance to the castle and Luned helped Walter and Meleri with their daily tasks. Walter must make sure Tegan's bed was shaken well away from the dwelling and that the large bowl made by Ninian himself from clay and paint was filled with the freshest water. Deris smiled as she mounded scraps of bread, meat, cheese for the patient animal and Walter watched as Tegan fed, then padded all round the house, workshop, sheds, before turning round and round on his bed and settling to sleep. Walter fondled the massive head and whispered a promise to take Tegan for a race through the woods before supper.

Meleri was anxious to be as much like her mother as possible. Deris smiled at the little maid, dressed as was Luned in a grey tunic, her kerchief holding back hair darker than her mother's but as soft and straight and without the hint of redness Luned had inherited from her father, hard to see now he had whitened with the passing years. His daughter took a cloth, wiping the few pieces of silver Ninian allowed to be displayed in his home. Meleri copied her mother, Luned smiling as she handed each goblet and small box to her daughter for a second busy rubbing. It was a happy, peaceful time for them all but no one failed to join in the prayers for William's safe return when Deris poured goat's milk and placed crumbled cheese and crusts of bread on the table at midday.

It was a day which warmed in spite of the rain but the light had begun to tire before Ninian returned to his home and Luned hurried to him.

"Father, you have been gone so long! Did you see Mistress Mabli? What did she say?" She helped her father remove the formal black cloak from his shoulders.

"Tcha! A wasted day!" Ninian was in a temper, unusual for him. "At the gate I was accosted by one of the shire reeve's men and he had me kicking my heels as I watched a steward cleaning the reeve's silver – much of which had been fashioned in my own workshop! The rest of the collection was tawdry stuff. Even at a distance I could tell there was more copper in the making of it than should have been."

"Mistress Mabli?" Luned reminded him.

Ninian smoothed his hair and made himself breathe more easily. It was a wry smile he had for his daughter and her patience with him.

"By the time the guard came for me the lady had already sailed. She went on the morning tide, without breaking her fast – water travel always makes her nauseous, I was told."

"I am sorry, Father, but she will be back one day and then you can ease your mind."

He was weary with a wasted day and sighed. "Aye, cariad, I trust in God it will be so. Nothing can help Margan now but I would have the answers to my questions and know if I was at fault in any way."

Luned placed a gentle hand on his cheek. "That is not so and in your heart you know it."

She was answered by sadness in the man. "Perhaps I do, cariad, but I would be sure." He stiffened. "I would also like to know why I was led round by the nose this day as if I was a stupid old fool."

"So much has been badly done in Pembroke since Gerald started building his new castle in Emlyn." Luned had tried to speak lightly but her deep bitterness did not escape the man who had loved her since her birth.

"You are right, child, and why the Constable chose this Roger fitzHugh to govern us in his absence I shall never understand. Even when young, Gerald de Windsor never could tolerate a stupid man and the reeve is often that. Gerald has been much occupied, I grant you, but he was always a man to look to his future."

Luned bent her head, remembering the younger Gerald, tall and strong, who had stormed into her life.

"When the captives are returned, Gerald will build again where Owain destroyed," her father assured her.

His daughter's eyes stung with unshed tears. "He builds it for her," she said quietly and Ninian caught and held her hands, warming them in his own.

"Not just the princess, cariad. His new estate will belong to your William in time – as Gerald's first-born."

"And the other William – hers – will have Carew and all her riches."

Ninian smiled. "It is why Gerald is so obsessed with his new land, his new castle. He is no longer young and would have a goodly portion of the world's wealth for his first child to inherit and enjoy."

Her father was trying so hard to cheer her and Luned forced a smile. "And you? Do you do the same?" she asked.

In the dimness of the passageway Ninian's eyes gleamed. "Aye, cariad. In my own humble way I try to amass a great fortune for my only child – which will make her the envy of all."

A small ship may have sailed early along the river to Carew, leaving Pembroke with little fuss, but a larger vessel docked at the quay as the sun was just past its highest. Sails were salt-stained and the crew rugged, with the look of men from the north. Cargoes from there had ceased to excite Pembroke townsfolk, they preferred the whiff of the east with its echoes of warmth and exotic smells.

The sailors new to Pembroke did not have the look of slaves, carrying themselves and their barrels of preserved foodstuffs with the ease and assurance of men unused to chains and the lash of a whip. They worked hard, the unloading of cargo and the taking on of supplies and bales of new wool rapidly accomplished. At a nod from the ship's master, the men surged into the long roadway between homes and shops of all kinds which was Pembroke town.

Wise men had already made sure their wives and daughters were behind solid doors barred from any attempt at intrusion. The sailors' strange tongue was not heard in any home but in the shops still open at the closing of the day guttural sounds and pointing resulted in sales. The leather shop was an attraction, fingers gnarled and toughened with salt gentle on the caskets, belts, scabbards, on display.

The busiest trading was in the beer shops, even wine being poured down throats in an endless stream. Women who earned their bread relieving men of their lusts tempted with smiles and by first light the seamen staggered from the corners in which they had slept, each with a sore head and an empty pouch. Not one wanted to stay behind, every man determined to go back to the challenges of the sea and the freedom it gave them from nagging women and mewling infants.

Pembroke began to shake itself awake at the beginning of a new day, tavern keepers sweeping up the shards of broken drinking cups and counting the copper and silver to be stored in secret places. The women who had been used were exhausted but the coins clinking in their tunics were music to make them smile even if many of them nursed bruises and sore ribs.

In the first hours of the day few had noticed a small band of the shire reeve's men, led by Roger fitzHugh, march the short distance from the castle to the home of Ninian, the silversmith. Red-faced, his mouth a thin line of determination, the reeve himself pounded on the heavy door of the dwelling, demanding entrance. He was impatient, relieving his temper a little by hammering on the wood with one fist, then two, until he heard the massive bar lifting and the latch begin to click. He shoved his full weight against the door, pushing it wide and seeing Ninian standing there in a nightshift, his spare figure made decent by a grey woollen shawl.

"What has happened? Is there news of William?" he asked, blinking in the early light.

"William be damned!" The reeve thrust the old man to one side and beckoned in his men. "You know what you seek. Find them!"

"Find what?" Ninian wanted to know as Luned came towards him, Tegan baring his teeth and growling beside her.

The dog would have leaped on to the shire reeve had not his mistress held him firmly by his collar. She could hear Deris in the kitchen complaining bitterly at the reckless way men were throwing around precious food.

"Look what you have done now!" Deris screamed at one man. "That was the best wheat flour and no way can it be saved! Who said you could do this?"

Luned could not understand the reply, its French arrogant and coarse, she was too busy preventing Tegan sinking his fangs into the nearest throat and reassuring Walter and Meleri all was well. The children found her words hard to believe as huge men stormed from one room in the house to another, wrecking everything they touched. Even the workshop, the sheds, the yard behind the house were being ravaged until a shout went up and Roger fitzHugh hurried to the source. Ninian's bedspace became filled with heaving bodies, each man intent on seeing what had been found.

A hand held high a silver goblet and there was a roar of triumph from all the Franks.

"Where is the other?" the shire reeve demanded to know but Ninian shook his head, clearly bemused by all that was happening.

"That is one of a pair I made for you, sir," he said, bewildered by all that had occurred.

Roger fitzHugh was not satisfied with the answer, pushing a face swollen with fury close to Ninian. "And now it is in your possession."

"No!" Ninian protested. "I swear it! Why would I steal from you?"

"To melt down and use for the priory's altar? You need much silver for that commission."

Ninian tried to answer but was not heard, Roger fitzHugh shouting at him again and again, demanding the return of the second goblet.

"Take him to the castle!" he shouted at his men. "A good flogging will loosen his tongue."

Luned clung to the shire reeve's arm. "Sir, I beg you. My father is an old man and an honest one. Something is wrong."

"Ma dame, your father is a thief. He has stolen from me and will pay for it – with his life if he is stubborn!"

Chapter Five

Unable to get to the workshop, Sulien had knocked hard at the main door until it was opened by Luned. She held the wood slightly ajar with one hand and Tegan's collar with the other. Even when she acknowledged the man waiting to enter her home, she still hesitated.

"Has something happened?" he asked, his voice gentle.

Luned turned away, freeing Tegan as she walked along the narrow passageway towards the kitchen. The dog paced between his mistress and the man hurrying after her until Sulien stood amongst the scattered furniture and food, amazed by what he saw.

"Who has done this?"

A defiant Deris stopped sweeping fallen flour to stare at him, her gaze matching Tegan's. "The shire reeve and his men. They have not long gone – it is a wonder you did not see them."

"Hardly, Deris, the town is filled with seamen lurching back towards their ship."

"So, you were too late to see the reeve take away the master to be flogged?"

"Deris!" Luned raised a shaking hand and her tears began again.

"I'm sorry, mistress," the girl said and hurried to her. When arms were tight around quivering shoulders she turned to Sulien. "The workshop is as bad, as are the store sheds and even the yard has been dug up. Gwri is already trying to tidy in the smithy and find out if those thieving rats stole anything as they searched. Two small silver boxes the master kept in the other room have already gone."

Sulien ignored the angry maidservant and bent to the stricken woman. "Luned," he began softly but her head came up fiercely and he realised his mistake. "Mistress, believe me, I will do all I can. Why did they take your father?"

"He stands accused by that accursed Frank for stealing two silver goblets. One was found hidden in my father's bedspace. The other is still missing and my father will be beaten until it is found," she told him, her voice steady but her hands trembling.

Sulien was all he should be to the grieving daughter, promising his help and his constant support of her and her family. Luned held herself proudly as he spoke and had never looked more lovely, her dark eyes huge in a pale face, distress pulling the skin tightly over shapely bones. She lifted a gracious hand, gesturing towards the workshop.

"There you can be of assistance and will have my gratitude for it. With Deris's help and that of my children, I will attend to my home."

Sulien bowed and was gone, Deris going to bar the door to the roadway from any other intruders before she returned to the wrecked kitchen. Luned went first to Meleri, the child struggling to restore her bed to its rightful place and tidiness. Tears streaked the small cheeks and Luned knelt and held her, waiting until sobs eased and the soft cheeks had been wiped dry.

"Tell me, cariad," her mother whispered.

"The horse my grandfather made for me." Meleri opened her small fists and showed shards of brightly painted clay. "See."

"We will keep these pieces until he returns to us – and that will be soon. Then your grandfather will shape you another horse before he does anything else."

"Promise?"

"I promise, cariad," Luned assured her with a hug, as well as a silent prayer the silversmith would return to them quickly and whole.

Walter was being more practical. As the man of the house he was righting all the furniture, inspecting the items carefully to see if any needed mending. What had been broken beyond repair he carried to the yard, piling the pieces tidily until he could get at them with an axe and ready them for the kitchen fire.

As midday approached, Deris called her mistress to show what food she had collected which could be eaten. The fire was burning briskly in the hearth, the floor and table swept and washed clear of flour. Wooden bowls and platters had been flung but were undamaged. Only the clay pots had suffered but Deris had found enough to hold the frothing milk she had persuaded from the nanny goat.

"Some of the cheese has been stolen, with the roasted meat left from last night's supper."

"You have worked wonders, Deris," Luned said and the girl's cheeks flushed with her mistress's praise. "I know you have not been able to bake or to get to the baker's shop, so we will toast the bread at the fire. That way it will not taste stale."

Meleri clapped her hands and hurried to find long sticks on which to impale the hardening pieces of an old loaf ignored by their despoilers. Luned's attention was with her children and their game of cooking the meagre meal so it was a cheerful atmosphere Sulien walked into and admired.

"Well done, Deris," he said, patting the girl's shoulder as he would a small child.

She bowed at his words but seethed inwardly at their

82

tone. It was that of a master praising a servant and he no better than she. Luned had not noticed, as she watched Meleri's attempts to crisp already dry bread. Walter had worked at his cheese until it was a ball on the end of a stick so when it met the fire it melted, flaring drops making him hurry to wipe it on his bread. Meleri would have some too and Luned watched as her children chattered, laughed. She thanked God for them and nibbled at a crust, knowing she must keep her strength. Her William gone, now her father. When would it end?

Life had been altered beyond reason when Gerald aided his master Arnulf's escape to Ireland and the new king in England must take possession of all Arnulf de Montgomery had owned. From a distance, King Henry had decreed a Welshman should hold Pembroke Castle and his choice had been Iorwerth ap Bleddyn, an uncle of the hated Owain. There had been instant fear in the town so often besieged by Iorwerth's brother, Cadwgan, but Iorwerth's tenure as the king's custodian was short-lived. It lasted only months before a band of his men attacked King Henry's soldiers and the king was again annoyed by what was happening in Pembroke.

The castle and its shire must have a Constable, he decided, and Sai had travelled as far west as man could go on land to establish the king's rule. Sai had been fair and gradually Pembroke and its shire once again became places in which to be safe and trade well. Only after Gerald had married the Princess Nest and returned to live in the shire did he find favour again with King Henry and become its next Constable, but Luned knew he would never look lovingly again at a silversmith's daughter.

The news of Ninian's imprisonment surged through Pembroke as does flame speeded by a gale. The curious and envious market wanderers with time to spare gathered in front of the silversmith's home and noise increased as they called to each other or shouted abuse at the inhabitants.

Gobbets of mud flew through the air, then stones, ordure, whatever came to hand which could hammer on the door and leave a mark of the filth in men's minds. Within the house Luned encouraged her children to be calm and carry out their small tasks as they would do on any ordinary day.

Deris worried in the kitchen, going again and again to the boxes and pots where food was stored and wondering how long they could stay shut away and not starve. Gwri was her ally, climbing the high wooden fence of the yard to a neighbour's house and running through the side passage from that home to get behind the crowd and to the baker's for fresh bread.

"Gwri! Come in, lad, come in," was Cynfan's welcome. "I can hear the visitors your mistress must endure but they are only the town's fools and sots. It will soon be over and can certainly not last past curfew," he added, refusing to try the French words. "Is it true the shire reeve's men wrecked Ninian's home?"

"Aye, sir, it is. Such a mess you have never seen. Stools and tables broken, beds torn apart and in the kitchen all the food the mistress had tossed everywhere."

"What did they seek?"

"Two silver goblets, the shire reeve said. I watched Margan and the master make them and when the reeve first came to Pembroke he inspected the ware in the master's shop and chose the goblets – said they were the best quality silver he had seen in a long time."

"Why would Ninian steal them back?"

Gwri was stunted by starvation and would always appear a scrawny, red-headed child but it was a man's frown he now wore. "I have never seen the master be aught but honest. Why does an honest man steal, sir?"

Cynfan was big and broad-chested, his hair whitened with flour making his face redder than ever. Silently, he pulled at his chin. "Strange it is, lad – if he did indeed thieve from the reeve."

Shaking his head, Gwri looked at Cynfan with sad eyes. "He must have done, sir. The reeve's men found one of them hidden amongst the master's old clothes."

"Did they indeed," Cynfan said softly. "And when was Ninian supposed to have removed two hefty pieces of silver from under the noses of a castle full of Franks?"

"Yesterday, sir. He went to the castle to see Mistress Mabli and was kept waiting where a steward was cleaning silver."

"Even more strange," Cynfan said slowly. "Did he return to his home burdened in any way?"

"No, nor did he go to where he sleeps and keeps his clothes."

"He must have gone to the yard before he slept."

"Aye, and the shire reeve insisted all must be dug up – even the privy pit."

"A real mystery, Gwri, one which leaves your mistress alone in the house with her children and only you and Deris to defend her."

"No, sir. Sulien is insisting he sleeps there now. The mistress does not want it but the crowd gathered and it made her cry, all the stones hitting her home and threatening her children."

"Has she agreed with Sulien's plan?"

Gwri shrugged his shoulders. "She is waiting until the evening to decide," he said, and Cynfan was silent for a long moment.

"Mistress Mabli?" he asked at last. "Did Ninian meet with her yesterday?"

"No, sir. She had already gone to Carew early – even before my master was admitted to the castle."

Cynfan smiled reassuringly at the little man who would always be treated as a boy. He put an arm round the narrow shoulders. "We must all endure unpleasantness when the

Constable is from home but he will return. Until then, carry all the bread you can back to your mistress. The smell of a good, fresh loaf will hearten her."

Cynfan was not the only one concerned for Luned and her children besieged in their own home. At the far end of Pembroke the roadway widened and wooden houses, some solidly built, fronted long gardens which reached the palisades of the east side of Pembroke. From one of these dwellings emerged a small, neat woman in a dove grey tunic, her kerchief white and wound round her hair and throat revealing plain but contented features.

Ceinwen was a familiar figure as she carried a covered basket and walked steadily through the loose crowd thronging the roadway leading towards the castle. Traders greeted her with respect, women nodded, some even bobbing a curtsy, while men cleared a path for her and one drunken farmer was clouted hard around the head to stop the flow of crude oaths spilling from dribbling lips.

When she reached the silversmith's home the rabble ceased its shouting and parted to allow her to reach the door, Ceinwen's thanks and a 'God be with you' easing her way. A gentle knocking and a quiet explanation of her visit had Luned lifting the bar and inviting her visitor to enter. Slowly, quietly, the crowd dwindled and peace was restored, the flotsam of Pembroke's trading day ebbing away.

"I heard your girl, Deris, was unable to get to market today so I have brought what may keep you all fed this night."

Ceinwen had gone straight to the kitchen, the heart of the home. From her basket came eggs, butter, fresh cheese of her own making, but it was Ceinwen's smile that was of the greatest benefit to Luned, yet was her undoing. She found it hard to hold back her tears, fighting to be as pleasant to her guest as she could.

Ceinwen understood but did not burden the sorrowing

woman with unnecessary words. "I know from Deris you have a nanny in milk so the children will thrive – and such fine children you have. How old is Meleri now? And Walter, such a tall boy and so like his father. You have every reason for pride in your little family."

"It will not be complete until William comes home – and my father."

"As they surely will, in God's good time," Ceinwen said quietly. "Is that what ails you?"

Luned clenched her fingers together, trying to still their shaking. "First William, then my father. Both are innocent yet now they are imprisoned and I can do nothing – nothing!"

Ceinwen led Luned to a stool near the fire, persuading her to sit while she knelt beside her. "William is with Nest, cariad. I know her and she will be caring for him as would you."

"How can she?" Luned protested. "She is not his mother!" Her voice was shrill, shaking with her fear.

Ceinwen's arms were around the distraught woman. "I have seen Nest with children she has not birthed. To her, every one is precious. As the years passed too many loved by Nest have been slain by their own kin – indeed, King Henry himself was not a good man to have as a brother. Nest saw death all around her as she grew and would have all the young ones growing in love and care of each other, whether brothers and sisters, cousins, whatever. She believes that only by following that path can we throw off the evils of the past."

Many had told Luned the princess would ensure William's safety but only now in the warmth of her own kitchen did the words of a quiet woman convince her.

"Then there is your father." Ceinwen was, above all, practical. "I have known Ninian since he first came to Pembroke and I respect the man he is. A thief? Never! There has been mischief done and he has been chosen to pay the price. Trust in the good Lord, my dear friend. Days and nights will be hard for everyone in this house but with God's help all will become clear."

"My father is not young – can he live that long?" Luned asked, her deep fear exposed.

Ceinwen smiled. "Remember, the shire reeve will have his goblet."

Luned was still, her thoughts sluggish but gradually allowing her to accept Ceinwen's reasoning. The younger woman shook her head. "He is an old man and was promised flogging until he confessed but if he is innocent, how can he give up what he does not have?"

"When I leave you I will go to the castle. The guards know me and my concern for the welfare of the prisoners they hold. I may not be able to speak with Ninian but it will be good for his jailers to know someone asks about him every day."

It was on such a mission more than ten years before that Ceinwen had encountered the pitiful wreck of a man who had been a glorious prince of Brycheiniog. Nest's brother, Hywel, had been captured at the battle of Aberdare, blinded and castrated to make him helpless and then sent to rot in the far west castle of Pembroke. Ceinwen had fed him, talked to him and helped Hywel regain his reason. She had cared for him as a mother and then loved him as a wife.

"Asks? Who asks?" Sulien demanded to know as he stood at the door leading into the kitchen from the workshop.

"I do," Ceinwen said quietly. "It is not unusual for me to do so and I am usually told the truth."

"There is no need, mistress. In Ninian's unfortunate absence I will take care of his family – and his business." There was no mistaking the easy assumption of authority, nor the man's natural arrogance.

Luned stiffened and was upright on her stool. "Thank you, Sulien, but this is my home and I will order it. I am grateful for your help with the silverworking and my father trusted you to do as he would, but how this family goes on from day to day will be my concern."

With difficulty, Sulien reined in his temper. "As you wish, mistress, but I must insist I sleep here tonight so you and your children are undisturbed by any violence from the crowd outside."

Tegan had padded towards Ceinwen and sat by her. He lifted his head, his eyes never leaving Sulien's face. Ceinwen put out a hand and laid it on the brow of the great hound. It was a gentle benison for a friend and Tegan was content.

"If your mistress does not wish it, there will be no need for you to stay away from your friends this night," Ceinwen told Sulien. "The angry horde outside is dispersing and Ninian has made this house a fortress so his family will be quite safe. I will go now and do what I can with those who have Ninian." Ceinwen stood and smiled at Luned. "Have no fear, cariad," she said, "the answer to this mystery will soon be found."

Only when Sulien had reluctantly left the kitchen did Luned unbar the main door. There was no one loitering outside, only a few people walking towards the slope which led down past the castle's palisades towards the water and waiting coracles.

Ceinwen stepped carefully across the ruts and holes which made up the road between Ninian's house and the castle. It was a short distance and the puzzle which caused her to frown had not been solved by the time she approached the gatehouse. 'Why,' she kept asking herself silently, 'was Sulien so angry the crowd had gone home?'

Roger fitzHugh was a very young man but one in great danger of an apoplexy. When he heard the woman, Ceinwen, was visiting the newest prisoner, his temper and his blood boiled until his men feared for him. It did not cool him to be told she was used to the stew of smells and degradation where the worst of men were chained, nor that she had the ear of the Constable.

"I govern here! It is my word which counts – and you would all do well to remember it!"

Fury was added to fury as the shire reeve struggled to find Welsh words which did not make his listeners laugh behind their hands. Did the idiots not realise they were a beaten people? They should be made to speak the good French as did he and everyone now of importance in this accursed country, yet it was not so. Welsh was still the language used each day and even the conquerors must turn their tongues around its strange sounds.

Striding about the great hall of Pembroke's castle, fitz-Hugh remembered the king's court of Westminster and the elegant French which hovered in the air like music. Outside the walls of Westminster Hall, the wretches who ran bare-foot through the streets of London cackled at each other in their barbaric English. Like these peasants in Pembroke, the ignorant fools refused to speak in the master tongue.

The shire reeve could no longer contain his anger and marched to the prison to confront the ignorant female who had so annoyed him. When the jailer unlooked the door and he entered it was to see a small woman helping the silver-smith cover his back.

"Ma dame!"

She took no notice of him, continuing to ease the rags of a nightshirt over the wounds left by a whip. Only when her task was complete and Ninian could sit in reasonable comfort did she stand erect and face Roger fitzHugh.

"Sir?"

Once more he struggled for the Welsh and told her, as harshly as he could, she intruded and risked being im-prisoned herself for displeasing him. He saw that she was a plain woman and that there was no change to her calm expression. "Do you understand?" he asked her in his awkward Welsh.

"Oh, yes, sir. You have the men and the force to imprison anyone you choose. You believe you answer to no one." She smiled. "There is always God, sir. Always."

"Do you try to teach me?"

"No, sir, there should be no need," she answered in passable French and surprised the reeve. Ceinwen allowed herself a small smile. "When the castle was first built here few of your people could talk as we do. I did what must be done."

"You suggest I do?" he asked her haughtily.

Ceinwen nodded. "There are two things of importance for you, sir. Firstly, should Ninian be whipped until he dies, his death will lose you your goblet – if he is the thief."

The shire reeve pulled at his chin, unwilling to let the woman see her words made sense. "And the other?" he asked, trying to sound bored.

"You know Sir Gerald de Windsor is a major strength in this part of the world. He has many influential friends in the shire – and at your king's court. Ninian houses and is kin to three of Sir Gerald's children and their mother."

Roger fitzHugh's upper lip curled in a sneer. "The Constable's concubine and his bastards!"

"Bastard," Ceinwen said quietly in her careful French. "The word is an insult in your world – yet your Conqueror was a bastard." It amused her to see the reeve's annoyance. "Here, our law allows that each child accepted by its father is a full member of that man's family – as though born in a Christian marriage, with all the rights that carries."

The reeve waved an impatient hand. "I have been told such ancient ways too often. It remains that the grandfather of the Constable's bastards is a thief!"

"Is he, sir? Ninian is a very clever man and has always been honest in his dealings. He would not steal from you." Ceinwen tilted her head a little and gazed at the shire reeve. "If you are right and he did take your goblets, you must remember he is not a fool – your men would never have found the silver piece in Ninian's own bedspace."

She was trying to tell him something but Roger fitzHugh could not understand her reasoning. "Ma dame?"

Ceinwen searched for the right French words. "Strange, is it not? Manon, wife of Gerwyn, the tanner." She watched the reeve become uneasy. "Someone would have used you, sir, to kill Manon for him."

Roger fitzHugh was restless, not meeting her gaze. "You say . . .?"

Ceinwen's small hand pointed beyond the castle's palisades. "Is there a man in the town who would use you again?"

"Never!"

"No, sir? It is wise for us all to be on guard during these days of treachery."

"Perhaps so – but Ninian remains in chains until my goblet is returned!"

By that evening's couvre feu, Ceinwen had found a respectable widow to stay with Luned and her children until Ninian was home again. Anwen had buried a husband who had worked at the tannery until age and a sudden illness robbed her of him. She lived in Pembroke with her son and his family, sleeping in a corner and helping with the children, but was glad to be of use in the silversmith's house and earn coppers which would help see her son's brood safely through the next winter.

It was a good arrangement. Deris had an extra pair of hands to help restore the home to its original order and Luned could be independent of any unwanted offers. Everyone was agreed it was to be for a short time, the shire reeve would come to his senses and send Ninian back where he belonged, but the days passed and Luned became a familiar figure waiting at the castle gates to be allowed through to carry food and clothes to her father.

Early on she had been distressed to see how much her

92

father suffered. The wounds on his back healed, thanks to a salve Ceinwen gave her for him. It was the fleas which added almost unbearably to his agony.

"Have no worry, mistress," Anwen insisted to Luned. "I will find ways for him to defeat the tiniest of God's creatures who aid the devil in making a man itch so."

She was as good as her word, bringing wormwood which had been soaked in seawater and then dried. Pounded and sprinkled amongst his clothes it led to fewer bites but the other inhabitants chained to posts along with Ninian were a very good source of strong and healthy vermin.

"I was at the leather shop and asked for help from young Nudd," Anwen explained. "My man talked of him and his ways with herbs after Gerwyn, the tanner, found the poor lad in the woods." She handed Luned a small clay pot. "A balm, mistress. Nudd says it will ease the burning around the bites. Yew and celandine beaten with stale piss, that young Nudd said it was. Wonderful what he knows. Before curfew, Nudd is coming with a hedgepig. He will show Gwri how to roast it out the back and collect all the fat running from the beast. If your father lays sticks and rags coated in the fat alongside him as he sleeps, the nasty little creatures will be drawn away from his skin. Mind you, if the master has such blood as is sweet to the little nippers, they may be loath to leave him."

Luned was bewildered by it all but did as she was bid and Ninian's days and nights became a little easier. She had followed Ceinwen's advice and carried food to her father each day, refusing Brede's offer to take it to the prisoner. Instinctively, she knew the reeve's man would sell off the victuals provided and her father would go hungry.

As far as she could, Luned kept abreast with all the work being carried on in the smithy. Much of the activity was familiar to her and had been since she was a small child peeping wide-eyed at her father's movements among the crucibles. Sulien did not object to her watching him, going out of his way to welcome her, be courteous. He was careful not to intrude while Anwen sat in the kitchen at mealtimes until the news came one morning that Anwen's son had been found by the reeve's men, breathing strangely after a savage blow to the head.

"They tell me my son was drunk in a tavern, mistress," she told Luned, "but he never spends a copper there, keeping every mite he earns for his young 'uns. I must go and be with them now. I have been happy with you all but my son –"

In the short time Anwen had been at the silversmith's, she had bloomed, enough food in her to fatten her a little and give a shine to her skin. Luned embraced her, said she understood and was sorry to see her go.

"I will pray for your son, as you have prayed for mine – and God go with you."

Also with the woman went coin to help the family through the next few days.

In the quiet of the kitchen, Deris shook her head. "If Anwen's son was never in a tavern in his life, how could he be found drunk in one? And who found him?"

"The reeve's men, after a brawl."

"Most of Pembroke will be hard put to believe that, mistress," Deris said with a snort as she raked the fire and piled it with fresh logs.

Luned collected clothes from Walter's shelf and began sorting them. He was growing fast and she must see about ordering him new tunics, shirts, hose. It would be sensible to let him wear his brother's old garments but it would be an acceptance William was not coming back to wear them and Luned was not prepared to take that irrevocable step. Instead she held up to the light tunics which were definitely badly worn, wondering about patches, darning, as her mind escaped to more pressing problems.

Should she replace Anwen? The extra company had been welcome in her father's absence and there had been no crowds at the door, no abuse shouted at her whenever she ventured forth. Her thoughts were disturbed by a banging at the door, Deris hurrying to find the cause. Luned heard voices, a man's, urgent, forceful.

"Two men from the priory, mistress," Deris thrust her hands into imaginary sleeves.

"Two of the holy brothers to see me?"

Deris nodded. "The ones who get the baskets filled with any food left on the stalls."

The baskets were propped just inside the passageway and Luned invited the two habited brothers into the formality of the living room. They would not sit and she faced them, wondering why she felt the need to be wary.

"Before I left my brothers this morning, I had speech with the prior," began the one she had heard demanding entrance. He was small and stout, his Welsh good but his manner pompous and offensive. "I am Brother Paulinus and this is Brother Martin," he said, indicating his companion who was tall, raw-boned and had the expression of a simpleton, although his dark habit and cowl gave him a aura of menace.

"Father Prior is most concerned, mistress," Brother Paulinus continued, apparently happy to reprimand his listener. "The silver ordered for the priory. With your father locked up a thief the sale to the holy father is in grave doubt."

"My father is not a thief!" Luned burst out.

"No? Then why has the shire reeve had him in chains these past days – or is it weeks? The prior has allowed ample time for the silversmith to be cleared of a wrong accusation but the time has come to tell you the holy father is most displeased."

"As I am, sir, that my father still languishes because of his enemy."

"Enemy, mistress?"

"Aye, brother, he who stole the reeve's goblets and placed one in my father's belongings."

Brother Paulinus was unaccustomed to laughing but his sneer was fast and well practised. "A useful story, mistress, but the reeve assures the prior the silversmith had opportunity on the day of the theft to remove two costly pieces of silverware. One has been found but not the other. Your father is more clever than we thought."

"Or innocent and badly served by someone with evil intentions!"

"Hardly likely," he said dismissively, "especially in such a household as this is."

"Sir!"

"You do have children?"

"Three," Luned said, holding herself proudly as she thought of the little ones who had made her life joyous. "One is at present a captive with the Princess Nest."

"Ah, yes, the king's whore. And you, mistress, you have borne children outside wedlock. You could be said to be the Constable's whore."

It was a moment of danger and Luned made sure there was no change in her expression. She made herself breathe slowly, steadily, as she kept her lips in a pleasant line and raised her eyes to stare at the fat little man.

"It is a measure of how your own mind works, brother, that you label me so. Sir Gerald has been all that is honourable to me and to his children. I would be grateful if you could, while you are in my house, at least attempt a modicum of courtesy."

He frowned, unsettled by her refusal to be riled by his words. "It still remains that you live here, kept by a man married to another, and with no protection from a husband now your father is imprisoned and likely to stay so because of his stubborn refusal to admit his crime."

"Your mind is more twisted than I thought, Brother Paulinus. Is this how you do the bidding of your superior?

Confuse and bedevil those you encounter? Tell me, do you do so at your master's behest?"

"No! Father Prior is all that is courteous. After matins he asked me to visit you today because you and your children would be alone in the world. I was to bring you comfort and suggest that marriage to a good man could establish you as a worthy citizen of this town and help maintain your father's trade and good will."

"So, if I marry to suit the prior, he will continue to buy silver from this workshop?"

"That is so – but not at the same price as when your father still had his freedom and his good name. Remember, it is important that when all are gathered at the altar in the priory, the silver used at that table must have come from a reputable establishment."

"As it does now," she reminded him. "Tell me, has the prior selected a husband for me?"

"The only one who comes to my mind is the journeyman working here. He is a capable silversmith and has good French so he is cultured enough for high standing in this new town."

"You know he speaks French well?"

"Aye, mistress, he always uses the proper language when talking with Father Prior."

It was with great relief that Luned shut the door behind her unwelcome visitors but the words 'after matins' returned again and again to haunt her. How could the prior have known then that she was alone again? It was as they sat at their midday meal men had rushed to the silversmith's to tell Anwen of the discovery of her son's unconscious body.

Chapter Six

Wherever she turned, Luned felt her life was menaced. Despairing, she shut herself away from everyone outside her family and its workers. Only Sulien tried to reach her, to insist he should stay for their protection, but Deris understood her mistress's misery and kept him away.

Luned stayed where she was until she heard the big door slam and the bars drop into place, only then could she trust herself to go to the kitchen and her children. They had been wary of her, unused to seeing their mother tight with a mixture of anger and fear. Deris had fed them all and as they were seated around the table, their prayers that night before bed included Anwen and her son.

"Nudd is looking after him," Gwri said in a quiet moment and surprised them all.

"Nudd? Your friend?" Luned asked.

Gwri nodded. "He is very good and will send a message to Mistress Mabli at Carew if he needs help."

"I did not think the mediciner so thick with Nudd," Deris said.

Gwri scraped his spoon round the bowl and Deris ladled more broth into it. "Nudd knows much," the boy added. "He finds plants Mistress Mabli needs and she shows him how she prepares them for use. Other things she teaches him, too."

"Such as?" Luned wanted to know.

A shrug of Gwri's shoulders was her answer. "They know," he said at last. "She did tell him her father would have wanted Nudd working with him."

"But Mistress Mabli's father was King Rhys's physician!"

"Aye," Gwri said cheerfully and finished his broth.

Only her children's arms about her after they had said their prayers before sleep eased the tightness in Luned. She lay in her bed and heard their breathing, Deris's distant snores, but still she lay unmoving, eyes seeing nothing in the darkness.

So many men seemed intent on squeezing her into a way of life she did not want. The fool, Roger fitzHugh, and his ridiculous story of her father being a thief. Such stupidity in a reeve, but because of him her father lay in chains in a hell-hole in the castle. Luned was anxious for Ninian, afraid the misery of the fleas would bring a fever and everyone knew fevers in prisons killed more than any hangman or axeman could. If he died, she would be alone. Did that thought please the prior? Alone, could she be persuaded to take less reward for the silver going to the priory altar? Surely no man in holy orders could behave so?

A dog fox barking in the woods beyond the stream was her companion in the dark, then the animal quietened and once more Luned was alone with her thoughts.

How had it all happened? Margan becoming ill, Sulien beginning work in the smithy, chance happenings which had led to the threat she now felt. And why was it now important she was married? Did no one understand? Great things, frightening things, were happening away from the small world which was the castle and the town of Pembroke. Her life and the lives of everyone she knew could be turned upside down and wrecked by the activities of those important ones who lived so far away.

Passing years had not eased the pain of that first loss of Gerald and now there was talk of her marrying. How could she? The part of her to which a husband had a right was a shrivelled wisp of what had been, its death throes the agony caused by the sight of the man she had loved with his wife. Nest was a king's daughter and had been a king's mistress, made wealthy by a royal dowry.

Luned turned restlessly on her pallet, the night warm and a thin blanket entangling. If only Nest could stay away but William was with Nest. If the princess never returned to Pembroke, neither would Luned's son. Her life and William's were enmeshed with Nest and those who would have her.

She remembered the day of William's birth, the baby warm in her arms and pain already forgotten. Gerald had taken the squirming bundle from her and held it high, his delight in his first-born son clear for all to see.

William.

William was the person who was most important. The prior might have power but not even he could dictate a different father for her son. Certainty invaded an exhausted woman and she slept.

The smell of freshly baked bread heartened Luned. It was a new day and the house already redolent with the knowledge men and women had been at work in Pembroke and all was well for them. Deris was unloading her basket, butter still damp from the farm. Gwri came in with a ewer of frothing milk from the nanny as Walter and Meleri, their faces scrubbed, their teeth scoured by hazel twigs, peered into Deris's deep basket.

"Anwen's daughter was at the bakeshop."

Luned turned to the girl with quick sympathy. "How was she? Did she say aught of her brother?"

"She was hopeful," Deris said slowly, "especially since Nudd took a knife to the wound."

Luned was shocked. "He did what?"

Everyone in the room was staring at Deris and the girl nodded.

"In the night. Eynon, Anwen's son, was making strange noises as he breathed so Nudd called for salt and hot water. When they were mixed he soaked in it his hands and the knife which he had sharpened. After that he called for extra candles and when he had all the light possible he made Anwen and her son's wife hold Eynon's head steady. When he was sure, Nudd slid the point of his knife into the place where the blow had been struck." Deris pointed to a spot on the back of her own head. "Nudd had already cut away the hair so he could see the size of the wound. Once the knife was inside Eynon's skull Nudd very slowly lifted the edge of the bone, easing it up until it was level with the rest."

"How long did it take?" Gwri asked.

"How did Nudd know what to do?" Walter echoed.

"I asked that myself," Deris said. "Gwen told me that when he lived in the wild Nudd had watched shepherds with sheep who stumbled and fell, the shepherds using a knife to open the front of the sheep's head and pull out the lump which they knew caused the animal such distress. I think Nudd must have helped some of the shepherds – he was so quick with Eynon."

"What then?" Luned wanted to know.

"A straw," Deris told her, frowning as she emptied the basket and began stowing its contents on the rightful shelves. "Nudd soaked a long piece of straw in the salt and water, then he put one end into the wound where the knife had been. He sucked the other end."

A variety of disbelieving noises resulted from her listeners.

"What came out he let flow into his hand, gazed at it, then tipped it into a basin he had ready. At first it was tiny chunks like liver, Eynon's sister said, then thin blood, then a clear liquid. After that Nudd cut the straw and held what was left in the wound with clean linen."

"Nudd?" Luned asked softly. For so long the boy had been regarded as the town's idiot, his looks and his manners

101

no encouragement to believe he had a mind of any kind. Only when the tanner's wife had been nearly done to death by the shire reeve and town gossip had Nudd begun to grow in stature. Now this. "Eynon. How is he?"

"His sister says he breathes like a baby and is sleeping. Nudd watches over him at all times and keeps changing the linen, staring at what discolours it. Anwen is so happy her son is better."

"What next?" Luned wondered aloud.

"Mistress Mabli. The Fleming from the castle was to ride for her. She will be in Pembroke again to look over Nudd's handiwork and to medicine Eynon – as good as any king could be."

"How strange," Luned began as she watched the others prepare to break their fasts, "we see the noisy rabble which floods through Pembroke when there is a market. Many are decent traders but they attract the feckless and the workshy who drift around looking for excitement as well as something for nothing."

"You are right, mistress," Deris agreed. "Those useless ones were the crowd who made your ears ring with foul language the day the shire reeve took away the master. Ashamed of living in Pembroke, I was."

"But they are not Pembroke people, are they? From the gwennies and the hedges around the town they come to see what they can scavenge, yet underneath all that activity is a web like that of many spiders. Have you watched a spider on its web, Deris? Our spiders are Pembroke's own people. They live in the town, work hard for it, maybe even love it. Eynon is injured and Nudd goes to help, the Fleming rides to fetch Mistress Mabli –"

"While Cynfan, the baker, gives her free bread and meat from his oven. Then there is Prince Hywel's woman, at Anwen's door as soon as she heard of the trouble, Sennen, the whore, too."

"So, there is another Pembroke," Luned said, "a town of good people who make little noise." She sighed. "I wish they could help my father."

For so long Luned and her father had kept themselves aloof, their lives lived apart from the rest of the town.

Gwri touched her arm. "Mistress, you and the master are real Pembroke."

"And will they help us, Gwri?"

The boy nodded, smiling shyly, and Luned was strangely reassured.

They heard a key turn in a lock, a door open and close, then strong footsteps in the passage before Sulien was with them. He bade them all a good morning.

"Today you look more content, mistress. Is there a reason?" She lifted her eyes to meet his and he saw a new colour in her skin enhancing her looks.

"We have all been thanking the good Lord," she told him. "Anwen's son, in God's good time, is like to recover."

A fleeting emotion rose and was hidden. "Good reason indeed, mistress. I join my thanks with yours. I had heard the man like to die very soon. It must be a miracle he lives."

"Aye, it is – a miracle called Nudd – and Mistress Mabli is to come and speed Eynon's return to health. Pembroke people are fortunate in their friends."

Sulien nodded his agreement and went directly to the workshop as Luned set her children their morning tasks. Meleri was to help Deris clear the table and begin to clean and chop the vegetables for the evening's pot while Walter saw to Tegan, feeding the dog, cleaning his water bowl and filling it. Gwri she sent to the yard to tidy the stack of firewood, so Luned was on her own when she pushed open the door of the workshop.

"You need me, mistress?" Sulien said with a frown. "I have asked to be left alone here to work as I should."

103

"You will admit I respected your wish – until I was visited yesterday by the prior's mouthpiece and much became clear."

Sulien waited. Used to the ways of the world and of women, he tried to decide what Luned intended but the face she presented was new to him.

Calm, beautiful, she showed no hesitations, no weaknesses. "You took it upon yourself to visit the prior on my behalf. Did I ask you to do so?" She gazed at him, silently demanding an honest answer.

"You have been much occupied with worry for your son, and now your father."

"And I trusted you. Do you know why?"

Again, Sulien waited.

"Because my father had faith in you and said you were a good silversmith. Amongst our people men – and women – who work with metal of any kind have a high standing. Indeed, in the old days, we even had our own god," she added lightly. "You have skill." Luned picked up a piece of silverware fresh from the mould and ready to be polished. "Take this piece." It was a large paten and she turned the dish over. "See, it already carries my father's mark – a sign known throughout Wales and indeed England too. It stands for value yet you talked to the prior of charging him less for it than would my father."

The tall man stepped towards her but Luned held up her hand.

"I grew up in this place," she said softly. "My father had no son to show the ways of his trade but as a child I learned at his side." Lifting the paten to her mouth she bit into it, her strong, white teeth firm against the silver rim. When she removed the paten she examined the marks she had left. "Hardly a trace, Sulien. With the high quality of the silver my father sells, the marks of my teeth should be clear. If the metal was pure, my bite would have gone deep indeed and the silver would be too soft for usage. I was very young when I learned copper is added to the molten metal to harden the silver and a man as careful as my father knew the best balance of metals. This silver is too hard, there is too much copper – far too much to be worthy of my father's mark."

Before Sulien could stop her, Luned reached for a sharp chisel and gouged deep marks across the upper surface of the paten, then she handed it to him.

"Melt it down and make spoons, large or small does not matter. They will sell well if you make moulds which have a saint on the handle – but do not use my father's mark! In his absence this is my silversmith's business and I am the guardian of his good name. Do you understand?"

"You are a woman," he reminded her, "and unable to manage alone."

Her head was held high and proud. "When you learned to speak as do the Franks you learned also their ways and their laws, but I am not a Frank. The women of our people have always been equal to any man whether it be in craft, in trade or in battle. You will make another mould for the paten and when it is ready I will come and watch you mix in the copper."

"There is no need –"

"There is every need," she reminded him. "I know better than anyone how my father decided the mix was right for his good silver. I will decide the moment and I will watch you pour the metals. Only when I am satisfied will I allow you to stamp my father's mark. After that, I will take it to the prior myself and see he pays the original price agreed with my father."

Deris was pleased with the change in her mistress but horrified Luned had every intention of facing the prior and telling him what she thought of his behaviour.

"No! He is a canny man and can harm you!" the little maid insisted. "Look what he nearly did to Mistress Manon, the tanner's wife — well, tanner's widow. Almost hanged, she was, and that only over a piece of land."

"Deris, since my father was taken away, I have been beset on all sides. It is enough. If the prior is as powerful as you say, then I will be starting with the biggest bully in Pembroke."

No arguments could persuade Luned to change her mind but she did agree that Walter should go with her to the monks' town and the priory. In a satchel Deris packed bread and cheese, "In case he keeps you waiting to annoy you."

Gwen from the leather shop was in the silversmith's kitchen to keep Deris company. Heledd, the daughter of Mistress Manon and her dead husband, Gerwyn, was already in the sitting room with Meleri, the girls playing at being grown-ups.

Walter was excited, escorting his mother while she talked to the head of the priory his father had helped build for his master, Sir Arnulf. He washed as carefully as he had been taught, put on his best shirt and tunic, cleaned the mud from his boots and was ready. Deris gasped when she saw him look so tall and manly and they both were silenced when Luned appeared, her purple tunic of the finest linen and the kerchief covering her head and throat held in place by an embroidered band.

"Mistress, you look so fine," Deris whispered. The girl was too young to remember when Luned was the Constable's love, dressed and jewelled to sup with the most important people in the shire. Today there was a glimpse of that Luned, her cheeks lit with a glow, not of love but a fierceness to defend her kin and her home.

Even the coracler wiped the seats of his small craft and helped Luned as she stepped in, watched by the idlers at the quay. Walter felt a sense of occasion, such as he had missed when William sailed with their father at the turn of the year and from his sickbed Walter could only hear the noise and the cheering as the vessel left Pembroke for the open sea and then the Teifi river.

On the far bank of the narrow river, the walk up to the priory was short but steep, the roadway rough with stones embedded in the solid earth. Walter carried the satchel and held his mother's hand as they made their way, every step of it gawped at by women in grubby tunics and kerchiefs, men toothless and ragged, all waiting for alms from the gatekeeper. The priory was a collection of small, squat wooden buildings set around the church built of stone and with a wooden roof. Little light penetrated the thick wall and when Luned had stated her business, mother and son must wait in the courtyard surrounded by indigents in a long line which would move only when the vast cauldrons of soup appeared.

"What do you think William is doing?" Walter wanted to know.

It was a favourite question and they played the game they had devised, imagining the captive's life so the family kept him in their minds and saw him happy.

"Meleri will be showing that child her dolls," the boy said dismissively.

His mother smiled. Sometimes he was so like his father. "Heledd is a nice child, Deris says, and Gwen is with them."

"The children will play and the servants will gossip," Walter decided, not knowing he had the expression of the Constable as well as his mannerisms.

Perhaps that was what persuaded the prior's clerk to fetch them to an audience. The room to which they were led was part of the church's structure, its stone walls comfortably cool on such a warm day. Large candles lit the desk at which sat the prior, his silvered head bent over his papers. The clerk ushered them to stools and still the prior ignored them. Walter was annoyed. How could any man be so rude to his mother, especially one who prided himself on his courtesy? Luned touched Walter's arm and when he turned to her he saw her smile. She knew the game and how to play it. Steepling her fingers she bent her head in prayer, oblivious to the movements of the prior.

"You wished to see me, ma dame?" he asked at last in his French which was of the king's court.

"I did, Father Prior, since you have taken the trouble to try and involve yourself in my life." Her French was not as polished as his, coming from Gerald and his friends.

"A woman alone, ma dame, I must do all I can to serve God's will and see you protected."

As the son of a Frank, Walter knew enough of their language to follow what was being said.

"My father trusted you, as you did him – or so I understood – yet you were prepared to deal with a servant to pay less for the silver you had ordered? Shame on you, sir."

Walter enjoyed the cut and thrust, never having seen his mother being so high-handed. He gathered 'Ninian's mark' was of special significance and was puzzled. It was on a tool his grandfather used and which he and William had played with many times. Now he understood it was a sign of quality, the mark as good as coin.

"The servant was mistaken," Luned informed the prior whose long, slender fingers had been clasped together gracefully but were now gripped tightly. "He could only offer you a lower price for goods containing less silver than my father would approve."

"But if it bears Ninian's mark –"

"No, sir! No silver objects of any kind will leave the workshop bearing that mark unless they contain their full quota of silver! You have been misled."

"How can you, a woman –"

"By the law of my people I am the silversmith in my father's absence."

The prior stood, his tall, lean, frame elegant in a habit

which did not look as coarse as those of his brothers. "How can you know what is good and bad silver?"

"As a child I grew in my father's workshop, watched as he tended his crucibles, made his moulds. A son learns as he stands beside his father and I learned. While my father lies in the castle there is no one better than I to prepare the best silver. Others may help, Father Prior, but I will decide as my father taught me."

The first morning Luned began work, Sulien was surprised to find her already at the crucibles when he arrived.

"You know I prefer to work on my own, mistress," he began, but she held up her hand.

"Like my father, I trusted you, Sulien, until you took it upon yourself to think of this establishment as your own. It was then I decided I must take my father's place, yet like him, and because of him, I shall continue to trust you."

Sulien's bow was courteous, as it should be, and it allowed him to hide his thoughts from Luned.

"Gwri has the fires growing hot and I have the pure silver melting," she said cheerfully. "Stand ready with the copper, if you will, and I will tell you how much is needed in a crucible."

Sulien held his flaring anger in check. This was a Luned garbed in the oldest of her tunics, grey wool and a thick leather apron protecting her from flames and sparks, a kerchief holding her hair and baring her face and neck. She was clearly in no mood to listen to any protests.

"Before we ready the silver to be poured, I must check the mould for the paten, mistress."

"I did that at first light. You have done a good job, as far as I can see. Once the paten has cooled and it is free of the mould, I can better determine what rasping and polishing is needed."

He had thought her quiet, a base metal easily turned his way, but this was a woman of iron and one who appeared to know what she was doing. If he said the wrong word now, she could have him walking jobless out into the roadway.

Meleri was chuckling as she helped Gwri sweep and tidy. Like her mother she was dressed for a work day in old clothes, no long hair to get caught in any tools or flames. Walter, too, had climbed into an old shirt and tunic of William's and was gazing at everything his mother did, a hand ready when she needed it. Ninian had taught them all well, Sulien decided. He did as asked and acted the part of journeyman and not silversmith.

Luned could have been an image of her father as she bent over the crucible, gesturing at exactly the right moment for Sulien to sprinkle in the copper. Turning her head slightly, she watched the molten liquid in the crucible seethe and spit and called, "Cease!" when the sputtering reached a certain sound. It was sooner than Sulien would have wished, it seeming more reasonable to him to add extra copper and make more money in the deal afterwards, but he did as he was bid and Luned was satisfied. She did allow him to use the thick gloves to hold the handles of the crucible, Gwri alongside to steady the equipment.

With the paten poured and cooling, Luned turned her attention to the workshop and the moulds to be made for the candlesticks. She inspected the clay, the sand, which would be used, explaining to Sulien the design she wanted for the largest pair of candle holders and the way the simple bands of pattern should be reduced for the smaller pair.

"Gwri will ready the workshop for the morning when you have finished the moulds you can make today. I will see them early in the morning and begin to prepare the silver needed. May I have the key? The one to the door through which you enter?"

Implacably she held out her hand, with a quiet, "Thank you" when she took the iron key. "Gwri will lock the door behind you and open it when you knock in the morning. Should any in the town make a comment as to my behaviour in my father's absence, you can now tell them I am safely locked in each night with only my children and two servants for company."

That set the pattern for the next days. As they worked together Luned learned a new respect for Sulien. Her father had been right, he was a promising silversmith. In turn, Sulien admired Luned for the grace with which she moved, the quickness of her mind, the understanding of the shining metal they birthed in the crucibles, letting it flow at their will. Together they admired the finished paten, the candlesticks, and as equals, discussed at length the design of the chalice.

In spite of the prior's wish to see her married to a man he could turn to his will, Luned was of the same mind she had always been. It was only Sulien who took hope from small signs. Increasingly, they shared smiles as a perfect form emerged first from the mould and then from the polishing. Luned let it be seen more often that she appreciated his work and he was once more sure his plan would be achieved. He was careful to keep his certainty hidden, there were still one or two matters which needed his touch.

Luned knew nothing of this, intent as she was in her new-found enjoyment of silver working. Each morning, after seeing to the precious metal and its pouring, Luned would change her clothes and take food to her father. Sometimes she was joined by Mistress Ceinwen, the two of them bringing comfort to a man despairing of his very existence amongst the criminals and the fleas packing the castle jail.

At every opportunity there were prayers for William, his grandfather's pleas especially heartfelt that the boy he loved should not know the same confinement as a captive as did he. Only in the evenings, when the children were in bed and asleep, Deris and Gwri gossiping by the embers in the kitchen, did Luned hold Tegan's head close to her and allow tears to flow.

*   *   *

111

It had been less than a week since she had visited the prior when Deris brought the news from early morning marketing that Eynon had woken and was beginning to talk normally. With a lighter heart, Luned tightened her kerchief to keep her hair safely stowed away and opened the door of the workshop. Moulds were as she wanted and she had turned to the store of raw silver, unlocking the casket holding it, when she heard a knocking at the main door.

Luned frowned. Sulien should not be trying to come in that way. Now Deris would have to leave the kitchen and see who demanded entry so early. She heard Deris cry out and Luned's breathing almost stopped. News from the castle? Her father?

"Mistress! Come! Come quickly!"

Luned ran and saw beyond Deris a tall, thin figure, its clothes hanging almost in rags. The head rose and Luned's breath failed her.

"William! Dear God be thanked!" she whispered.

Joy and relief illumined her but she held back from clutching William to her when she saw his eyes. With a gesture she silenced Deris and in the quiet of the early morning she held out her hand to her son. Slowly, the boy reached for it and Luned drew him over the threshold. By now Walter and Meleri were close by and she nodded to Deris to close the door. Only when it was barred again did William slowly release his breath. Even in the dimness of the passageway he could see gathered there features he had struggled to remember in the worst of his despair.

"You are safe now, cariad," Luned said gently as she stood close to her son and opened her arms.

He leaned against his mother, smelling her and knowing at last he was home. Luned cradled him, crooning as she rocked. The first of her babies was in her arms at last. Walter and Meleri came close, the boy touching William's shoulder to reassure himself his brother had returned, while Meleri's small hands reached as far as they could around William

112

and her mother, happy her little world was almost complete again.

Deris wiped away her tears, sniffed and became brisk. From the state of William and his clothes, the mistress would soon be demanding hot water in great quantities. She hurried to the kitchen fire, blowing flames from the embers and feeding them with the driest wood. Gwri came from the workshop to see what was happening and gave a little skip of delight. Without being told he hurried to bring in more firewood and fill the largest crocks with water from the rain barrel. Deris sharpened her favourite knife and began cutting slices from a hanging ham until she heard a knocking.

"The side door. Let Sulien in and then go to Cynfan for the first of his bread." She stopped slicing to reach in a pot and hand Gwri coppers for the bread.

"Will I tell Cynfan?"

"It is the best news ever! Tell the whole world, boy!" she exclaimed, tears running afresh as she returned to the ham.

Sulien sensed unexpected happiness, excitement even, and he frowned. "What is happening? Gwri was like a madman, nearly knocking me over in his haste to get out the door – and where is he going? He is supposed to be under my orders in the workshop."

"William is home," Deris said calmly, noticing for the first time that in spite of his scowling Sulien seemed to be in a very cheerful mood already. Usually, he woke with the devil on his back.

Sulien turned and would have gone to see for himself but his way was barred by Deris, brandishing the knife with which she had just sliced cured pig meat.

"Leave them be!"

"No! I should be there."

As the first of the ham slices spat and curled on the skillet, Deris stood firm. A tiny fury in her brown tunic and

113

enveloping apron, she aimed the point of the well-honed knife Sulien's gut.

"The only person William needs to see now is his grand-father and that is not possible, is it?" she hissed at him.

The man was instantly wary, alerted by something in Deris's voice he could not fathom. "Perhaps Ninian may return one day but William should have a man with him."

"Aye, he does, but it must be a man he knows and can trust."

Gwri came running in with hot bread and gasped out the excitement of the news he had taken to Cynfan. He stopped when he saw Deris, her knife pointing with a deadly firmness at Sulien's belly. Silently, Gwri went to stand by Deris.

"Hot bread? Good." Sulien reached for a loaf, tore off a huge crust and picked up the largest slice of ham from the skillet. "Cut more ham, Deris, I am ravenous this morning."

Chapter Seven

Early morning mist had shrouded a ship as it sailed to Pembroke's quay. From the bank on which was the monks' town, coracles crossed the stream, each filled with men and women clutching their wares for market. That time of day there was a steady flow of people and goods up alongside the castle and on to the road through Pembroke town. There they would join with and fight for space with farmers and their wives trudging towards the town from lands towards Lamphey and Stackpole. No one had paid much attention to two men with the look of poorly clad servants, nor the woman with them, her features almost completely obscured by her veil, the boy beside her young, bedraggled and drooping with weariness.

When they had reached the top of the rise from the river, the woman touched the boy on the shoulder, urging him towards the shops and houses to their right. He hesitated, then caught the woman's hand, holding it tightly in both of his before he turned away and walked to the iron-studded door of the largest house.

Nest waited until William's knock was answered. She heard a scream of delight and there was a pause which seemed interminable until she saw a woman's hand reach out to him. Slowly, William stepped forward and inside the house, the door closed. The boy was safe in the haven he had spoken of so longingly when they were alone. She prayed he was prepared to be unmanly enough and cry as a child should when he has despaired. She stifled a sigh and her companions were at first anxious for her but she smiled at them and they knew the boy she had protected for so long was with his family at last.

Henin and Endaf waited for their princess. They were short and stubby, more alike than most brothers, with coarse dark hair blowing in the breeze from the river which even on an early summer morning chilled bones laid bare by little food through their years as slaves. Torn tunics and shirts did little to warm them and their bare feet were gnarled and muddied by such a long journey.

"Come," Nest said to them, "let us go home too."

Above them the guard on the castle gate shouted a warning to his comrades: strangers were approaching, a woman amongst them. They could be spies as Sir Odo had warned, pathetic travellers trying to have the gates opened to let in a horde of raiders!

The woman understood their strange language only too well, having learned it long ago in English castles. She walked up to the main gate and allowed Endaf to beat on it with the stick he had used along the way. There was no sound of bars being lifted, or a key turned in a lock. He beat again, Henin helping his brother with his bare fists. They had all endured so much to reach this place and they would not now be denied.

At last the massive woods yielded and a guard Nest did not recognise strode out. He made sure he was backed by armed men before he approached the odd-looking trio and demanded their names and their business that early in the morning.

Nest explained, first in French and then in Welsh, but the man was puzzled and would not stand aside to let them enter.

"Rolfe! You halfwit!" An older man pushed through the

116

rank of anxious soldiers and was on one knee before his princess. "I have prayed for this moment," he said in Welsh. "Welcome home, my lady."

She did not look like a princess, the hem of her tunic torn by much travel, her boots worn and split, but the tunic was of velvet and the boots of fine leather. Her kerchief was dulled by much washing but it still swathed the face and throat of a great beauty, albeit one who was tired and travel-worn.

"I know you," she said. "Puw, is it not? Your welcome is indeed – welcome," she added and laughed, a gentle sound but with an echo of tears. "Who is in the castle? The Constable?"

Puw shook his head. "No, my lady. He has driven himself and everyone around him to find you. No one is to sleep until you are safe and many a horse has died under its rider in the search for you and the children."

"Where are they?" she asked and he heard the urgency of her need to know.

"Safe, my lady. In Carew. They are well, to be sure, and need only your return to be content."

Nest was relieved and almost sagged as she stood. "So, Mabli is with them?"

"The mistress was, my lady, but she is here, in the town."

The princess was finding it hard to hold back tears. "Dear Mabli, making the sick well – as always. If she can come, I need her now, Puw."

"I will bring her to you –"

Rolfe pushed forward, furious events were happening outside his control. "You stay where you are!" he ordered Puw. "No one moves until I say so."

Puw stood and glared at the man. Struggling with what little French he had he told Rolfe who was at the gate. Reverting to his native Welsh he used few words but even Rolfe understood their meaning. "You hinder this lady and

I will tell the Constable of your stupidity to his wife – then may God help you stay alive!"

There was no more delay. Nest might not be garbed as a princess in King Henry's court, nor even as she once was when the first lady of Pembroke's shire, but servants of every rank heard the whisper racing around the castle and ran to the outer bailey to greet her. Shouts, cheers, clapping, tears, each expressed their relief and delight in their own way. Kitchen boys gawped, stewards beamed, to see the woman who had enchanted them all walk once more towards the curtain of wood which surrounded the inner bailey with its great hall.

Nest called on all her strength to smile at her people, remember names, have her hands grabbed, kissed, watered with tears. Used to captivity, she longed for peace and the solitude she would find in her own room but those who loved her would not let her go.

It seemed an age passed before she stood in the jewel-coloured space which had been hers, but she was still not alone. Maids scurried in with clean towels and clothes hastily removed from a chest. From the kitchens cauldrons of water appeared to be followed by food quickly cooked, the freshest eggs coddled for a lady who must be starving after all the deprivation she had endured. More food was promised as soon as the cooks could prepare it.

Nest smiled her thanks, insisted Henin and Endaf were taken to the kitchens and fed first, then new clothes found for them and a quiet place for sleep. They had guarded her well and ensured she reached Pembroke safely. The man who had been chief steward when Sir Gerald ruled made his promises, silently delighted the jumped-up toad who was the shire reeve's man could stand aside for once.

The door closed and only Nest stood in her room, seeing the tapestries Gerald had found for her, the bed, tables, chairs and stools Pembroke carvers had made beautiful. Thick woollen blankets were waiting for her as were sheepskins made fragrant with washing and perfumed oils. Nest wandered around the space, touching first one thing, then another. The door opened and she turned to see a broad figure in a brown tunic, kerchief firmly draped about an aged and kindly face with a twisted cheek.

"The children?"

Mabli was ever practical, folding her arms upon a sturdy belly. "They are well. William is as angry as his father until you return."

"Maurice? His cough was so bad when he left."

"Good food in the day, hyssop and honey at night – he is recovered."

"Angharad? She was so young to endure it all."

"In body she is well but too quiet and we do not see her smile. For that she needs you, cariad – as we all do. Sir Gerald is a shadow of himself, never stopping for food or sleep. What of his son?"

"Safe with his mother. I saw William go to her. He is – untouched."

Mabli was surprised. "Dear God, cariad, how did you manage that?"

"A bargain made and kept," was all Nest would say.

Mabli opened her arms and Nest walked into an embrace with a sigh. Tears flowed from her, not from sobbing but with the knowledge she need no longer fight to survive nor struggle to keep safe Gerald's son, William.

Not everyone was pleased she had returned. Roger fitzHugh had woken late, as was his habit. Kicking a servant girl from his bed, he demanded hot water before he broke his fast, then dozed until his orders were obeyed.

A noise, noises, woke him. No one had brought his water, and where was the food he expected? Throwing a cloak around his shoulders he put his head out of the door and saw guards, servants, stewards, cooks, hurrying this way and that. No matter what he shouted, he was ignored, and very quickly the shire reeve was ready to whip anyone who came within reach.

The water was scented with herbs and oils, Nest moving luxuriously in the heat. Mabli had fed her the coddled eggs while they were still warm, keeping dishes ready for the table on braziers brought into a room filled with steam. Before she left her bath, Mabli washed Nest's hair, sad to see it so dull and neglected. She made up her mind Nudd must find her the herbs she wanted, until then the precious store of oils must be raided.

"You carry fewer passengers than I feared," Mabli said as she used a fine comb to catch fleas, lice, eggs.

"The raiders took some of my things with us – nothing sensible like fur boots on a night as cold as was that one, but amongst what they grabbed in a hurry was one of your special combs. It helped pass the time."

"Then let us get busy and you dried, my lady. Much longer in that water and you will be as wrinkled as a walnut fresh from its shell."

"I am loath to leave something for which I have longed," Nest told her and Mabli smiled.

"If I promise one each day?"

"Agreed!" Nest stood as she spoke, waiting to be wrapped in the largest of the towels, but Mabli was stricken.

Bruises had developed as if by magic in the hot water and the mediciner could see the brutality with which Owain had shown his captive what he called 'his love for her'. Mabli was careful to make no mention of the marks but held her charge in the towel and very gently patted her dry.

Nest smelled the fragrance left in a familiar old robe and was content to sit, eyes closed, as Mabli rubbed her hair until a thunderous knocking on the door disturbed their peace.

"Reeve Roger, may God be with you," was Mabli's greeting for the very irate young man breathing heavily at the door. She stepped outside the room, pulling the wood close to give Nest privacy.

"Ma dame, the Constable's wife has returned to the castle and I am the last to know?"

"Perhaps no one liked to waken you, reeve. You have a reputation of throwing heavy objects at any who do so."

"I act as castellan! I should have been the first told!"

"No action was needed from you, sir. You could be left to your slumbers."

Swearing at her in French, the shire reeve attempted to push past Mabli, realising too late such a move was not possible.

"Did you wish to speak to the princess?" she asked smoothly.

"Wish, ma dame? I insist!"

"A moment then," she said and opened the door a crack. "The shire reeve would speak with you – if you will allow?"

He did not hear the answer but Mabli swung the door wide and he could see Nest sitting in a carved chair as though on a throne. Her bath still steamed and there were the remains of the food with which she had broken her fast. A dish smeared with egg yolks. Thinly sliced ham curled amongst fresh bread. He looked again. One of his special rolls was all that was left of what should have been his meal!

"It would have been a matter of courtesy for you to have come to me when you arrived in the castle!"

Nest fought hard to hide a smile. The little court popinjay was offended. "Had you been with your men, I would have done so, sir. You could have been of such assistance in informing my husband of our return. The captain of the ship bringing us from St David's made sure messengers were sent in all directions to reach Sir Gerald. I am sure he will be – interested – to hear of the reception I have had from you."

Mabli coughed and turned away to fold towels and napkins. Her lady had learned many ways to deal with men but since being in Owain's care she had sharpened her claws to deadly points.

"I would be grateful if you could send someone to Manorbier," Nest continued. "I would like to see Sir Odo as soon as it can be arranged and I thank you for your welcome, sir."

The princess turned away, picked up a bronzed mirror and examined one side of her face in detail while Mabli made sure she did not look at the discomfited shire reeve. He was about to swing away from the room when there was a disturbance nearby, shouts, cries of alarm, racing footsteps.

Nest gazed at him. "I would like to believe you considered my safe return was good news, sir, but now you may have tidings less fortunate?"

Mabli followed the shire reeve as he went towards the source of the disturbance in the outer bailey. He pushed through a group of his men huddling over something on the ground but did not stay near its centre for long, reeling back through the crowd as if desperate for air. He did not see Mabli as he raced for seclusion behind the walls of a shed from where she could hear him throwing up what food he had enjoyed. Intrigued, the mediciner tried to see what was on the ground.

"Puw?" she called, unwilling to heave aside the crowd.

He straightened and came to her, wiping his face with his hand as he did so. Short and grizzled, he was an able bowman and had fought for King Rhys in his day. "Mistress?"

"The body, who is it?"

"Brede, mistress. The early patrol found him, cooling but the blood still wet. He was lying against a tavern door – the one almost opposite Cynfan's bakeshop."

"So near the castle?"

He nodded. As the men ringed around the dead Brede began to shuffle away awkwardly, Mabli was able to push through and look down on the corpse, studying it carefully. Faces turned towards her, words were mumbled, questions became insistent.

"It was a very keen knife," she said. "The deepest part of the cut across his neck means the man was right-handed."

"Brede was sharp, mistress," a gruff voice said. "Who could take 'im like that?"

"See the top of his head?" The men bent forward, gazing where she pointed. "A mass of loosened hairs. Someone stood behind him and pulled his head back suddenly, exposing the neck. One clean slice and he was gone, all the blood spurting forward. If the attacker immediately pushed the body away, he would have no blood on him."

"Like a slaughterman?" she was asked.

"Aye," Mabli sighed. "Just like a slaughterman, but who?"

"A husband! Brede took any woman he fancied," said one.

"A woman?" suggested another.

Mabli shook her head. "The killer was very tall – look how that hair is pulled up and away."

"Sennen is tall," a gruff voice said slowly, "and, by God, she hated Brede."

"With good reason," another added.

"Who had good reason?" the shire reeve demanded to be told.

"Half the husbands in Pembroke," a young man offered, the shakiness of his words betraying his unease, "and Sennen. She carries a knife."

"Then bring her to me! At once!"

"Wait!" Mabli's voice, deep for a woman, rang in the morning air. "No woman carries a knife as sharp as the one used on this man, and is this Sennen not the woman who stood up to Brede when he was determined to break her spirit? If gossip is true, she bested him so why kill him? No, reeve, if Sennen was lying there dead I would say Brede had killed her because he had a reason – revenge. Who wanted your man dead? What has he been doing which would earn him the ending of a sheep or a pig?"

All eyes turned to Rolfe, who had been Brede's friend. He was taller than the shire reeve and lanky, with greasy black hair around a face marred by a long scar down the left cheek. "How should I know? He was his own man."

"Was he earning silver some way? Silver he would not share with you?" Mabli asked softly.

Rolfe stared at her, wondering if she was a witch.

"I will search Brede's quarters myself," the shire reeve decided, and Mabli hoped the man's stomach could stand the smell he must encounter. "You – and you, come with me," he ordered two of the younger men, and the mediciner guessed who would actually do the dirtiest of the work.

"Puw, something puzzles you?"

"Two things, mistress. One of the coraclers came to the castle before Brede's body was first found. Someone has stolen his coracle."

"He tied it properly last night?"

"Aye, he swears it."

"So, we are supposed to think the killer has escaped Pembroke. The other matter?"

"That wound," he said, pointing towards the corpse. "I have seen one like it."

Mabli stiffened, like an old hound scenting quarry. "Who died?"

"That is what is puzzling, mistress. We never knew. Just the body of a man no one had seen before. It was near a tavern but it was after sailors from the north had just gone downriver. Again, it was a sharp knife – sharp like sailors use to gut fish. The shire reeve decided the murderer was on board the north men's ship and that was the end of it."

124

"Describe the man who died."

Puw did so and Mabli was very thoughtful as she made her way back to Nest, encountering a jubilant shire reeve holding high a small pouch which rattled as he shook it.

"Silver!" he shouted at Mabli. "Now I know why he was killed. It was for his money."

"Indeed, reeve? Then why are you holding it? Is it not more likely Brede was draining someone's purse? Someone who did not want to pay any more?"

Deris wiped her face. It had been a busy morning and time now to feed Gwri and Sulien. The kitchen was warm, tidy, the stools around the table neat, orderly. The girl wiped the surfaces, crumbs from the table swept into Tegan's food bowl. The dog raised his head and she could almost think he smiled at her before settling to sleep, all the children safe with their mother.

"Gwri!" she called. "Tell Sulien."

Gwri never needed telling twice food was going on the table and he hurried in, wiping his hands on the leather apron he wore and which was speckled with tiny burns from white hot sparks. Seated, he waited for Deris to hand him his platter with a goodly share of the dark barley bread he found so much nicer than the white stuff the cracach enjoyed. Cheese was there too, sliced onion beside it, and Gwri licked his lips, ready to eat.

"Better wait for Sulien – you know what he is like," Deris warned.

There were few heartbeats before the man strode into the kitchen, smiling broadly. "It has been a good morning, mistress –" he began and then realised Luned was not there. At the table Gwri sat staring at his platter and only two more waited, one filled with bread and cheese, one with a much smaller helping. Gazing at them allowed Sulien to gain some control.

"Mistress Luned and her children have had their meal," Deris said, trying not to look too smug. "They are together in the other room."

"I warned you –"

"And I told you. William needs to be with his family, not with strangers. He has seen too many of those these last months."

"And much good they did him," Gwri muttered into his bread as he bit deep.

"What did you say, boy?"

Deris was a small fury, banging the table with her fist, the edges of her kerchief dancing. "Leave him alone! Today of all days the family need to be private together and give their thanks to the good Lord. You should be man enough to see that."

"Man enough? If you only knew . . ."

"What should I know?" Deris asked and Tegan, aware of the unease in the room, gave a low growl and began to rise.

"You, you stupid girl? You know nothing! You are a fool and you are keeping me from my rightful place."

Sulien's face flushed a dark red and he lifted his hand, clenching it in a fist as it rose. With one bound, Tegan was at Deris's side, his teeth bared. The sight of the dog was the final insult. Sulien's boot rose in an instant but Tegan caught the toe of it in his jaws, swinging Sulien off balance. The man was superbly fit and writhed, freeing his boot and standing to face the animal, enraged by the dog's defence of the girl.

"Get that beast out of my sight!"

Afraid for the dog, Gwri clutched at the hairs standing up on Tegan's neck and led him outside, shutting the back door. In an instant, they all heard Tegan scraping at the wood of the door and howling to be let in.

"After all I have done to help this family in its bad times –" Sulien began. He snatched the bread and cheese from his platter and turned to thrust his way from the kitchen, catching sight of Tegan's water bowl as he went. Again he lifted his boot and the bowl crashed across the room, water spilling everywhere. The bowl hit the solidity of a table leg and a huge chunk of hardened clay fell off the base, smaller shards scattering on the floor.

"It was an ugly thing – better on the rubbish heap," Sulien said. "I work here to help Ninian and his family and since you have made it plain to me I do not belong, I work no more today. You can explain to your mistress why the polishing of the largest candlesticks must wait until tomorrow."

Gwri had already started collecting up the pieces of the bowl while Deris searched for an old, shallow crock which would hold Tegan's water. She let the dog back into the kitchen and he bounded around the room, sniffing for his enemy.

"Poor Tegan," Deris said as she pulled at his ears and stroked flat the hair on his head. "The man has gone for the day and we can have a little peace now." She smiled to herself. "I did show him his place, did I not?" she whispered into Tegan's nearest ear.

"Deris, do I put all this on the rubbish tip?" Gwri held all that remained of the bowl in his apron.

"No, we do not take orders from Sulien." She thought for a moment. "I will find some old linen to wrap it in and you can hide it all underneath the firewood."

Gwri nodded, pleased Sulien's will was to be thwarted.

"The master made the bowl. When he returns, he can repair it," Deris said firmly and set about wiping up the water.

Luned was unaware of the storm in the kitchen. With Walter and Meleri, she sat in silence watching William. The boy had said little since coming home, content to be hugged by his family, cleansed, reclothed and fed. Questions clearly bothered him and Meleri had played with a little wooden horse carved for her in the town while Walter slipped pieces of kindling into the small fire on the hearth. William had been sitting cross-legged on a sheepskin until he had curled in a ball like a hedgepig and slept.

"Will he ever talk to us, Mother?" Walter whispered, his eyes huge and sad. He had missed William so much but it was a stranger who had come among them, a stranger who looked like his brother.

"Be patient, cariad. William has endured much. He needs time to be sure he is safe at home with us all. Remember, it distressed him greatly to know of your grandfather's plight." She looked down at her sleeping son and saw in the curve of his defenceless neck, the baby he had been. "When William has had enough good food, and sleep, and the peace of his home, he will be himself again. Until then, let us join hands around him and give our thanks to God and His Son for William's safe return."

They were praying quietly when the latch on the door was lifted and Deris's anxious face appeared. "Mistress? It is Tegan – he would be with you."

Luned beckoned them both in. The hound padded quietly to the sleeping boy, lying beside him and nudging William's hand with his nose until sleeping fingers stirred and curled into a familiar warmth of skin and hair.

"The poor wee man," Deris whispered. "May God grant him sweet dreams now he is safe," she added, creeping away.

In the castle Nest slept, but not like William with the deep stillness of relieved exhaustion. Constantly, she twitched, murmured, cried out in distress and Mabli soothed her with a gentle hand, a few words or a melody from Nest's days in the cradle. The old woman knew it would take many broken nights before Nest had faced all the demons rising unbidden when sleep held her. Poppy juice might help but only when Nest was ready for the dreamless hours which would help her return to her normal sanity. Those hours would come at Carew.

Almost sobbing, Nest sat upright and held her hands out, palms stretched to an imaginary monster. "No! No!"

"Hush, cariad, you are safe," Mabli whispered and held fingers cold and rigid as stone.

Nest woke and stared at her surroundings, turning her head this way and that as though she could not believe where she was.

"Yes, cariad, you are safe in your own bed and I have no doubt you are hungry." The mediciner kept her voice warmly practical. "Nothing has passed your lips since you broke your fast, and by those sticks you call your limbs I would swear you did not sup too well while you were away."

The smile Nest saw was almost her undoing. "Oh, Mabli! I thank God you are here!"

The old woman held Nest's hands, returned now to their softness. "The kitchen boys have been vying with each other as to who cooks your supper." She chuckled. "I fear the shire reeve will be starving again – they are saving all the best meats for you."

"Do I have to eat?"

"Aye, cariad, you do. Now, you want to go to Carew and see your babies? Then you must empty all the bowls of broth I put in front of you." She went to the door, almost falling over a youth with his ear to the wood. "You, boy. Ask the cook for the scraped meat broth with the tiny vegetables. Now."

Nest laughed, an unsteady sound, as the boy scampered away. "Tell me, were you not at a sickbed when I first came?"

"Aye, I was. Young Eynon who works at the tannery. A blow to the head near killed him."

"Should you not be with him now?"

129

"No. I have a good helper, young Nudd, who took his knife and treated Eynon as he would a shambling sheep. A good job he made of it – indeed he saved the life of poor Eynon. You rest easy, cariad, the invalid is in good hands."

"Nudd? Is he not the strange child Gerwyn rescued from the woods and took with him to live in his own home?"

Mabli nodded. "He is the boy. You remember he was good with plants as medicines?"

"I do, but he was the town's halfwit. What has happened while I have been away?"

Carefully, Mabli told of Gerwyn's murder, the suspicions aroused in the town that Manon was guilty, her subsequent trial.

Nest was devastated by the news of her friend. "She could never have had him killed, Mabli, she loved him so – he was her life!"

"Aye, cariad, and nearly her death but she had friends, as did Gerwyn. His killer was one of Owain's men and was slaughtered in Maelienydd for his crime against you. He had been tended here by his brother Iolo – husband of Gerwyn's own sister. He was hanged the same day Manon went back to her children."

"I must see her! Can she come to me? I do not want to go into the town this soon. People will stare and I am not ready for that yet."

"In the morning, sweet one, I will send a message – and you should also see Ceinwen because your poor brother has been frantic and his woman scarce off her knees with her prayers for your safe return."

"Dear Ceinwen, she is so good. Hywel is well?"

"He is. Your brother may even come to the castle to be with you."

"Hywel? He hates this place – after all, it was here he endured such hardship."

"And met Ceinwen. It is also where you are," Mabli said gently.

With a long sigh, Nest leaned back against her pillows. Mabli sent for more broth and some wine, slipping into the goblet a few drops of poppy juice. Her charge would have fewer bad dreams this night.

Chapter Eight

It was too soon for daylight. Luned opened the shutters which faced the castle and breathed air fresh from the woods and the river, dampness in it cooling and refreshing. The fire she had kept smouldering all night still had redness in its heart and she used an iron rod to stir it and shake out a little ash, feeding the feeble glow into a tiny flame which took hold and gave her brightness, something for which she thanked God.

Through the darkest hours she had kept watch over her son, seeing him breathe gently, silently. At other times he was restless and frowning, troubles chasing him even into his sleep. Each time he moved Tegan raised his head and stared at his young master, not disturbed by fingers clenching in the soft hair and skin under the dog's neck.

When William had opened his eyes he was still stunned with sleep and Luned had urged him to bathe himself with cool water in the silence before dawn when no others stirred. He had taken a candle to do as she asked, finding clean clothes she had left for him to wear. Seated beside the small fire which was now burning steadily, she waited for him to return to her.

The boy who entered shocked her. He had changed from the son she had bade farewell such a short time before. He was taller, lean but even so his tunic strained tight across his chest. The main change, she realised, was in his face, the expression set, careful, his eyes wary. Luned beckoned William to sit beside her but he ignored the stool and knelt against her knees as he stared into the flickering life of the fire.

The mother put an arm around the son's shoulders and at first she felt a stiffening, then he softened and let the arm stay. How long they were like that Luned could not guess but it was comfortable, reassuring, to have him close to her. Wood in the fire settled and with a matching sigh William bent his head until it rested in her lap. Again, she was content to wait. His face moved closer until it was buried in her and she held him, feeling the dampness of his tears through her nightshift. The boy's sobs were quiet at first, then deep, tearing, reaching up from the depth of his soul.

A sudden draught made Luned realise the door had been pushed aside. Deris stood in the opening and Luned looked at her, shaking her head. The girl turned and pulled the thick wood in place but not before Luned had heard her stop Walter and Meleri from disturbing William and his mother.

As Luned rocked her first-born and crooned to him, her anger grew. Her child had suffered so much, as they all had because of 'that woman'. Her bitterness was a weight which increased in her very being and would have no release.

Time passed and William quietened, was calm. He lifted his tear-streaked face to his mother and she held it between her hands, kissing his brow, then his eyes which had lost some of their suspicions.

"Are you well, cariad?"

"If it had not been for the Lady Nest –" he began, then tears flowed, more easily now.

Luned was puzzled. "She helped you?"

His head nodded against her. "Every day – even when Father's castle burned. After she had made him go for help she kept us all together and protected us from the wild men.

She was so strong, Mother, you should have seen her. She would not let them touch us or harm us in any way, listing all her kinsmen who would rend them in pieces if any of us children was wounded."

William nestled into his mother and she guessed he was living again the flames, the fear, the danger. He shivered and she knew he was once more in the snow surrounding that attack.

"Next day we were in Cadwgan's maenor in Ceredigion and Owain was drunk with wine. She was so brave, Mother, the Lady Nest. Owain dragged her away and we heard him grunting as he beat her and she tried not to cry."

Luned was puzzled. What she was hearing of the woman who had taken Gerald from her was at odds with the resentment which had deepened in her as each year passed.

William rambled on, telling of stables in which he slept, men who came near him and were driven away by the force of the princess's tongue and her threats. The more he talked, the more his mother knew he was keeping silent something dreadful which seared his mind like an inflamed fester. Noises from the road outside swelled and faded, footsteps paraded the passageway but did not intrude, the stillness of the familiar room working its healing on the boy.

"What is it, William? Tell me, cariad," Luned said, determined to keep her tone even.

"Owain . . ."

Instinctively, she tightened her arms around him. "Owain can no longer reach you, cariad. You are safe."

"It was her, Mother. The Lady Nest."

Luned waited.

"Her children had been sent away with Menna and Owain was always angry. I heard whispers my father was near and we would be moved. Always, there was gossip and Owain's men were afraid. They whispered together my father was a soldier and never gave up in any fight. 'Remem-

134

ber the Pembroke sieges,' they would tell each other. One night the whispers were very bad and the men jumpy, like cats when a dog is near. Owain returned from hunting and he was so angry, Mother. He started drinking, on and on. Then he was deadly quiet and reached for the princess. She turned her face away from his breath and he was like a thunderstorm, screaming and raging. He would gouge my eyes out and make me like the Franks made her brother, Hywel, if she was not willing to go to his bed that instant."

William clutched at his mother, pulling her nightshirt tight against her neck. Luned felt no pain, only a desire to send Owain to the devil.

"You should have seen her, Mother. The lady sat so still and gradually everyone was quiet, holding their breath – as was I. Then she spoke – so softly – but we all heard her tell him, 'Yet again I must remind you, sir. If the boy is harmed in any way, you will know it is my knife in your heart before you draw another breath.'"

The boy leaned against his mother, drained by all he had remembered and recounted.

"What happened than, cariad?"

"A messenger came, his horse badly lathered. There was a lot of shouting which went on through the night. Next morning, Owain was gone. We never saw him again."

Mother and son sat together, no words passing between them. From the direction of the castle came shouted orders, the clanking of iron, neighing and snorting of horses, then hooves clattering on the stones of the roadway through the town. Traders who had crossed the stream in coracles from the direction of the monks' town called to each other in the strengthening sunlight and Luned knew the market which was held at the far end of the town would soon be taking shape.

Gradually, the smell of fresh bread intruded and William sat up, sniffing, smiling at his mother as he knew he could go out to the kitchen and eat his fill. It delighted her to see her boy hungry, eager to break his fast.

"After we have eaten, we will all go to the workshop and get the silver ready to pour in the mould for the prior's chalice. Sulien has done good work preparing the mould. We tested the pattern with less valuable silver and we will try to sell it to a benefactor for one of the poorer churches."

"That is what my grandfather would have done."

"Indeed it is. Today, the new mould should be even better – and you will be there to help."

"I must change my clothes now," William said, anxious to start.

"No, cariad. Today you will wear your grandfather's leather apron. It has protected his clothes well and will do the same for yours."

William looked at his mother and she saw a shadow across his face.

"What is it troubles you?"

"Grandfather will return safely from the castle?"

"Yes, he will," she promised and felt assurance rise in her. She had bargained with the prior, prevented Sulien from riding roughshod, and William was home. Her help-lessness gone, Luned felt able to deal with even the shallow man inside the shire reeve. William nodded, trusting her word, but still he hesitated.

"There is more?" she asked.

He nodded. "The coin my grandfather gave me before I went to Caenarth Bychan. I have lost it."

"The silver coin?"

"Aye, from ancient Greece. Do you remember, Mother, it had the head of a god of theirs on one side and the name Herakles on the other – so Grandfather told me when he gave it to me."

"It was a coin for your safe return and your grandfather will be pleased to have paid it. One day, someone will find

136

it. Now, Deris will have newly churned butter and honey she kept for you. You will break your fast as does a king and, like a king, you will be able to thank God for His blessings."

The meal was quickly eaten and a happy group surged into the workshop to be met by a beaming Gwri. He helped with the silversmith's apron, tying it round William who was at pains not to trip over its length. He was not a newcomer to the work and, like his mother, had learned well from a master.

"We have another helper today?" a deep voice asked and William turned to take his measure of Sulien.

The months spent with Owain and his supporters had given William a hard grounding in the characters of men. They had also taught him to keep a pleasant face. The man he examined saw the apron William wore and was annoyed, although he did his best to hide it.

"William has spent much time here with my father," Luned explained. "It is the way in our family, the silver working handed from father to son – or to daughter. William knows he must understand all that is done here, as does Walter and so will Meleri. Whoever inherits will oversee this smithy with knowledge as well as care."

Sulien held back a comment as he bowed courteously and smiled at Luned, William noting his every move. "Such experience is useful when we have a difficult task ahead."

Getting the silver ready to pour was achieved, both William and his mother raising their hands at the same instant to stop the addition of copper. Luned left the pouring to William, Sulien at hand with thick gloves to help him steady the crucible. Walter and Meleri watched silently, as did Luned, and the slightest mistake on anyone's part would have been noticed. Nothing occurred to mark the pouring and a very satisfied group stood upright and heaved sighs of relief.

"It is finished!" Walter said and butted his head against William's shoulder.

"Not quite, cariad," his mother reminded him. "The chalice must still be polished as your grandfather would expect and then the base must have his mark."

"I had forgotten, Mother," the boy said. "May William put on the mark? To celebrate his return?"

Tears began to threaten Luned's composure. "Of course. It would be most apt if that is done. When it is complete we will take the set to the priory – all of us."

Sulien stepped closer to Luned. "Surely that is not wise, mistress? I will carry the silver and have a man or two with me as guards."

"You have been so kind to us all, Sulien," Luned assured him. "I thank you for your offer but the set ordered by the prior was from my father's workshop. It is only fitting that those Ninian trained through their childhoods should carry such valuable work bearing his mark. When he is restored to us, then he may carry on his own traditions."

"It is too great a risk you impose on your family!"

All the children gazed at the man, only William not showing any surprise at the outburst. Luned unfastened her apron, tidying it away as she had been taught.

"I thank you for your warning. When we go to the priory, we will not be unprotected."

"Me, too, Mother?" Meleri asked.

"Aye, cariad, you, too. You have been very good keeping everything orderly and clean."

"Gwri helped me and showed me what to do."

"Of course he did. He had a good master," her mother said with a smile before turning her attention to the journeyman. "We have all achieved much this morning, Sulien," she said. "While the silver cools, Gwri will keep watch and you shall have a free day."

"I will stay and see to the silver," the man insisted, determined not to be seen taking orders from a woman.

"No, Gwri will also see to the fire – make it safe – and clean what is necessary. Here . . ." She reached into the pouch at her belt, handing Sulien coins. "My father would wish you to have this and I do so for him. I will tell him when I see him later today, what a help you have been – to us all."

It interested William to notice the man's cheeks as he accepted the money. The boy had seen that tightness before and knew what it meant. As Gwri helped him discard the silversmith's apron, William thought of the hard months which had passed. They had changed him, given him knowledge of men and their ambitions as well as their goodness and their greeds.

While Luned and her family were shut away, busy about Ninian's business, the rest of Pembroke was buzzing with excitement and news. Their princess was home and safe.

"And the Constable's boy?" one would ask.

"Aye, him too – and all intact!"

Traders, farmers, egg women and the like sold their produce well, the day's smile easing coppers from pouches or resulting in favourable barter. Nest had endeared herself to the people of the town and her loss had not just been the Constable's. In her absence, Pembroke lacked lustre and the whole town's prosperity had waned. With her return, every man and woman hoped riches would again flow through the hands of the inhabitants.

"Remember," a wizened old man said, "Sir Gerald will need himself a new castle."

"Aye, and furniture to sit and sleep on," said another, thinking of the carving the Lady Nest had once ordered and might do so again.

With dreams of work to come and coins to stow under the hearths, all of Pembroke gave thanks for God's mercy.

*   *   *

Mabli thanked the steward who had carried a pitcher of fresh milk. "This will hearten both of you," she said as she poured cups of the creamy liquid.

Nest's hair flowed free, gleaming and curling about her shoulders. She was wrapped in a favoured robe of rose pink velvet and her feet, in their embroidered slippers, were raised on a footstool. Manon, too, sat in comfort, her head-dress discarded to help tendrils of hair dry against her neck in a cool breeze. The swell of her belly was her pride beneath a dark blue linen tunic and one hand cradled the baby there.

"The baby grows well?" Nest asked gently.

"Aye, he does and Gerwyn is very proud of him."

Nest was startled by Manon's answer and looked at Mabli who smiled reassuringly.

"No, Nest, I am not seeing and hearing what I should not. It is the raven." Manon told of the big black bird waiting for her on the roof of the leather shop when she returned a free woman after her recent trial. "Gerwyn was a man who had earned the right to come back as a sign of his love for us. The raven watches all who come to our home and I can talk to him in the quiet darkness of the night."

"She tells you the truth, Nest," Mabli said. "Indeed, because the raven watches over all in the leather shop, even those who possess tongues like daggers are sure, as is Manon, it is Gerwyn's child she carries. No bird with the soul of such a loved man would cherish a woman who has sinned."

Manon's contentment confirmed Mabli's words. "He is still with us, Nest," she said almost in a whisper.

"Then God is good," Nest said as she cradled her cup between her hands, looking at Manon and then at Mabli. "While I was with Owain there was no great one returned in the form of the sacred bird to comfort me but when I was low I dreamed of being here, like this."

Mabli nodded. "And it came to pass," she said softly.

"You have told each other the worst of your tidings and your tears have helped wash you. It is time to nourish yourselves as the Good Lord intended. I must go to Nudd and be sure he has all he needs. Can I trust you two to behave?"

With their mothers, Mabli had watched Nest and Manon run headlong through the woods on the banks of the Gwaun river. Such happiness, such freedom, was soon to end, Nest to grow in the court of her father, King Rhys, and Manon to escape the sheltering village with her own father after her brothers had been enslaved, her mother and sister killed there. Since the turn of the year both their lives had hung on the slenderest of threads yet they had been stoical in times of hardship, never faltering in their will for their children to survive.

"Something is wrong," Nest said after they had been left alone. "Mabli's mind is sometimes far away."

"I think it is to do with Nudd," Manon said slowly. "He has walked to Carew to see her, more than once. The first time she even took ship and was rowed, with Nudd, back to Pembroke."

"Mabli away from the children and on the water? She must have been deeply concerned. What mystery is there which takes so much of Mabli's attention?"

"No one has said but I believe it has something to do with Ninian."

"The silversmith?"

"Aye." Manon sipped her milk. "The first visit was made when Ninian's man, Margan, was so sick. I was told Nudd had gone to Carew to get medicine for him."

"Is this Margan well again?"

"Neither Mabli nor Nudd could help him. The boy was taken home to his mother and there he died."

Nest watched Manon as she finished her milk and used both her hands to caress the child she carried. "That was not all?"

141

"No. Soon after, Ninian was accused of theft by the shire reeve. The old man was dragged off to the castle to be whipped and left in chains until a silver goblet of the reeve's was surrendered."

"Manon, you jest! Ninian is an honest man."

"Indeed – and his daughter left alone in her home, with her children."

"And William with me. Poor Luned, she must have despaired."

"Her servant talked to Gwen and to me of Luned's danger. With the help of Ceinwen we asked Anwen to help, she whose husband worked for Gerwyn at the tannery. Anwen went to the silversmith's house and was company for Luned – an ageing widow to give respectability in a town full of gossips." Manon was frowning, unhappy.

"What changed?"

"Anwen's son was found near dead. His mother must leave Luned's side and return to her family."

"So Luned was left alone again?"

"Aye, and Gwen tells me that was not her only problem."

Nest listened as Manon recounted Luned's disagreement with the prior, his determination she should be married, the suggestion she wed the young silversmith aiding her father or lose the trade offered by the priory and anyone dependent on Father Prior's goodwill.

"The prior really said that?" Nest asked, hardly believing such a thing possible.

"Oh, he is very careful – as I found to my cost. He would have seen me hanged to take possession of tannery land but he uses Brother Paulinus, a smug toad in a habit, to put into words what would benefit the foundation. Father Prior keeps his own hands clean but he does not cease his plotting."

Nest was intrigued. The prior had always been most

courteous to her, yet Manon was not a liar, nor was she ever tricked into believing a lie. "What next?"

Manon explained the gift of tannery land she was now supposed to make to the church.

"That is not possible! Our own scribe, here in the castle, wrote down for you that it was Gerwyn's and then would pass to his first son, Meurig."

When told of the monks visiting Meurig daily and talking of the rich reward to be found in entering the priory as a novice and then a brother, Nest became incensed, calming only when Manon smiled and pursed her lips. A greater power than the prior's scheming mind was at work, she told Nest. Meurig had become enchanted by Buddyg's eldest daughter and would have her as a wife.

"The Buddyg who is neighbour to my brother, Hywel?"

"Aye. His woman, Ceinwen, has been of great help to Buddyg when the girls were laid low by the coughing sickness. They are delightful little women and marriage to the elder girl is one arrangement I would be willing to agree for Meurig."

"Would the tannery land make a good mill?" Nest asked.

"Indeed so, but you have my word the prior will not have it as long as I breathe."

Nest was thoughtful. "A mill needs a licence from the king and the prior is well placed for such a favour. A mill for the priory – it would earn him much praise from his bishop. Do not forget Arnulf's foundation of Benedictines is very young." Nest used her fingers to count. "Eleven years."

"So, the prior needs to show a profit." Manon smiled slowly and as of old, Nest recognised mischief. "A licence is no use without the land."

"You are right, cariad. We must put our heads together and see the licence and the land go to the right man."

Manon's smile grew. "I have heard from Ugo, the Fleming, that Cynfan the baker longs to be a miller. He would charge the townspeople less for their flour than the prior."

Nest sighed. "Oh, Manon, do you remember the women in the village – how much of each day was spent grinding barley?"

"The querns used were so heavy!"

"Indeed they were. Do you mind the day we tried, the two of us? Together we were still too weak to get enough meal for a loaf!"

The friends sat in companionable silence. "So much has changed," Manon said at last. "A miller uses great wheels and water to grind enough barley meal and wheaten flour for a whole town and all the women must do is hand over money."

"Money," Nest said and shook her head. "It is useful and buys so much in goods and work but it is yet another thing which gives men an excuse to fight."

"And love?" Manon asked, thinking of her friend's recent tribulations.

"No, not that. I was meant to be Owain's way to power. He has slept in the beds of too many women to know love."

The friends idled away time quite contentedly, gossiping, making plans, spinning schemes. Nest had been so long from Pembroke she had felt apart from the town and its people, an outsider as much as any Saxon or Fleming. With Manon's visit her interest grew in what had happened in her absence and, as she poured more milk for Manon, ideas began to foment.

"Manon's chatter has done you good," was Mabli's decision when she returned to Nest's side. "You have more colour. Would I be right to guess you have spun mischief between you?"

"Mabli! How could you think so little of us?" Manon

144

protested. "Nest may have supplied some of the threads but all I have done is tell of Pembroke happenings."

"I am glad to hear it, cariad." She sighed. "There are some flying devils who need to be caught and devoured."

Nest was concerned by Mabli's mood. "The man from the tannery? Is he worse?"

"No, praise God – and thanks be to Nudd, bless his soul. He used his knife and the man still lives. Today we drained and dressed the wound which I stitched for him and already young Eynon wakes and talks to his wife and his children. He knows each one of them and names them. With care – and a judicious use of the right salves and tinctures – he will recover."

Nest saw the mediciner was still despondent. "Yet still you worry?"

Mabli called a steward to carry away the cups and the empty milk ewer. Only when the room was as neat as she approved did she settle by the fire, low in the hearth as was appropriate in the warmer weather. A spot of grease on the front of her tunic held her attention and she licked a finger, rubbing away at the dark brown wool.

"It was Nudd who came to me with a problem. Together we understood what was happening but there was not one thing we could do."

"You were prevented?"

"In a way. When the Constable returns it may be possible to tell him all and let him take action. "

"Roger fitzHugh is responsible?"

"No, cariad," Mabli said, shaking her head, "although he is the shire reeve."

"You are not able to tell him – as you would Gerald?"

Again, there was a shake of Mabli's head and in the light from an open shutter Nest saw how the soft skin of the older woman's cheeks was more deeply lined than she remembered.

"When you tell Gerald what is amiss, can you convince him your thoughts are true?"

"Without doubt. It should all be easy . . ."

Nest did not want to press Mabli to explain her indecision but she was unhappy the woman she had known all her life should be so disturbed. "Tell me."

"With Nudd's help, there is a collection of materials which would make clear who is behind all this but the shire reeve would not be able to comprehend – he is too young and ignorant," she said at last.

"You want to wait for Gerald to come to Pembroke?"

Mabli let out her breath in a long, slow sigh. "There is a great darkness behind it all. Even Nudd looks over his shoulder all the time."

"Carew. You will not come with me?" Nest grasped Mabli's hand. "I must see the children, Mabli – I must! You insisted I stay here until I was recovered. Was it so you may stay, too?"

"No, cariad! Never! Your William and Maurice were shamed to have left you in the grasp of that devil, Owain. The last time they saw you is carved into their minds, the torn tunic, your kerchief rent from you and your hair wild about a bruised face. I wanted you to stay here long enough for me to get you clean and whole again so they see the mother they worship step from the ship."

"You did not mention Angharad."

"No. The boys would talk to me but not the little one. It has taken great patience to be with her and wait for her to speak. Young Menna has been all you would wish in a nursemaid, Angharad her particular care. At last the child whispers an odd word or two but she has never laughed – never even smiled since she came back home. Tonight I will dress your hair with a special mixture of my oils and let them soak in overnight. Then there is the lotion which I mix for your face. After you have bathed tomorrow and your hair has been washed again, you will be ready to meet your children."

On her knees in front of Mabli, Nest hugged the body which had shielded her from so much. "Forgive me, please!"

"Hush, cariad. You will see your children soon and if it pleases you, I will stay here until your husband is home."

"Home? Perhaps – but he may not make haste." Nest's mood was resigned. "Gerald will not seek my bed until he is sure I carry no child of Owain's."

Mabli held Nest's face in her hands. "Should he fret?"

Nest's laugh was a harsh sound. "Remember that woman in King William's court who was brought in bonds from the hot lands beyond Greece? Little did we know how useful it would become to listen to the gossip of some stupid Frankish women and their slaves. Because of that Gerald has nothing to fear. When I sailed north at the turn of the year, I was determined no child began in a new, cold castle so my ball of wax was within me – as it was the night Owain took us from Cenarth Bychan."

"Aye, we learned many things in those filthy and freezing pigsties the Franks call castles. You soon copied the Franks' way of talking – and made me sweat over it, too – always pretending we were ignorant of what they said but learning much. The slave girl was wise beyond her years. Beeswax and herbs – a potent mix in the right place."

Laying her head in Mabli's lap, Nest submitted to her hair being oiled, the perfume of the mixture soothing, but the mediciner was still not easy.

"Whatever dangers we faced then, cariad, I swear I feel them now as I did then."

"You! Where do you presume to go?"

The shire reeve stood squarely in front of Luned, preventing her progress.

"To speak with the Constable's wife, reeve, if it please you?"

"Never!" he spluttered. "She does not hold court here, in my castle!" He lifted his chin to try and look along his nose at her, but the woman was tall. She faced him calmly, the light brown linen of her tunic draped softly around the lines of her body.

Luned stared at the man, his soft round body encased in shiny purple silk, the cut of the tunic spoiled by droplets of food and wine which had missed his mouth. She realised his hair was thin; long before he had aged he would be bald. Fat and with a gleaming skull? He reminded her of when she was a small child in Shrewsbury. There was just such a man there, a sergeant in the pay of Earl Robert, who enjoyed his master's cruelty and added to it.

"Were I a courtier," Luned said in the best French she could muster, "I would understand, sir, but I come as a mother to talk to a woman who helped my child live."

"Huh! One whore to another? You will have much to discuss – bedded by the same man!"

It was his mood reminded Luned of that long-ago sergeant. Whenever he was angered he must pick on someone weaker than himself and make them suffer. It took only a moment for her to reason with herself. Such a short time ago she had been weak, helpless, but no longer. Luned held herself proudly and stared at the paunchy little boy, for that was what he was.

"It is wise for you to remember, reeve, this castle is held by its Constable for the defence of the whole shire. However much you may strut within its bounds, this castle is not yours. Both the Lady Nest and I have the ear of Sir Gerald, the Constable, and we are used to speaking the truth – and afraid of no man for so doing."

"You? A whore and mother of bastards? The daughter of a thief –"

"Thief? My father never stole from anyone!"

Roger fitzHugh's sneer was unpleasant. "No? With my precious goblet wrapped in his bedding? Indeed, I am sure you will tell me it was put there without his knowledge. If it was, it must have been by a man with the run of your sleeping spaces –"

"Or," Luned interrupted, "by one of your own men you had sent on a false search. Who was it found it, reeve? I know the cry when the goblet was seen came some time after your gallant troopers stormed into our home. Any one of them could have hidden it, hoping you would do as you did – blame my father instead of the real sinner."

The shire reeve began to stutter with fury but part of his weasel's mind accepted what she said could be true.

"The day before these events, my father was kept waiting and put where a steward was cleaning your silver. Why there? Why for so long? Who made it so? You?" she demanded of him.

It was enough to cause him to erupt in a fury of spittle and words she did not comprehend. Neither Gerald nor his Frankish friends had ever uttered such foulness in her hearing but she could not mistake the pointing finger, shaking as he indicated the gate.

She tossed her head, disgust of him clear in her expression. "I will return in the morning and then I will talk to the Lady Nest."

Chapter Nine

The man was unkempt, his eyes bleary, hair and beard awry. What had been a decent brown wool tunic was stained and his boots were a mess of mud and worse. Groaning, he leaned against the open doorway until one of the servants pushed him out of the way so she might sweep what she could from the tavern on to the roadway.

"Serves you right," she muttered, banging her besom against him in her annoyance. Time after time he had banged his cup for more beer until broken shards made him look owlishly at his handiwork. He was not the only one who had revelled inside the wooden walls which bore a cut bush above the door. She had got rid of the broken pottery but heaving grown men too drunk to walk into the roughness of the track was beyond her.

"Trouble?" the deep voice of a woman called.

The girl looked up at Sennen, tidy and with her face washed early in the day. "They were all inside by curfew but drank empty every barrel the master had in the place."

"Cheering on a new soul in hell, I expect."

"Aye, Brede. He had caused such pain, they just had to honour his sudden departure from this world."

"Brede – a devil to so many. There will be those who miss him."

The servant girl was startled. "Not him."

150

Sennen smiled. "There were probably those who used him – the shire reeve for one." She had seen the reeve's man Brede whispering in dark corners to half-seen faces.

"The shire reeve? He never sliced Brede to eternity!"

"No," Sennen agreed, "nor wanted it – but someone did."

With a snort of disbelief, the tired little maid tried to push the unwanted customer from the doorway. Sennen went to help, kicking the man's feet from under him and propping the loose-boned body against a wall. "Any more like him inside?" she asked and, at the girl's weary nod, went with her into the tavern, providing entertainment for early morning housewives and farmers as, one by one, drunken vestiges of husbands, fathers, sons were lifted out of the stench of the beer house by Sennen and arranged in a line. She looked at them and shook her head.

"Each greets news of a death in their own way. Me? I thanked God for His wisdom and slept like a baby."

Luned examined her best tunic carefully. Was that a stain, she wondered? Opening wide the shutters of her room she peered more closely, sighing with relief it had been just a shadow. A warm iron and a thorough pressing would make the April green linen as fresh as new. An unworn kerchief came next from the coffer, still holding the fragrance of dried rose heads. Yes, she decided, it was clean and the same iron would have it draping gracefully around her head and throat. An embroidered headband? Luned drew out one which had been a favourite of her mother, a strip of dark green velvet stitched with a design as ancient as their people.

The evening before, the urge to visit the princess was a moment's folly after Luned had left her father's food with the guard. Carrying her empty basket she had begun to walk towards the gate in the outer bailey when she had turned and gone towards the inner bailey and the living quarters she had known so well. That was when she had fallen foul of Reeve Roger, his unpleasantness designed to cow her into submission as a mere woman. Luned allowed herself a small smile. Once, she would have surrendered to the reeve's will but no longer.

As Gerald's new family increased with healthy children, Luned had watched from the windows facing the castle, the shutters half closed so she might not be seen. She had shut herself away from others, her life the daily work of a home, the constant care and love for her children with servants like Deris to go out amongst the townspeople. Meleri might stay with her forever but Luned had known that William and Walter must one day take a greater part in their father's life. Building his new castle in Emlyn, Gerald had made it possible for them to be recognised as his heirs, and the time was so much closer when they would leave Luned. A string of familiar prayers helped, each one a pleading for God's good grace to care for William and Walter when they must leave and learn the trade of fighting men. Lost in her thoughts she was startled by a boy's noisy entrance.

"Grandfather's workshop – what would you have us do today, Mother?" William wanted to know, Walter at his shoulder and Meleri following.

She took time to think. William should visit the princess but today she would see the woman alone. "The polishing of the pieces for the priory, cariad. When we all agree the silverware for the prior is the best it can be, it will receive the mark due to it."

Meleri and her brothers solemnly nodded their understanding.

"You would do well to watch Sulien, how he works. He is a fine craftsman and you must learn what you can from him."

William and Walter grinned at each other. They were being trusted as men. "Do we decide when it is ready, Mother?" William asked.

152

"You are the head of this family for a while," she answered, trying to sound cheerful. "It is your duty."

Walter was nervous. "Sulien . . .?"

"Is a good silversmith and we are indeed fortunate to have him with us in the workshop but he is not of your grandfather's family." Luned began tidying the table with unusual firmness.

The children gazed at their mother. There was something they did not understand and yet they could not put their unease into words.

"Where will you be?" Meleri wanted to know.

"I must visit the Lady Nest and thank her for all she did for William. Now, let us bow our heads and thank God for the food he has given us this day and that Willliam is here to share it with us."

A flash of colour at the gateway to the inner bailey caught Roger fitzHugh's eye. He frowned, puzzled. A well-dressed woman, holding herself proudly, was walking towards him as if she owned the place. Beside her scuttled Puw, one he considered the least of his men and unable to speak any but the tongue of the conquered savages. "Ninian's daughter!" he spat out angrily but she was too far away to hear him.

Fuming with impotent rage, Roger fitzHugh considered himself ill served. He had been persuaded against his will to stop the flogging of the silversmith and now this woman dressed like a lady walked about the castle without his permission. Who did these people think they were?

"Rolfe!" Brede's usefulness might have been cut short but his ansel, Rolfe, knew only too well who paid him. "Rolfe!" was bellowed across the inner bailey and Rolfe came running.

Unkempt, unfit, the man was breathing heavily by the time he reached his master. "Sir?"

"Ninian, the silversmith – has he spoken yet?" It added to the reeve's annoyance that he must use the stupid tongue of the countryside as well as his native French.

"No, sir. He gets the odd kicking when we go near but never when his daughter or the Lady Ceinwen are about."

"They are favoured by the Constable," Roger fitzHugh muttered, "and with his wife taking her ease in my quarters, it is a matter of days – hours – before the great Sir Gerald rides in and thwarts me – yet I will not be denied my goblet! Ninian may be a thief but his making of an object does give it value." The reeve gnawed at a knuckle, the pain he induced keeping him sharply aware. "So, he must have no beatings? And the other criminals make Ninian's life unpleasant with their oaths and their fleas?" He straightened and was pleased with an idea. "Take Ninian to the cave beneath us. Chain him there and give him no food and no water. Tell him again and again he will be alone, starving and thirsty. It is how I say he will spend his days and nights – if he can tell which is which in the darkness."

"Sir?" Rolfe was uneasy. "He is an old man and already sick from his wounds. He will die."

"Tell that to him," the reeve advised. "He shall drink, eat, see his daughter, stand in the sunlight, only when he tells me where is the goblet he stole from me."

Luned had held herself proudly as she walked to the gate of the inner bailey. There was no need for her to demand entry: a man she recognised from the old days bade her enter when he swung wide the wood, then one of the reeve's chosen men hastened towards her. He opened his mouth to protest until she raised a hand, staring him into silence. Briefly, in French and then in Welsh, she told him she was on her way to visit Princess Nest.

Rolfe was uneasy, shifting from foot to foot as he tried to shape an answer. The shire reeve would be angry if this woman learned of the new way her father was to be induced to confess. The man groaned and wished Brede still lived. He had always been a wily fellow and would have kept the lady ignorant but Brede lay dead in his shroud.

"You!" A woman called to him from the far side of the chapel. "Bring Mistress Luned to me – and waste no more time."

Mabli was well used to dealing with stupid men and this one took no risks, almost grabbing Luned by the arm to pull her towards the distant mediciner. The lower part of Luned's face was covered by her kerchief but above it her eyes blazed with warning and Rolfe became respectful. He had never seen her like this and had learned to be wary of women in such a mood.

"I am glad to see you, mistress. " Mabli surveyed Luned from head to toe, seeing the careful dressing, the well-draped kerchief with its jewel-coloured headband. The mother of the Constable's first children had prepared with great care to meet the mother of his present family. "Your son, William, is recovered?"

"Indeed he is, Mistress Mabli, and I thank you for your enquiry – as I thank the Good Lord for His care of my son. William has told me all the Lady Nest did to ensure his safety and I wish to tell her of my gratiutude. One mother to another."

Mabli bowed, keeping her thoughts private. She doubted the young William had any real idea of the evil which Owain was capable of inflicting on a child. Menna, the nursemaid taken from Cenarth Bychan with the princess and the children, had told Mabli of Owain's glee when faced with a child of his enemy unrelated by blood to Nest.

"My lady has talked of your boy. He has much spirit and a good heart. He has not come with you to pay his respects?"

"I needed to talk with the Lady Nest alone. William is in his grandfather's workshop as he has long been trained to do."

A gracious nod from Mabli made it clear she approved of the boy's occupation. "We should all learn what we can of honest labour. If you will follow me, I will take you to the princess."

Luned smiled and shook her head. "There is no need, Mistress Mabli. I have known the way these many years."

Luned did not speak for a moment, gazing at the woman who had greeted her and then sat facing her in the light from an opened shutter. Swathes of colour surrounded them in the tapestries hanging on the walls. The wood had been bare when Luned occupied this same space with Gerald but they were the signs of Nest which surrounded them. The woman's legendary beauty was undimmed but Luned could see faint lines in the creamy skin, a new tautness around the eyes. The rich, purple velvet of a robe covered Nest's body and her hair hung loose, curling tendrils still damp from her bath.

"William is well?" the princess asked.

Luned bent her head for a moment. "I prayed to God to protect him and bring him home safely and the Good Lord heard my pleas." She gazed steadily at Nest, feeling hatred begin to shrivel. "William has told me of all you did – and suffered – to keep him alive and whole." Luned was silent, searching for words. "I do not know how I can begin to thank you." She reached into the pouch at her belt and drew out a small, calfskin bag. "Please," she said and handed it to Nest.

Slowly, Nest undid the drawstring of the bag and drew from it a small silver box with the same design on its lid as was on Luned's headband. It was exquisite, its tiny hinges perfectly made and allowing Nest to open it and find inside a curl of baby's hair.

"My father made it for my mother when I was born. The hair you see there is William's. This little box will outlive me but I give it to you as a reminder of the gratitude I am not able to speak."

There were tears in Luned's eyes and Nest's delight was not dimmed by her own tears.

"All my days," Luned went on, "I will think of you, pray for you – be glad you were with my boy at a time when he was so in need."

Nest had clasped the little box to her and now she reached out a hand to Luned. "You are so kind," she said, "but I am in William's debt." She looked down at the tress in the opened box. "When my children were taken away from me I was told they were being returned to their father," Nest said quietly. "I had hoped and fought for such a moment but I did not trust my captors. I watched my William lead his little sister by the hand, Maurice following behind and helping Menna – she was their nursemaid and could barely walk she had been so badly used by Owain's men. Before they had gone far I could no longer see them, I was crying so much, and it was then that William put an arm round my shoulders and bade me dry my tears. 'They will be safe,' he insisted and I believed him – I had to believe him. We clung together and I drew strength from him. Then Owain wrenched us apart and William was sent back to the stables," Nest said and shuddered as she relived what followed.

Luned waited for a moment for Nest to regain her composure. "When do you go on to Carew and your children?"

"As soon as Mabli has decided I have been scoured clean," Nest said with a smile. "She was right to keep me here. As I was, I would have frightened my little ones even more than did their kinsman, Owain."

"They know you are safe?"

"At once." Nest looked down at her hands. Strong, shapely, they were bereft of jewellery. "I sent them a ring I always wore so they knew news of me to be true but I long to see them for myself – hold them – and know for sure God is good."

"When William came to the door I did not know whether to wash him or feed him," Luned admitted.

Nest chuckled. "And which did you do?"

157

"I do not remember," William's mother confessed.

"Nor I when Mabli found me, but I was desperate to sink in deep water and wash away Owain and his ways. Each day Mabli has soaked me and scrubbed me – washed my hair and dressed it with oils and her fine comb until I can almost recall what it was like to be clean. Do you know," she said in a whisper, "I think I shall never feel empty of Owain as long as he lives."

It humbled Luned to think she had so loathed this woman. "I will pray you find peace before then, Nest. Gerald will return to you and you will soon see your children. Owain would have destroyed all you hold dear in Cenarth Bychan but you had the strength to defy him there. With God's help and your own courage you will destroy the shadow the evil one still casts over you."

"You remind me of Ceinwen," Nest said, her smile gentle and muted with tears. "She has been good to my family."

"And to mine." Luned could see Nest's deep sadness. "The day your three children reached Pembroke, the town went mad, rejoicing to see them once more. Mistress Mabli brought them to the castle gate for everyone to see and I watched with Walter and Meleri from behind the shutters of our house. There was cheering but it quietened when Mistress Ceinwen knelt to pray for you and for William. I saw her – but I was already on my knees."

"Dear Ceinwen, her thoughts are always for others."

Luned nodded. "When my father was dragged here from his workshop and flogged, she was the one who stopped the punishment and salved his wounds."

Nest shook her head. "Ninian – that good old man flogged. It is beyond belief."

"Aye – it was on the orders of the shire reeve. Silver of his had been stolen and a goblet was found wrapped in an old shirt of my father's. The reeve is ready to kill him to get back what he has lost and my father must endure all the reeve spits at him because he was not the thief."

Nest frowned, was puzzled. "I wonder if this is what concerns Mabli? I go to Carew as soon as a ship is ready but Mabli remains in Pembroke. Only a matter of great urgency would stop her being with the children again." She patted Luned's hand. "If Mabli is concerned for Ninian, she will see he is safe from whatever Roger fitzHugh can devise."

"I pray it will be so."

"Be sure of it." Nest sat against the comfort of her cushions and studied Luned. "You know, over the years I have watched you with Ninian and envied the love he has for you."

Luned was so startled she could not speak.

Nest smiled. "Gerald once told me your father had a marriage planned for you – a rich merchant in Cardiff, a fine man who would have given you everything your heart desired – but you loved Gerald and Ninian put aside his scheme so you could be happy."

"I never knew!"

"No, Gerald said your father had not burdened you." Nest sighed. "Then the king needed a husband for me to keep me safe from his queen's friends – and from ambitious warriors amongst our own people. He married me to Gerald, kept my dearest little Henry with him in England and sent us back to the protection of Pembroke. It was a hard time for us all," she said and bowed her head, remembering grief. Then she straightened and forced a smile for Luned. "I wanted to meet you, talk to you, but Gerald forbade it. He wanted no more hurt for you and your little ones. With Ninian he conspired to do all they could to give you peace."

There was so much to hear, to understand, and Luned was bemused by it all.

"From William I learned what a loving home he had come from," Nest said, and there was envy in her voice. "He and Walter and Meleri have much for which they may thank you and Ninian."

159

"Of course! Your own father – you were so young when he died."

Nest nodded. "The age of your Meleri, but my father was a king – always in the distance. At times he must go to Ireland for safety and my mother took us girls to an old friend deep in the Gwaun valley where we could be hidden until my father returned. When he held court he was surrounded by so many important people he had no time for little girls. Oh, he was proud of me. I resembled my mother and would make a fine trade one day with a chief – a wife for a warrior who could follow my father into battle. The last time he spoke to me he was annoyed I was too young for a marriage bed but next morning I stood with my mother as she held Gruffydd, my little brother."

Luned realised Nest was lost in the past, living again a day which had meant so much to her.

"It was Easter time and there was a mist in the early morning. Around the court at Dynevor the trees are tall and that day they were wreathed with white. It was the noise, beginning while it was still dark. Men shouting, horses stamping and neighing, the clank of metal, cart wheels creaking. To this day I remember every sound. When all was ready my father checked his armour and his weapons, then mounted his horse, my older brothers alongside him. Cynan, Gronow and Hywel," Nest said softly and for a moment she was lost in her memories. "My brothers – they were young and ready for the fighting to come. All the horses were restless, wheeling and rearing, their riders cursing as they pulled them into line. At last my father raised his hand and began the ride along the woodland road." Nest brushed a hand across her eyes. "There was a glimpse of sunlight and it shone on my father, his helmet glistening. It was covered in silver and fitted with a golden circlet so every man with him would know he was in the forefront of any skirmishing. Within a heartbeat he was lost in the trees but it was a long time before the last wagon trundled out of sight. I was so proud of my father that day and I could not understand why my mother wept."

"They were riding to Aberdare?"

Nest nodded. "And only poor Hywel have I ever seen again."

Guards whispered behind their hands as she passed but Luned was oblivious to them all. She had so much on her mind yet the movement of a chain nearby took her thoughts to her father. From the beginning, the accusations hurled at him had been ludicrous yet he lay nearby and she was helpless. If Nest's mediciner was determined to stay in Pembroke, perhaps there was hope her father might soon be released. Luned's steps quickened. Nest was not the ogress she had hated for so long and this new knowledge freed her.

Nest. Gerald had always been careful to keep them apart. Luned had seen her from a distance, her proud stride as she walked in the town, her tunics and cloaks the envy of all women. They had never spoken and Luned had understood Gerald wanted no unseemly quarrel between women to reach the ears of King Henry.

Luned lifted her chin and breathed deeply, smelling woodsmoke from fires in the bailey. It was so familiar, yet it was of the past. She lengthened her stride. There was so much for her to do.

"They are all in the workshop, mistress," Deris said. She knew Sulien had been furious that William and Walter were to be in charge, but he had been careful to hide his temper, encouraging the boys as they worked and even helping Meleri with the back of the paten.

Once in her father's workplace Luned breathed in its familiar smells and was soon lost in the final stages of bringing the prior's order to perfection. Sulien had done a good job with his moulds and the pieces which emerged needed little finishing. Item by item she examined every part of the silver, noting only a slight roughness here and there which needed extra work. When all was ready they stood back and saw the magnificence which had been created in the dark cavern hung about with instruments and lit by the fires beneath crucibles.

Breath escaped from Luned in a sigh. The prior would have no excuses to argue but she knew he would. She also knew he would covet what Ninian's training had produced.

"It is time for your grandfather's mark."

Gwri scuttled forward. In his hand he held a shaft of iron, the insignia of Ninian standing proud.

"William, the chalice," his mother decided.

The boy stood the chalice upside down as he had seen his grandfather prepare others, handling it with the same care and soft linen. When it was as solidly set on the bench as he could make it, he raised a mallet and looked at his mother.

"When you are ready, remember what you were taught."

"Look at the place you want the mark, strike the end of the shaft with the mallet, thinking only of the quality of the silver and the smiths who made it. Then hit sure and swift, lifting back the mallet as soon as it has landed," chanted all the children and Gwri.

There was laughter and Luned joined in, almost able to see the silversmith as he had made very little boys and girls recite the process. When William was solemn once more she nodded. He took a deep breath, gazed at the base of the chalice, his blow swift and its recovery neatly done. Everyone crowded round, inspected the result and beamed at William.

"My turn," Walter said and took the instruments from William. He dealt with a large candlestick and a smaller one, both marks receiving full approval. Meleri, with her mother's help, marked the paten and then the mallet and iron bar with the insignia were handed to Sulien.

"It would please us for you to mark a candlestick," Luned said, not knowing her gentle words roused a silent fury in the man.

He was calm, pleasant and struck well but his mark was not as clear as those of the children. Luned examined it carefully and decided the 'N' of the brand was deep enough. Gwri dealt with the remaining candleholder and Luned was relieved the valuable collection was ready for the priory.

Deris had watched from the doorway. From there she could hear many voices and shouts from near the castle which drew her to the front shutters and a good view of whatever was occurring. "The princess is going to Carew!" she cried on her return to the workshop and William turned to his mother with an unspoken question.

"Go, cariad – but not in your apron!" she called to his back as he ran.

Walter and Meleri hurried from the smithy, Gwri and Deris following when Luned waved them away. Sulien began handling the silver which had just been marked until Luned stopped him, giving him the soft old linen which was to be used to give the final polishing. As he completed the work, she found the pile of linen pieces which could be used as wrapping, putting the articles into leather satchels.

"Come, Sulien, there is time to eat before the children and I journey to the priory," she told him as she led the way to the kitchen and the food Deris had ready.

"I still believe I should accompany you. Such treasures could be tempting for a thief."

"We will be safe enough," Luned assured him as she washed her hands in a basin on the bench near the back door. Slicing bread from a loaf, she used her knife to cut cheese, ham which Deris had boiled, urging Sulien to eat.

"William knelt to the princess and kissed her hand," an excited Meleri said as she raced to tell her mother the news.

"Aye, and the lady lifted him and kissed him on both cheeks, Mother. She seemed very pleased to see him," Walter added, surprised any woman could think well of his brother, "even insisted he walk with her to the ship."

"He will be back – and hungry," his mother said. "Make sure there is enough left to feed him when he comes home."

'Comes home' echoed silently in her mind as she imagined Nest and William walking to the quay. Once, she would have been consumed with jealousy that Nest should be so close to William but since she had at last met and talked with the woman who had haunted her dreams for so many years, her fears had gone. "Like mist when the sun rises," she said, not realising she had spoken out loud.

"Mother?" Walter queried.

He had startled Luned, then she smiled. "William will be home soon."

The day was well advanced when they returned and supper was ready for them, Luned smelling a potage Deris had made from the ham stock.

"Did all go well, mistress?"

"God be thanked, Deris, it did."

William and Walter were hungry but carried the empty satchels to the workshop. Meleri was tired, drooping a little as she leaned against Deris. Luned changed her clothes as the children helped Deris prepare the table and after a hasty prayer the potage was ladled out, the children silent for once as they ate. By the time their mother returned to the kitchen, the boys and Meleri had eaten their fill so Luned urged thanks to God for his blessings, the prayers of thanks still ringing in their ears as Deris cleared the empty bowls to the scullery.

In the kitchen Luned and Meleri watched the boys move Tegan's bedding, his makeshift water bowl, emptied now after the hound had drunk his fill. Lifting part of a plank which had been left bare by their activities, Luned revealed

164

a hole into which she placed a heavy pouch chinking with the prior's silver coin. When all was restored and Tegan once more on his bed, Deris came back to sweep crumbs from the table.

"You should have seen Mother argue with the prior, Deris," Walter said, chuckling as he remembered the man's expression. "At first he said the quality of the silver was not what he expected and he would pay less. Mother had us set out all we had carried and then she lifted a small crucifix and placed it in the middle."

"What for?" the little maid wanted to know and Luned smiled.

"I knew the crucifix was but a poor copy of one my father had made for Lord Arnulf before he went to Ireland. Amongst the silverware produced here, it looked dull and insignificant. Candlelight is very good at showing the difference between the best silver in the world and the cheaper kind which contains much more copper. Even the prior had to admit his purchases were the best money could buy."

"He still argued the price, Mother," William reminded her.

"So Mother made us wrap up all the pieces and put them back in the satchels. Then she said the prior could have his silver – when he was ready to keep his word," Walter told Deris.

William frowned. "He raised his voice to Mother, trying to order her to do what he wanted – leave the silver with him and return home empty-handed."

"What did you do?" Deris asked her mistress.

"I began to lead my family away and Tegan growled." She fondled the head of the great dog. "My father had trained him well to protect me and the prior ceased his arguing. Aye, Tegan has earned his supper this day and no mistake. He guarded the silver all the way there and the price money all the way home. Deris, a goodly helping from the pot for our friend."

"When it is cooled he will eat like a king, mistress."

Deris busied herself at the fire. One day she would tell her mistress how Sulien had looked when he learned the dog was the one to protect the family and its silver. "Thieves have tried," she had told the man thwarted in his attempt to be part of the family. "One has had a useless hand ever since and another limped from Tegan's bite until the day he died."

"My father's meal, Deris. I must make sure he is fed before I sit to my own supper."

In her workaday tunic and kerchief, Luned carried the basket with its bowl of soup, slices of cold ham, bread from Cynfan's shop and wheatcakes fresh from Deris's bakestone. There was goat's milk in a ewer, honey in a crock and all was covered with a cloth whitened by being dried in the sun.

It had been a good day, Luned decided as she walked the short distance to the castle gates. Once there she knocked and waited to be admitted but no one stirred. She knocked again. And again.

"Is there no guard on duty?" she called at last.

A head emerged from between shutters in the room above the gate. "Aye, there is," a voice shouted in French.

Luned recognised Rolfe, the shire reeve's preferred man. "Why am I not admitted to take my father his food?"

"Orders!"

Another time Luned would have been meek but the events of the day had changed her. "Let me in at once or the Constable shall be told." There was a silence and then she could hear muttering amongst the guards above.

"Shire reeve, ma dame. You are not to see your father or bring him food and drink until the goblet is returned."

Luned was insulted as much by the man's lack of courtesy as by Roger fitzHugh's order. "How dare you!"

Rolfe heard the voice of a woman with authority but the shire reeve could do him more immediate damage. "No, ma dame. I dare not. Everyone has been told to keep you out of the castle and your father starved until he tells the hiding place of the reeve's silver."

Wave after wave flowed through Luned, almost drowning her in despair. At last she had begun to fight back and the one to suffer most would be her own father. She knew his frailty, so did the shire reeve. The orders against Ninian were a death sentence.

Chapter Ten

Luned's senses swirled and she leaned against the castle gates for support. Hardly aware of running footsteps, she only knew strong arms held her.

"Mistress! What has happened?"

Deris's voice was a familiar comfort but Luned could only shake her head in despair as the basket was taken from her.

"Come, Mother, we will get you home," William said, reminding her of the strength of his father.

Between them, William and Deris half dragged, half carried Luned's limp body. Walter raced from the house and took the basket, flinging questions at William which he could only answer with a shake of his head. Meleri was at the door and behind her, Gwri, his pinched little face as anxious as the rest.

In the warmth of the kitchen, Luned was made to sit on a stool by the fire as she shivered, unable to stop even to cry. Meleri hugged her mother, rocking her as she would a baby, while Deris was busy with the stew pan and a bowl.

"Mistress, you must eat, you are faint from hunger," the maid insisted when she came at Luned with a bowl of broth from the pan and a spoon.

Luned was frantic, pushing away Deris's hand. "How can

I eat when my father is being starved to his death?" she cried and there was a horrified silence.

"You must tell us what happened," William insisted.

Slowly, the shivering lessened and Luned spoke of the man shouting at her from the gatehouse and telling the whole world Ninian was to stay in darkness, alone and unfed.

"Who was the man?" William wanted to know, and when Luned told them it had been Rolfe there were exclamations from Deris and Gwri.

"The shire reeve's man – if you can call him a man," Deris explained to the others, barely noticing Gwri slip away.

The broth was urged on Luned. "Mistress, you only nibbled a little cheese when we broke our fast this morning – and at noon time you would not stop for food, so busy you were with the silver."

"She is right, Mother," Walter added. "When we returned from the priory you would not have supper, saying you would eat later."

"Now it is later, Mother," Meleri said and would have helped Deris but Luned pushed the spoon away.

"That is enough!" William decided, his voice strong and sure. "You do not help Grandfather by becoming weak. He needs you to be more able than the fool who is the shire reeve and for that, Deris's good cooking is the best weapon you could have."

Luned gazed at her son, seeing not the young boy who had marched to the ship behind his father almost half a year ago, but the man in him. William had suffered the same fate as his grandfather, locked away from all who loved him, yet he had returned stronger with all the signs of the good man he would soon become. She held out her hand to him and he grasped it, warm fingers about hers dragging her back into the battle ahead.

Deris and Meleri fed Luned spoonful by spoonful, the little girl deciding meat should be added to the bowl and bread in her mother's hand. "After this you will have the wheaten cakes we kept warm for you, Mother, and honey. You always make us eat honey if we are ill. If it can fight illnesses as you say, perhaps it can see off Roger fitzHugh."

From the kitchen Walter could be heard making safe all the doors and shutters, ready for couvre feu. He was frowning when he returned to the candlelit kitchen. "There is no sign of Gwri and soon the patrols will be out."

Deris stood, pleased the bowl she held was empty and the mistress watching Meleri smear honey. "Have no fear for Gwri. He has ways of getting around Pembroke at night. No one will see him but the person he visits."

It was a long night for Luned. She heard the dog fox bark as it hunted for prey or for its mate in the darkness. Shouts came from the castle as a patrol leader demanded entry. When she could bear no longer to lie idle and restless, she crept down to the kitchen, feeling for an old cloak of her father's he kept hanging behind the door. Wrapped in its warmth Luned huddled by the muted glow of the fire and used dry kindling to encourage a flame. She fed the leaping light quietly, stick by stick, and was absorbed in the life building under her fingers when she heard a rustling from the back of the house, a door opening.

Grasping the poker Deris always left ready for the fire, Luned waited for the first sight of her enemy. The kitchen door slowly opened and she stood, prepared to strike and angry enough now to strike hard.

"Mistress!" It was Gwri, crouched and frightened, his eyes huge.

Luned lowered her weapon, trying not to shake with relief. "Where have you been?"

The boy did not answer but stood to one side and let his friend be seen.

"Nudd!"

"Aye, mistress, and sad I am if you are afeared of me."

170

"No, no – but surprised. Aye, I am that."

Gwri pulled Nudd towards the light of the fire and Luned wondered again at the changes in the young friend of their sweeping boy. After Gerwyn, the tanner, had rescued him from a life in the woods, Luned had watched as the pathetic little scrap grew with good feeding and kindness, even beginning to laugh when he was with Gerwyn's children. The growths on Nudd's face still repulsed many but he stood straight, as a man should. His hair bushed like straw ready for cattle as it always did but his words were sharp and clear, his eyes knowing and direct.

Luned gazed at Nudd and he nodded, understanding the question she was about to ask and answering it with a smile. She felt the cloak drop from her shoulders, taking with it the weight of agony. He had brought her hope.

"The doors to the front, are they barred?" Nudd asked Gwri and the boy ran to see. He was back in an instant, nodding hard, and Nudd knelt in front of Luned. "First, your father. At dawn, Mistress Mabli will find Ninian and take him food and milk. It will take time to get him from the cave and free of chains but Ugo, the Fleming, is ready to ride at first light. He will go to Manorbier and return with Sir Odo."

"How?"

An excited Gwri could keep still no longer. "Nudd went to the castle for Mistress Mabli to come to Eynon. His head wound needed her care."

Luned's fingers clenched with a sudden fear. "He is worse?"

"Not at all," Gwri assured her cheerfully, "but Nudd needed to speak with the mediciner and while she was with Eynon, she inspected his wound, told Nudd he had done well and dressed it with fresh salve."

"Mistress Mabli already knows of matters here and in the town which have affected Ninian," Nudd said, his voice deeper than Luned remembered. "It was urgent she knew of

171

the reeve's latest orders for your father so she might help him. There is something I must have from you, mistress."

"Anything!"

"Gwri, you know where to find it?" Nudd asked and with a nod the boy scurried away, a lighted candle in his hand.

There was a soft yawn from the doorway. "What is all this?" Deris demanded as she rubbed sleep from her eyes.

"Come to the fire," Luned urged. "We will explain, but softly so the children do not yet wake."

Gwri crept back to the kitchen, a wooden box under one arm, its lid hinged with leather. He handed it to Nudd who opened the casket and examined the contents. His expression became hard, grim.

"Where was it?" Nudd asked.

"Where it has always been – in a far corner under a box of old moulds."

"Was it disturbed when the reeve's men came and searched?"

Gwri shook his head, the movement slowing as he thought. "I did not think so but look at the box. Where is the dust on the lid?"

Nudd's smile for his little friend was warm and bright. "Well done, Gwri. Mistress Mabli will be proud of you." He turned to Deris. "Have you a means of tying this box and sealing it?"

Blinking her eyes as she thought hard, Deris reached into a basket under the dresser where were kept old cloths for cleaning. She pulled out a length of what had been a nighshift and tore from it a strip long enough for Nudd's needs. Meanwhile, Gwri had gone back to the workshop, returning in triumph with red wax.

"The master seals his precious packages with this," he said with a grin, "and with this," he added, holding up the iron rod with Ninian's mark.

The box was soon dealt with. "Now, where can it be

hidden in greatest safety? I must not be caught with it on my way home or we shall never see it again."

"It is so important?" Luned asked.

"Aye, mistress, it is."

"Give it to me," Deris ordered Gwri. "I will put it with Tegan's old water bowl."

Luned was astonished. So much seemed to be happening in her home of which she had no knowledge, yet everyone there was determined to help her and get her father freed. "I thought Tegan's bowl was beyond repair."

"No, mistress," Deris said with a sly grin, "only beyond another kicking from a heavy boot. I hid it so the master could repair it when he returns." She took the box from Nudd. "This will go with it."

Nudd disappeared into the night, Gwri to the workshop, as Deris was heard moving around in the woodshed. Luned was left in peace but not for long. First William came to her, then Meleri, followed by Walter, yawning as he stumbled, not really awake and scratching himself under his night-shirt. William lifted the poker and raked the fire, watching ashes settle and logs flare, feeding the flames carefully so the bakestone would be hot for Deris. Still yawning, Walter went along the passageway to unbar the door ready for Sulien, and Meleri climbed on a stool to reach the honey jar.

"Did you sleep well, Mother?" William asked as he stood erect again.

She smiled, more at peace than for some time. "I think it has been a good night."

"Thanks be to God," William said with great feeling.

"And to our friends – the ones we know and the ones we do not," Luned added so softly William did not hear.

Mabli waited.

Summoned to the great hall, the reeve's man, Rolfe, had ordered Mabli to stand. She understood but ignored the French words, gesturing imperiously until a stool was

173

brought. Carefully, she lowered her stiffness into comfort and folded her arms on her stomach, relishing the battle to come. She could hear the noises of a busy day in the castle and there was the smell of hot meat. Sniffing, she decided pork turned on a spit and thought back to how the morning had begun.

As the first fingers of dawn pushed into the sky, Mabli had gone to the kitchens, harrying sleepy cooks until the fire was hot and meat warmed, bread freshened. With that in a basket as well as cheese and a pitcher of milk, her next target was the guard above the cave housing Ninian. The man did his best to obey the shire reeve's firm instructions but he was no match for Mabli in her most determined mood.

Lifting away the hatch over the cavity he tied the basket handle to a rope and lowered it into the abyss. Mabli had taken a flare from a sconce in the wall and by its light she could see the gleam of Ninian's white hair and then his face. The agony of desolation was in every line of him but she spoke cheerfully to him in their common tongue, regretting she could not have him lifted out but happy that at least she could ensure he was warm and fed.

It took time for Ninian to realise he was being encouraged to live. Eventually, his hands scrabbled in the basket and he found the milk, drinking deeply before taking another breath. When he spoke again his words were clearer, stronger and she knew the will to live had been rekindled.

"Here," she said to the guard as she handed him what he thought was her cloak. It was an old one of the Constable's, its tight weave of thick wool promising warmth and sleep to the prisoner. "Now, lower the flare," she ordered when she had seen Ninian find the candles she had secreted for him.

The jailer was worried, protesting the dreadful things which would happen to him when the shire reeve discovered what had been done.

"Leave him to me," Mabli said in French and Welsh, a light in her eyes which promised a stormy meeting.

As the man was replacing the cover over Ninian's prison, Mabli had seen movement across the bailey. A saddled horse was being led out, its rider mounting and walking it on grass towards the gates, thereby muffling the hoofbeats. She lifted a hand to the man in the saddle and he responded with a grin and a wave. Once the main gates shut behind him, Ugo feared no more discovery and in the clear morning air she heard him canter and then break into a gallop along the road from Pembroke which led to Manorbier and Sir Odo.

Mabli returned her attention to the present as she heard the sound of footsteps clattering towards her. "Those silly heels of his – he might as well have men shouting his advance," she muttered in disgust.

Roger fitzHugh hurried into the great hall, waving an imperious hand to empty the place except for his guard and the mediciner. Mabli sat unmoved as he waited for her to rise at his entry. Instead she inspected him from his boots with the extra slices of thick leather on the heels to make him look taller, along the lines of his bedrobe, thick velvet in a strange green which reminded her of invalids she had treated. His hair was awry with his haste to reach her and his face red with anger.

"Later, Reeve Roger," Mabli said calmly in French, "I will prepare you a salve which may quieten those spots of yours. They must cause you great distress."

He stopped as though slapped hard with a heavy gauntlet, his breathing ragged, his temper almost beyond control.

Mabli's smile for him was serene. She guessed he had already forgotten Ninian. "You wished to see me?"

A steward ran to the reeve with a cup of wine, another pushed forward the carved chair which dwarfed him but gave him a certain dignity. The wine was gulped at first, then sipped more slowly.

"You, ma dame," he spat at her, his lips and chin spattered with wine, "you have taken it upon yourself to defy my orders!"

"They were, sir?"

"The thief, Ninian, is to stay alone in the darkness, without food or water, until he confesses the theft and where the remaining goblet may be found. My goblet."

Mabli nodded as she considered his words. "I understand what you are trying to do and your plan is worthy of success."

Roger fitzHugh held out his cup for more wine, satisfied the small storm was ended. The mediciner waited until he had begun to drink again.

"The punishment you have devised will be very effective, I have no doubt, but one thing puzzles me."

"Quoi?"

"If Ninian is guilty, as you believe, who will hear him speak before he dies?"

Suspecting a trick, the shire reeve stared at Mabli, her words hammering into his mind as they echoed and re-echoed.

"A frail man in the darkness and alone, he must already be near death. His jailers do not hear him, even should he shout out where he has hidden your silver." She shook her head at him, tutting sorrowfully. "All the Constable, or even Sir Odo, will see is a man dead and you responsible for his murder."

"No! No! I have only been strong as I must be in this damned hell!"

"As you say, Reeve Roger, and I have only been trying to keep yet another prisoner of yours alive until the truth is known!" Mabli was no longer the submissive servant he wished to see. She stood and dwarfed the little man in the big chair. "This is not the first time evil ones beyond the castle walls have used you to kill where they must be seen to have no blood on their hands. You would have it happen again?"

The woman's command of the French language amazed Roger fitzHugh, then he recalled she had spent almost ten years in the English court with her whore of a mistress, the Princess Nest. He hugged his thick robe around him, needing its warmth to hide the chill of his fear. The princess still had the ear of King Henry, his threats alone enough to have Owain squeezed out of Wales and exiled to Ireland. Then there was the Constable. With his wife and son returned and no castle of his own left standing, he would be back any day to live in Carew and Pembroke and he would not take kindly to finding the grandfather of his children dead or in a dungeon.

"I am in control here! What I say must be done! The Constable would not allow any weakness to be shown – how often have I been told that?"

Mabli had once seen a wolfcub cornered by a pack of hounds. It had spat and snarled at its tormentors, not looking for any means of escape, nor any way of fighting. Like that other cub, the shire reeve could only spit and snarl helplessly. She bowed to him, hiding a smile.

"Then leave Ninian where he is," she said and turned to leave the great hall.

"Wait! What if he dies?"

Mabli said nothing, merely shrugging her shoulders and raising her hands, palms uppermost. Roger fitzHugh read the message. Ninian's fate was not in her hands.

It was hard for Mabli not to chuckle as she walked across the inner bailey to her hut and her medicines. Ninian had to be found in the cave by the Constable's friend. It was the only way the shire reeve's stupidity could be evident to all. The silversmith now had hope as well as food, warmth, light. He could endure until Sir Odo arrived.

*   *   *

177

Cynfan's sweeping boy led the horse carefully through the narrow alley to the yard at the back of the bakeshop. There, he held a pail of water for the thirsty animal, fed it oats and piled sweet hay before he used a wisp of the dried grass to groom sweat-matted hair.

In the room behind the shop, Cynfan poured beer from a jug and Ugo drank as deeply as his horse.

"It is good of you, my friend," he said as Cynfan refilled the cup. "Not many in Pembroke would be as glad to house a Fleming."

"Nonsense! You are welcome here – and you know it. There is much you have done to aid our people in a quiet way and they are grateful." The baker smiled. "You have become one of us."

"You honour me, Cynfan. I believed when my home and all in it were gone there was no place for me while I lived, but Pembroke is a good town for an outlander like me to settle."

Cynfan inspected his own cup and added to it. "In a way, Ugo, we are all outlanders, coming to the trade from the castle – aye, and to its safety when raiders are near." He saw Ugo's expression darken. "There is something amiss in the town?"

Ugo said nothing for a while then, "It may be so."

"You and Sir Odo. I heard you had ridden that way at first light and he galloped back with a pack of his troopers, all armed to the teeth – oh, news travels fast along this little stretch of road."

"As well I know!"

"And you need to be outside the castle walls. Free to do what, my friend?"

"Wait. That is all I can do. Wait."

Sir Odo had less success finding his bed for the night. On reaching the gates of Pembroke Castle he had demanded entry and found it denied. Almost speechless with rage he was detailing which parts of the gatekeeper's body should hang from the walls if he was kept waiting when a braver soul poked his head out of the opening and squeaked that it was on the order of the shire reeve that no one be admitted. No one, the man had emphasised.

When the knight could breathe calmly enough not to stutter, he insisted Roger fitzHugh should be brought from whatever he was doing and answer for his decision. It was a long wait.

By the time there was movement in the gatehouse, Sir Odo was near to an apoplexy.

"Sir Odo! A thousand pardons for your discomfiture but it was you yourself who insisted the gate was not opened to one and all."

The patronising tone of the young man's French did not help matters.

"Get this gate opened!"

There was a further delay but at last the bars were lifted and the studded wood creaked on its hinges. With barely enough room to pass, Sir Odo thrust his mount at the gap and forced his way through, his men following in short order.

"Well?" Sir Odo demanded when he stood face to face with the shire reeve. "What is your explanation for keeping me waiting?" In the corner of an eye he caught a movement amongst the men manning the gate and realised there had been a purpose to the delay.

Roger fitzHugh would have no such thing admitted. Smoothness itself, he gave a long-winded reason for the extra security he had ordered. "As you have said, Sir Odo – and the Constable – we must always be alert for spies and their like."

Across the darkening bailey Sir Odo saw two of the castle guards hurry away. They appeared to be carrying something between them and he was certain the young reeve had kept him outside a locked gate until some mess or other was cleared.

"Stop those men!" he ordered the shire reeve.

Roger fitzHugh would have tried to talk Sir Odo out of his curiosity until he realised the knight was ready to explode with fury. For the moment it was enough for Sir Odo that the two men waited in the distance with their burden.

"Disturbing news has reached me that Ninian the silversmith has been held by you as a thief," he said when satisfied the men were at a standstill.

"How could you have heard such a thing, Sir Odo?" Roger fitzHugh asked smoothly, trying to convey the idea that the castle and its inhabitants were completely under his control.

"Friends who wished to buy goods from him enquired why he was no longer in his place of work." The knight gestured to the town beyond the gates. "You should have realised by now there is little goes on behind the palisades which is not known to the least of Pembroke's people. Do you hold Ninian?"

The shire reeve nodded. "He was found with silver stolen from me in his possession."

"Which is why you had him dragged here and flogged?"

Even in the twilight, the reeve was uneasy with the grimness of Sir Odo's expression and his voice. "He was dealt with as should be a thief."

"And you would have had him beaten to death because you believed he stole from you – a man never before known to steal?"

"No man should risk punishment he is unable to stand," Roger blustered.

"Fair words, shire reeve," Sir Odo said, "and they apply to any man – high born or low, silversmith or shire reeve."

"Sir! I protest!"

"Protest away! I will have your chamber while I am here," Sir Odo said in his clearest French , "and see the silversmith is brought to me immediately. When your patrols go out into the town tonight, let them spread the news Ninian is safely in my care."

"Sir Odo! You will be weakening my authority! I demand you leave this matter to me."

"Left to you," the knight said softly, "we will have one dead silversmith and a town ready to turn on us. You might think that of no consequence but for our enemies it would be a gift from heaven – or hell. Now, is there a physician of any kind in the castle?"

An uneasy Roger admitted to Mistress Mabli being there.

"Good. Send her to me. She can tend Ninian and your men can pass on the gossip the silversmith is still held in the castle but well cared for. It might just save your skin."

The shire reeve held on to his temper with great difficulty, bowing to Sir Odo and preparing to do as he was bid.

"I must also tell you," Sir Odo went on, "that Sir Walter, the king's justice for Gloucester, is in the shire. I was able to tell him the Lady Nest was safe home and in her castle at Carew. He has gone there to see her and learn all he can of the outlaw, Owain. I am sure he will come here, to Pembroke, as soon as he deems it necessary."

Roger had been sweating with anxiety but now he began to shiver. Unable to trust his barons, King Henry had appointed sound men to travel the country and establish equally fair justice for all. Sir Walter had a reputation at court for being shrewd as well as ruthless. He was the last person the shire reeve wanted enquiring into all that went on inside the walls of Pembroke Castle.

"When will we be honoured with his visit?" he croaked at last.

"That, I do not know. He will travel here when it suits him. Now, Ninian?"

Just before couvre feu that evening, a quiet knock on the door was answered by William, Walter at his back for safety.

The message they received was whispered, the hunched figure delivering it disappearing fast into the gathering night.

"Mother!" both boys called as they ran back to the family assembled around the table. "Grandfather is safe with Sir Odo and Mistress Mabli is to tend his needs!"

Luned's relief almost overcame her. "Is he coming home?"

"Not yet," William said, "but he is safe at last. The man said to be patient, the truth would soon be known – but we must tell no one of this message."

"Why not?" Deris wanted to know.

William and Walter had no answer for her but Luned had begun to wonder. "It was the same with Manon, the tanner's wife. When an injustice was being done, her friends – and her husband's friends – worked secretly to put right a wrong." She smiled at them all. "Could it be we, too, have friends?"

Time jerked past slowly. Another message from a stranger advised Luned not to try and see her father. The words puzzled her. If he was free why was he not allowed to return to his own home? Luned swayed and leaned against a wall for support, wondering why she had recently felt so strong and sure of herself and was now as helpless as a mewling kitten. Reason ranged through her thoughts and she realised she was on the point of fainting through lack of food.

When she had first heard her father was to be starved into a confession, she had found herself unable to eat. Deris and Meleri did all they could to coax her, the boys to argue with her. She had fought them but finally she acknowledged her children were right. Slowly, and holding on to the wall of the passage, Luned made her way to the kitchen. She could not see the shapely bones of her face stood proud, increasingly unencumbered by flesh, but when surrounded by her children she struggled to eat.

Another day dragged past and as that evening approached she bade good night to Sulien, watched William bar the doors and Walter feed Tegan before the household settled to enjoy one of Deris's meals. Luned was tired and decided she must try to eat again, accepting a ladle of the fragrant meat and broth in her bowl.

There was a thundering at the door and she dropped her spoon, her children looking to her, needing to know if it was a summons which should be answered.

"I will go," she said and stood, shaking a little and grasping at the table for support.

With her sons behind her, Luned walked to the door, hearing it beaten again. She lifted the bar, finding it surprisingly heavy, then swung wide the wood. A familiar figure stood there, looking at her, then past her to William. She put out her hands and felt them held in a warm, strong, clasp before she swooned.

Chapter Eleven

"She refused food since told her father was to be starved until he talked."

Deris's words reached Luned through a swirling mist, sound coming and going as did the waves of the sea.

"On whose orders?" a deep, vibrant voice asked and Luned, her eyes still closed, was puzzled.

She knew the man but he could not be in her home, not holding her as she remembered. An awful smell was under her nose and she drew back but the arms around her held her steady in the smoke. Coughing, she struggled to be free and was awake.

"She is with us again," the man said and waved away Walter, who had been holding burning hen feathers under his mother's nose.

"Gerald?" she whispered, wondering if she dreamed.

"Aye, cariad, and about time too, I think. Now, if you can be persuaded to drink some milk – sup some broth – I will have the full account of what has been going on in my absence. Meleri, will you help the girl with the food? Walter, bar the door, we must not be disturbed. As for you, William, help me get your mother comfortable while there is talk I must hear."

Gerald de Windsor was a man used to giving orders which would be instantly obeyed. In this house, surrounded by children of his siring, there would be no exception. Luned found herself propped at the table, held there by Meleri who urged her mother to sip milk. When Luned could drink no more, her young daughter tore bread from a loaf and dipped small pieces in warm broth, feeding the sops to her mother until Luned had the strength to lift a spoon and feed herself. Deris watched and ladled more into the bowl until Luned could not manage another mouthful.

The Constable had smelled the good supper and he was served with a bowl and bread, taking very little time to eat his fill and thank Deris for her cooking. The little maid flushed with shyness at the praise but sat at the table as directed by the Constable's finger. Gwri was allowed to hover in the background, watching the family assemble.

"Now, who will begin?" Gerald wanted to know.

They all looked at each other but it was Walter who spoke. He told his father of the despair in the house when William was taken by Owain and how his grandfather, Ninian, kept them all busy in the house and the smithy. Margan, who had been a quiet part of the household, had sickened and no one knew why. Sometimes, Walter told his father, Margan had seemed better and then he worsened again.

Gerald was puzzled. "Who did his work? I know Ninian was training you all, as he did your mother, but –"

A chorus of voices told him of Sulien's visits to Ninian, his offer of help, his many kindnesses to them all. As his children talked, Gerald looked first at Luned, then at Deris, noticing a movement behind her which he saw was the sweeping boy's agitation.

"Then there was the day Grandfather went to the castle to see Mistress Mabli," Walter said, "but she had already gone. He had been kept waiting for a long time where a steward was cleaning silver –"

"And next day, Father, men came before we were dressed," Meleri told him. "They searched everywhere so roughly they broke things." There were tears in her eyes as she remembered her little horse.

"Aye, and they stole silver, too," Walter added.

"Did they hurt you?" Gerald asked Luned and she saw again in his expression the gentleness in him few had ever seen but which was so familiar to her.

"We were pushed a little, but when a man found the goblet in my father's bedspace –"

"He said Grandfather was a thief!" Walter burst out.

"Who was he?" Gerald asked.

"Brede," Luned said. "I learned his name later – and that he is well known in the town for his harshness to all he meets." She was still for a moment, confused. "But he is dead now and it was after that I was stopped from visiting my father – even from taking him food."

"On whose orders?" There was the chill of a building anger in the Constable's words.

When Luned told him what he wanted to know, Gerald rose, kissed Meleri, gripped his sons' shoulders and turned to look at Luned. He gazed at her for an age, then sighed and was ready to leave. "There is much for me to do, it would seem – much to put right."

Behind Luned, Gwri's agitation was frantic as he whispered again and again to Deris.

"What is wrong with the boy?" Gerald demanded to know and they all stared at Gwri.

"Sir, Mistress Mabli!"

"Aye, aye, she is in the castle. I have come from Carew and was told the mediciner must stay here to tend some poor wretch near death."

"No!" Gwri burst out. "Eynon recovers but she says that so she may come and go freely. Sir, ask Mistress Mabli first. She and Nudd have been working –" The boy stopped, realising all eyes were on him.

"Thank you," the great man said quietly. "I will do as you suggest and I will return soon. William, a king's justice is in

Carmarthen and will visit Pembroke. He will want to talk to you, hear what you have to say of the time you spent away from us. Sir William is a good man and you may speak freely to him."

With one last, long look at Luned, he was gone. They heard the bar lifted and his sons raced to fling wide a shutter and watch him cross the short distance to the castle and its open gate.

In the morning, Luned rose very early and with a lighter heart, dressing in one of her newest tunics in her favourite green. The children slept and she gazed at each in turn, rejoicing in them. As for her father, Gerald had assured her he would be safe and have all the food he needed. 'Be patient,' he had said, and she was happy to be so, going towards the kitchen and her daily tasks.

Gwri stirred from his bed near the woodpile. His grin for her was a sleepy one and she realised she had neglected the boy. Hazel twigs, she thought. Gwri must be encouraged to use them every day and keep whole and fresh the teeth God had given him. Deris was already busy, her workaday tunic twitched out of the way and held by her belt, an apron spanning her small body.

"Good day, mistress!"

"And to you, Deris. Aye, and thanks be to God, it is a good day."

"With the Constable back among us all can be put right now and the master will soon be in his own bed and waiting for Cynfan's hot bread."

Luned nodded. Blood had raced to her cheeks at the mere mention of Gerald. She had thought him lost to her forever but from his grasp of her, the way he had stared at her last evening, she knew he had not forgotten what had been between them. The love they had shared still leaped and flared, even if it could no longer be admitted. She drifted through her first chores, seeing everything she touched with new eyes. The cheese from market, had it always looked so moist and creamy, the butter, too? Bowls on the table were inspected carefully, Luned's finger exploring the twists and turns of the grain lines in the wood.

Distantly she heard Gwri and Deris chattering as the outer door was unbarred and Deris went to Cynfan's for the first bread and the first gossip of the day. Luned went to open the shutters of the gracious living room first made beautiful by her mother. There was time to relive quiet and enduring love as well as peace to stand in the light and look at the castle opposite, watch little figures scurry above the gates and see the huge wooden masses swing open to let out the first of the servants and the troopers who must deal with the people of the town, the girls and women to the market growing at the far end of the roadway, the armed men to deal with drunks in the alleys alongside the taverns.

Deris came to find Luned as she dreamed by the window. "Food is on the table, mistress. The boys are in the yard washing and Meleri is slicing the cheese. Gwri has milked the goat for me this morning – he is becoming very helpful."

"I am glad to hear it," Luned said with a smile and followed Deris to the familiar sounds of the kitchen.

The first meal of this day was almost a celebration, each person at the table eating well, including Luned.

"Bread is the food of life and we are lucky to have such a good craftsman as Cynfan," she said as she helped herself to another piece of his baking and spread it liberally with butter.

"He might be changing his work," Deris told her and Luned turned to the girl in surprise. "Aye, there is talk he dreams of buying the tannery land from Manon, the widow of Gerwyn the tanner, and building a mill beside the stream there."

"Once all the ponds and sluices are cleared away, it would be simple to build a dam to hold the water coming down. A millwheel would ensure Cynfan could grind whenever he chose." William was very knowledgeable about country matters, especially since his father had promised he would inherit the estate at Cenarth Bychan. He said no more, wondering if the Constable would be able to rebuild the castle there. It had all burned so fiercely that terrible night.

Luned was puzzled. "Surely Cynfan must get permission from the king for such a venture?"

"Aye, he must," Walter said.

"Talk in the town is of the prior wanting that land for his own mill – for the benefit of the church, he says," Deris added. "You wait and see. If that man of God gets what he wants, we will all have to pay more for our bread."

"For the benefit of the church," Gwri muttered.

He surprised Luned, not only with his words but with the bitter tone of his voice. Gwri was changing, becoming a grown man inside his small body. She watched him eat his fill, wondering what had made it happen.

"How is it Cynfan might get the land – and the king's permission?" Walter wondered. "Surely the prior would have the ear of all the people useful to him?"

Willliam smiled and Luned saw again a little boy full of mischief. "Perhaps there are others who have influence and do not approve of Father Prior's bullying."

"William! How can you say such a thing?" his mother protested.

He looked at her and smiled. Another had grown to manhood without her seeing it and there was a coldness in her. As a man, Willliam must leave her for good.

"It is true, Mother. I have listened to all that happened while I was away from Pembroke. The wife of Gerwyn the tanner nearly hanged by the shire reeve? Why? Because her husband was murdered and Roger fitzHugh must have someone to hang. So, why the widow? The prior went to

189

her before her trial and tried to persuade her to confess. He offered her sanctuary – if she gave him the land."

"How do you know all this?"

The boy-man chewed a piece of cheese. "I listen to all and then I make up my own mind," he said, and his mother heard his father's voice echoing in the words. "Did you know two brothers from the priory daily visit Gerwyn's son, the one now running the tannery?" he asked his mother. "Each time they try to persuade Meurig to join them in the monastery."

"With the land as a benefice?" Luned said slowly.

"Aye, but the prior is a fool. He ignores what any who walk the town may see," William said loftily.

"And what is that?" Luned asked.

"There is a lady at the far end of the town who sews. She has two daughters and Meurig would have one of them in bed – even if it means he must wait to wed her," William said calmly.

"William!" Luned's cry fell on deaf ears as all around the table joined in the laughter.

Walter was the first to become practical. "How does that help Cynfan get the tannery land?" he wanted to know.

"Father Prior is a man who has made enemies with his ambitions while Cynfan is a good man and gives freely of all he has to help the people of the town," William explained. "There are those in Pembroke who notice such things."

Deris began to gather up the discarded bowls and cups. "Mistress," she whispered, "later this morning, when Pembroke is at its busiest, will you please go to the leather shop?"

"Why?" Luned asked, concerned by Deris's earnest plea.

"It is necessary. When you get there, ask to see Mistress Manon – to find out when the new boots you ordered for William will be ready."

"I know that already – in a day or so."

190

Deris nodded hard. "Aye, but will you go? Please? It is important."

With her daily tasks completed, Luned prepared for her short journey alone into the town. She had kept herself apart from everyone for so long her fingers trembled as she swathed her kerchief around her throat and lower face, anchoring it in a plain headband. All morning she had been intrigued by Deris's message, hoping she might begin to find some answers to all the mysteries. Deris was to keep Meleri busy making cakes from the precious white wheat flour while the boys were taking turns at the crucibles in the workshop.

A stranger to most in the town, Luned had rarely ventured along the street of shops and houses since her father had been imprisoned. When she did she was greeted with silence and stares. Today was easier, the occasional half smile and a nod from acquaintances cheering her. Was it the warmer weather, she wondered, looking above the rooftops to a blue sky and sunshine, or had the people of Pembroke accepted at last that their silversmith was still the honest man he had always been? Luned could not see that her choice of tunic in a becoming dark blue linen and the swathing of white linen around her head and neck showed her pride as she walked. Her obvious confidence in her family was the greatest proof of her father's innocence.

The leather shop was soon reached and Luned paused for a moment as the crowd drawn by the market swirled around her. Gwri's friend Nudd was behind the trestles fronting the roadway, watching the boots, pouches, belts arrayed there with a keen eye. Behind him shelves held caskets for which Manon's family was becoming famed, the colours and intricate designs on the leather-covered wood catching every eye. Luned gazed at the patterns set there by a crafstsman's hand: some of the curves and symbols she remembered from her mother's stitching, while others were from afar and entrancing in their complexity.

191

"Good day to you, mistress," Nudd said quietly when he realised Luned had looked her fill. "I will tell Mistress Manon you are here."

"Thank you, Nudd – and may God bless you for all you have done for Eynon. His family will be always in your debt, as am I. I feel a sense of guilt his mother was with me when he had need of her."

Nudd's strange green eyes flashed and were quickly shuttered. "There is no need for you to feel guilt, mistress. No, not you."

She was left bewildered as Nudd went to the back door of the shop and called for the tanner's wife. He had sounded so sure, Luned thought, as if there was someone to blame. Who?

There was no time for more as Manon appeared, hands outstretched to greet her customer. "Welcome!"

The greeting and the smile brought tears to Luned's eyes but she held herself erect and walked into the warmth and firmness of Manon's grip.

"Come!" Manon invited, and Luned followed her along the narrow passage between the workshop and the house to a door leading into the big kitchen which was the heart of the house. Gwen was kneeling by the fire, turning small cakes on a bakestone, her cheeks flushed as she tried to persuade a very small boy to stay away from the heat and the food.

"If his mother permits, you should take him to see the juggler I am told is in the market today," a woman said.

"Go, Gwen. The cakes will wait for your return," Manon insisted and smiled at Luned who had been surprised to see Princess Nest's mediciner seated in a dim corner of the kitchen.

"Mistress Mabli?"

"Aye, and a good day to you, Mistress Luned," the older woman said as she rose stiffly to her feet and adjusted the belt around the fine brown wool of her tunic. "I have a need

192

to speak with you – but where no one can see we have met. Manon has been my conspirator – as have Nudd and your own Gwri. Believe me, we have the safety of you and your father at heart."

"All this secrecy," Luned said at last. "Why such a need for it?"

Mabli gestured towards the noise from the roadway. "Pembroke on a market day. All can be seen – and heard. Yet in Pembroke there are some who prefer to do their good works and not be noticed except by the Good Lord who guides them always. Among such company are those who are afraid for you and for your father."

A sudden fear tightened Luned's throat and in the heat of the kitchen she shivered. "You have brought me here to tell me he is dead?"

"No, child." Mabli said and smiled. "Ninian is well. He has bathed this morning and suffers much less from the small companions who have blighted his existence. The Constable broke his fast with Ninian and they talked until the tide was turning and Sir Gerald sailed for Carew and his family."

Shutters at the far end of the room opened to the garden beyond the kitchen. By the light which streamed in, Mabli could see Luned's mouth tighten when there was talk of the family at Carew.

"Manon, would you be so good as to leave us, cariad?" Mabli asked.

Without a word, Manon rose from the bakestone, placed a platter of fresh cakes on the table between the two women, moved into Mabli's reach a pitcher of fresh milk and went to the workshop.

"You need have no fear, Luned. Nothing you had with Sir Gerald has been taken from you. When my lady must be sent from the court and return to Wales she had to leave behind a son who was her delight."

"Henry – she told me he was called Henry."

"Aye," Mabli said with a sigh, "after his father – a father who was forced to send Nest away, yet would keep his child by her. It near broke my poor lamb's heart. Then she must marry, the king decreed in his wisdom. He knew of Sir Gerald – of his courage, the strength of the friendship between their fathers. Henry also knew of you and your children as well as the care Sir Gerald had of you. You were not wed so the king had found a man free to marry my Nest, a man who knew what it was to love and care for a woman and her children."

"Gerald was taken from me to keep a king happy?"

"You are right to be bitter but Henry is a king. He wanted his kingdom quietened, his queen and her followers appeased and Nest under the protection of a man he knew he could trust to be faithful."

"My man," Luned said so softly, Mabli could barely hear her.

"Aye, he was, but I watched as the two of them made the best of their lot. My lady has her home at Carew and wealth enough for comfort –"

"While Gerald became Constable of Pembroke and was to have his own castle in due course. Must he love her as well?"

Mabli put a large hand over the knotted fingers of Luned. "Not the love he had for you. He gave Nest what she craved most – children. It is a man's way, to sow seed easily, but he has been loyal to his wife. I have seen that – and no one has watched more carefully than have I – but his love for the children you gave him is untouched. Never forget, Sir Gerald's new castle in Emlyn was to pass to your son, William. He is his father's true heir."

She had heard it all before. Luned closed her eyes, her head bent almost as if in prayer, and Mabli waited. With a sigh, the younger woman straightened on her stool and looked directly at Mabli. "Was that what you brought me here to tell me? All the secrecy was for that?"

"No, cariad. That was the past as well as the present. I am concerned for the present and the future. Tell me, the dreadful events for your family, when did they start?"

A dainty snort of disgust was Luned's immediate reply. "When my son went with his father after the Nativity. I watched him sail from the quay."

"But you were not afraid then?"

Luned's brow furrowed. "Not more than any mother whose son leaves her to journey on the sea."

"Then came the dreadful news of the destruction of Cenarth Bychan – Nest and the children with Owain?"

Breathing was difficult for Luned. "Aye. Nights without sleep – all I could do was pray and be thankful Walter had been too ill with the hooping cough to go with William."

"Many could not understand Sir Gerald leaving his wife and children in the burning castle while he escaped. Did you?"

Luned was puzzled and frowned but she wanted above all to be honest. "As you know, I had been with Gerald through the sieges and knew, better than any, his courage and his determination to fight to the death."

"So if he left, he must have had a reason?"

"Aye, a good one."

"The best. His children's lives, especially your William's. Sir Gerald dead, Owain would have wasted no time killing your son when he might have spared Nest's children – for a while. You and your children, you are very important to the Constable."

"Is that why I am here?"

"In a way. Now, in more recent times, can you think of a pattern of disaster?"

Luned tried hard, images scudding through her mind, backwards and forwards, as she tried to arrange them in a sensible order. "Margan. It was when he sickened, that was first."

"Aye, that was indeed the start. First, Margan. Then your father is taken from you and you are alone. What did you do?"

"Argued with the prior." The memory still haunted Luned and she was sure she would pay the price of her defiance when she met her maker.

"I am glad to hear it. Apart from paying less for his silver, what else did the prior want you to do?"

"Marry."

"You were not willing?"

"No."

"Was a bridegroom suggested?"

"The journeyman helping in the workshop. I think the prior was anxious for cheaper silverware."

"I have no doubt he was, determined as he is to amass treasure for so young a foundation."

Luned was annoyed. "At the expense of my family."

"It is the way of some men who choose Mother Church for their ambitions. Was that when you were made aware of how vulnerable you were and when it was arranged for Eynon's mother to move in with you?"

"Anwen? Aye, it was. She was a good person to have in the house and I am grateful to Mistress Manon for arranging it."

"Until Eynon, the son, was attacked and left for dead."

"Poor Anwen! She was prompt in going to his family and helping them at such a terrible time."

"And you were once more vulnerable. Was any suggestion made to you of a remedy?"

Luned thought for a moment. "Aye, Sulien offered marriage but only as a means of protecting my good name. It was reasonable, my father having such trust in him. As for me, I have always known Sulien to be considerate of me. When he suggested we wed, he was only being very kind."

"You refused."

"Of course. The father of my children lives, I am not free."

Mabli nodded, understanding Luned's reason. "Next, your father is thrown into a dungeon in chains and is to be starved to death." The twisting of her fingers told Mabli all she needed to know of Luned's distress. "Now you see it, cariad," she said gently. "There is a pattern, a pattern which involves you. I asked to meet with you today so I might warn you of the danger but do not be afraid, nor for your father. He is secure in the castle and there are those around you who have your safety at heart. They will protect you."

"I do not understand!"

"There is no need. Go home, look after your family and take the greatest care. Be sure to do all the things your father must have taught you to keep your home safe. You have two fine sons to help. They will bar doors and keep stout wood to hand. Young Gwri can get about the town, day or night, without being seen and you may trust him completely, Deris too. Should Nudd come to you, do all he asks."

She was aware of a greater sense of peace than for some time but Luned knew all was not yet resolved. "How long must this go on?"

"Sir Gerald is at Carew. Then there is Sir Walter, one of King Henry's justices. When those two men next come to Pembroke, we may have the means to settle all your disquiets."

Manon came at Mabli's call, smiling as she prepared to escort Luned out of the leather shop. The two women stopped to watch Old Twm at work on the final stitching of a boot.

"See," Manon said. "We promised your son his boots. Let the boy come when he is ready to wear them."

Luned went into the workroom. It was long and narrow, lit by open shutters into the yard behind the leather shop, tallow lights burning in dark corners so nothing was hidden. At the far end a great table held a pile of tanned skins

197

ready for cutting, a smaller pile of softer calfskin sorted into the various muted colours which had become the mark of Gerwyn's work before his death when he used dyes made from rare plants brought to him by Nudd.

A dark-skinned man was bent over a stretch of fine green leather, a template of a hand helping him cut the material accurately for a lady's glove. To his left a wizened figure was engrossed in his deft stitches.

"Kamal is our artist," Manon explained. "He is responsible for so much of the beauty which leaves here to go far and wide."

Luned bowed to the man and his craftsmanship. "I have one of your caskets," she said, "a present from my father. In it I keep the brooches and rings my father made for my mother – or I did until our home was searched and some went missing."

"Oh, no!" Manon was distressed. "How callous of the reeve's men!"

"Aye," Luned agreed, "but it was the least of our worries that day – and since."

Manon clasped Luned's hand. "Take heart and put your trust in God and the people of Pembroke."

Surprised, Luned turned to her. "The ones who have stood at the door and shouted words at me I did not even understand?"

Manon's chuckle was refreshing. "No, not those, the flotsam tossed here by every tide and wind. I mean the real Pembroke folk who live year by year in the shadow of the castle and have learned to trust each other. Keep always in mind you are of them, as is your father."

"You are so kind, helping me as you do."

"Kind? No. Grateful, I will be always. There are many like me who gathered in the castle when Cadwgan's men surrounded it and bayed for our blood. You were always at Sir Gerald's right hand and kept us in hope."

Luned was bemused. "I? I did nothing."

Manon smiled. "You were one of us and lived with us, your trust in Sir Gerald shining for all to see. Then there was your gentleness as you helped many a woman in those dreadful days – but enough of past miseries. Now, these boots. Old Twm is working on them – come and see."

Luned inspected the boot she could see and praised the old man for his workmanship. Old Twm grinned his toothless smile and Manon was pleased to see Luned had no awkward pride talking to the bootmaker, listening to what he had to say and what advice he offered for care of his handiwork.

She nodded her understanding and assured him William would attend to his new boots with the grease and the hard polishing Twm suggested.

"I must pay you for the boots now," Luned insisted, reaching into her pouch, but Manon would have none of it.

"Wait until the boy has tried them in the morning – or the next day – and made them his own, then call in when you are passing. There is no hurry."

The short walk back to her home passed in a daze for Luned. She neither saw nor heard any around her, being pushed out of the way by a helpful hand when almost run into by a farmer in a hurry to get home as he whipped the horse pulling his cart.

"Thank you," Luned said and added, "May God bless you for your kindness," realising it was the big woman, Sennen, who had helped her.

"Thank you for your words, mistress and may God be with you also. He will need to be if you are to get home safe!"

All Luned could think about as she continued on her way was Gerald. For so many years she had been so angry and bitter, his love cut from her life. Nest had been her unseen enemy and Luned had centred every iota of her hatred on the woman. Learning what she had done for William had opened a crack in Luned's armour of loathing. Meeting Nest had wrenched wide her antipathy and now she heard again Mabli's words, words of Gerald's love for her and her children undimmed by all he had shared with Nest. 'Remember, the new castle in Emlyn will be for your William, not Nest's' echoed and re-echoed, proof that the love she had shared with Gerald had remained whole.

"It is a pity you do not have your new boots to go a-visiting," Walter chided his brother in the darkness before dawn.

Their mother had wakened them and they must dress, William in his best, because of the journey he must make to Carew. The ship would leave on the first tide and the orders had come from the Constable late the day before. William was to go and greet his other family and then answer the questions of the king's man, Sir Walter.

Luned had dressed quickly, uneasy to lose William again so soon, but glad he would be with his father, at least for a day. Deris had risen before dawn, as had Gwri, and the fire in the kitchen burned brightly. In the brightness Deris toasted yesterday's bread for William to break his fast while a sleepy Meleri, wrapped in a shawl, urged honey on her brother. Walter joined in, teasing William on his visit to the crachach. He wanted to make sure his brother minded his manners and did not shame them all, he said, reaching for hot toast as Deris brought it from the fire and spreading it liberally with butter and honey. Gwri had milked the goat early, the poor animal still sleeping as she was drained, but William must be well fed before he left his home, on that they were all agreed.

Walter, as full of good food now as his brother, begged his mother to let him take Tegan and walk with William to the quay.

"He could do with a good walk, Mother, and when William has sailed I can make sure those awkward-looking legs of his are made to run for a change."

Luned hesitated but it was very early and the flood of pickpockets and thieves would still be asleep, inside the town and out. She smiled her permission and the two boys set off , Luned waiting to bar the door again when they were out of sight. That done, she returned to the kitchen and sighed as she sat on her stool.

"Mistress, he will be back – and soon – after he has made sure those brothers of his, and his little sister, are well and happy. He needs to see them again – in their home and safe."

"You are right, Deris, as always, but I was not grieving for William. It is that our day has finished and it is not even light!"

Deris was pleased to see her mistress smile. "Just you wait. This is Pembroke, where no one knows what is to happen after they say their first prayers of the day."

Chapter Twelve

"Keep a tight hold on that dog!"

The deep voice with its strangely accented Welsh came from the dimness of the earliest dawning. William and Walter heard the clop of hooves and a dark mass resolved itself into two men and a horse, the horse without a saddle and the taller of the men carrying a foal. Walter recognised him.

"I have Tegan safe, Master Ugo. Are you for sailing to Carew?"

The two groups merged and faces became clear in the first light. "With this much wind, young Walter, I fear the rowers will be forced to work up a sweat. Do you journey with me?"

"No, sir, not I – my brother William. You will not have met him of late, Master Ugo. He has been away from home."

The man was very tall and laden but he bowed most courteously to William. "I am pleased to make your acquaintance, young master, and like everyone in Pembroke I thank God for your safe return home."

"You are kind, sir. Is your home and family in Pembroke or in other parts?"

"I regret I have no family now and my home is wherever your father, the Constable, needs me. Today, it is in Carew where this young lady is to grow strong." Ugo smiled as he turned to show the boys the face of the foal nestling in his arms, a narrow white flash down the length of its strong, proud nose. "Your sister, Angharad, is too silent since she has been once more with her family and it is hoped caring for this little beauty will help her return to the happy creature we all remember."

William stiffened. He remembered the child in his father's castle in Emlyn before the raid, her laughter seasoning all their days. It was one more crime for which Owain must pay and a hasty prayer that it should be so rose silently.

At the quay the ship lay waiting, its sails furled, its sailors standing ready at the oars. Planks of wood were laid on to the vessel and from the rail to the deck. Ugo gestured to William to wait with the mare while he went on board and placed his burden gently within a ring of straw tied in bales. That done, Ugo walked back to the mare and talked to her quietly, lifting her head that he might look into her eyes and breathe softly in her nostrils. He stood closer, letting the beast smell the foal on him before he took the halter rope and moved a step backwards. The mare followed. Another step by the man and then the anxious mother and so it continued until he could turn and tread steadily, carefully, up the planks and then down to the deck. William ran on board and moved aside a bale, allowing mare and foal to be reunited.

"Ready, sir?" the captain called.

Ugo checked the mare's tethers at the prow then gestured to William to bid his brother farewell. "As you will, captain."

Walter helped untie the moorings and pushed at the side of the ship which eased its way from the quay. Oars dipped into the water, the mainsail was unfurled to catch even the slightest breeze and William was on his way to Carew.

* * *

203

Deris finished clearing crumbs from the table, wiping the wood with a clean, damp cloth and beckoning to Gwri to bring his besom and sweep the floor. Meleri moved from her stool and settled by the fire at her mother's invitation.

"Have you thought more of what I said last evening?"

Meleri nodded. "Aye, Mother. It would be a kindness to make a silver toy for the new baby when it is born. It has already lost its father and Mistress Manon will be grieved again when she can see the baby's face and know it can only ever smile at its mother."

"I thought, perhaps, a silver rattle?" Luned was anxious for her daughter's approval but she smiled, remembering. "As I know to my cost, babies are attracted to anything which makes a noise."

Meleri nodded her agreement. "Mistress Manon will like it, I am sure." The child frowned. "You said it would help to use up the silver mixed by Sulien. Will such a metal be safe for a baby?"

"Of course, cariad. It will be harder than your grand-father's usual custom but then he is keeping to a standard – the highest proportion of silver to copper which is yet hard enough for use."

"Sulien's silver is stronger?"

"Aye, it will be, but it does not have enough silver for your grandfather's mark."

"So, it can be sold more cheaply?"

Luned was pleased. This young lady would have a good head for trading.

"Could other toys be made?" Meleri asked. "Surely they would be stronger than any we saw in the market? Then there's the horse Grandfather made for me which was broken when the reeve's men raided us. One like it but made of this new mixture could not be shattered into pieces."

"What a good idea! When he returns your grandfather can

carve a mould and we will be able to cast toys which can withstand even the shire reeve of Pembroke's worst efforts!"

Deris was beaming at her two charges. The mistress had been a changed person when she had returned from the leather shop the previous noonday. Now she was making plans for work the silversmith was to do. She whispered, "Please God he comes home soon."

"Can you think of any tool you use here in the kitchen which could be made of a workaday silver and sell well?" Luned asked the little maid.

Deris stood in front of the fire, arms akimbo, her brow furrowed as she thought. "Rich folks like supping their broth from silver spoons – I have no idea why because surely they must burn their lips. Ordinary men and women would copy them if they could – were the price right."

"Excellent. Gwri, have you a suggestion how we can expand our trade?"

The boy leaned on his besom and hesitated.

"Please, Gwri," Luned said. "You help in the smithy, you know more about silver than most men twice and thrice your age. What would you say we should do?"

They watched him summon up all his courage. "Buckles," he said at last. "Belt buckles in silver for ladies – and made into belts with the softest, brightest leather Kamal can provide for you."

"That is inspired, Gwri! Such articles would need the hardest of silver – and we have some waiting in the work-shop already!"

"Mistress, the light has grown and I must be to Cynfan's if I am to get the first baking," Deris said. "After the boys finished up all I had in the basket, I must get more bread as soon as possible."

"Aye, and the freshest of the gossip," Gwri added with a grin, dodging Deris's outflung cloth as he did so.

"Go, girl. We have been so busy thinking this morning, I swear we will need to break our fast again!" Luned laughed and shooed Deris away.

"Will you be secure, mistress?" the girl asked. "The boys away – and Tegan. I expected Walter to be home again before I must go to town."

"I gave him coin for a coracle. It is a long time since Tegan had a good run and Walter must feel he can have an adventure today – as well as his brother."

"Then I will stay – Cynfan will keep the bread for me."

"No, no, Deris. I will bar the door behind you and be as safe as a mouse in its hole."

Meleri went to her bedspace to look for other toys in wood and in pottery, trying to decide which, if any, could be usefully cast in silver. Downstairs, Gwri was still sweeping and Luned wandered her home, seeing all was in order and planning work to come which would add interest to her father's days as well as augmenting the coin hidden from all but her and the children.

A loud knocking at the main door disturbed her progress. She stood for a moment, puzzled. Deris would still be learning all the news in the bakeshop and it was far too early for Walter and the dog to return. Her father's strictures returned to haunt her. Alone with Meleri and Gwri who was little more than a boy, she should ignore the summons.

The knocking was repeated. It echoed along the passage and made her think of a soldier demanding entrance. Perhaps it was Gerald? Her cheeks burned and she ran like a girl to the door, lifting the bar of wood which held it firm.

Before she could move of her own will, the great mass of iron-studded wood was slammed back and almost knocked her off balance. Early light streaming in was blocked by a figure, not massive but skinny, its clothes ragged and smelling of fish. It was a man, she decided, even if his face was obscured by a ragged scarf. He moved a hand and Luned's blood froze. He was holding a knife and she had time to see it was old, the handle held firm by twisted fibres, its blade gleaming and curved by much use and sharpening.

"Ninian's coin! Give it to me!"

The voice was hoarse, the words in Welsh, but Luned knew from the sound he was not from Pembroke or its surrounding villages.

"No. Only my father may pay out his coin."

The knife mesmerised her as the ruffian turned it this way and that in front of Luned's face, at one point laying it against her cheek.

"There is much coin from the priory. Take me to it – or I will carve up you and that little one you call your daughter."

She realised he relished the thoughts of what he might do and for an instant Luned could not move, could not speak. This excuse for a man must have watched to see when the silversmith's house was undefended and he was ready to maim or kill anyone who stood in his way. Such a coward should not be given what he wanted and blood which had chilled began to warm and then to boil.

"Get out of my house!" Luned shouted as loud as she could and realised she still held the wooden bar. It was heavy but strength flooded through her and she lifted it, knocking aside the hand with the knife as she told the man exactly what she thought of his craven attempt to harm them and steal what had been earned by hard work.

Gwri came running, his besom aimed like a lance, the myriad stiff twigs pointing at the coward's eyes. The first hit caused the man to scream with pain and lash out with the knife but all he could slice at was the besom's handle. The boy kept his head, poking with the twigs and catching the man where and when he least expected while Luned slammed the wooden bar into raiding flesh at every opportunity.

"Mistress Luned! What is happening?"

It was Sulien at the door and she was very relieved to see him. He grabbed the intruder by the relics of clothing at the back of the neck and dragged him from the doorway, throwing him like discarded rubbish into the roadway. Skinny legs and rotting boots carried the creature away as he dodged this way and that through the crowds gathering for market. Gwri made to follow him, besom at the ready, but Sulien held him back.

"Enough, boy. You have done well but he may have friends hiding in the nearest alley and we do not want you sliced up this morning. Go and see Meleri is safe and knows all is well. Keep her in the kitchen."

Luned was shaking. Gently, Sulien took from her the wood with which she had belaboured the would-be robber. He shut and locked the door, sealing it with the wooden bar, then he led Luned into the quietness of the family room. For Luned it was as though she was in her mother's presence, feeling her in the very air. Slowly, the breaths she took became less ragged, then even.

"It is as I feared, Mistress Luned. With your father in chains you are helpless here – and known to be so. One robber was defeated today but when will the next come? Will it be two? A band of three or more? However brave you and your children, there are rogues enough loose in Pembroke to take what they want if they have a mind to it."

"You speak the truth, Sulien, but my father will be home soon – I feel it."

He shook his head and she could see a gentle sorrow for her. "You are a loving daughter and have done all you can but once the news of this attack spreads through the town, others will decide to try their hand at taking Ninian's wealth from you. The silver in his smithy is well known to be encased in the strongest iron and locked against any man, but can you be sure there are not minds planning to rob you even as we speak?"

She leaned back against the strength of the settle which

had held her parents and her children in comfort. At her side was a small cushion stitched by her mother in the last winter of her life, and Luned stroked it. She remembered times when she was young and life was hard but her mother had never wavered in her love for Ninian and their daughter.

"I will be content here, Sulien, until my father returns. If we must, I will barricade all the doors and refuse entry to all until that time."

"There is another way." He kneeled in front of her and held her hands in his. "Marry me, Mistress Luned. It need only be a – a trade – if you like. You would be known to have a husband to defend you. I can go and see the prior today and I am sure he would help us quell this unease as soon as possible."

There was one weak moment when it would have been so easy to agree and be safe. Sulien was a handsome man and he had the smell of cleanliness about him which was the pride of the best of their people. Luned almost began to lean close to him then reason was uppermost. "You are very kind, Sulien. You have done so much to help my family but I must not expect you to give up your freedom for me."

"Believe me, Luned, it is no hardship – the thought of being your husband." His gaze was earnest, flattering her as he tightened his grip on her fingers.

"You do not understand," she said. "Firstly, I could never wed anyone while my father is a prisoner, then there are my children. Their father still lives. I made my promises to him and they remain."

"But he did not marry you."

"There was no need. Under our old laws he is the acknowledged father of my children and that is what is important to me. I will not throw away my promises to him for my protection, whether it be for a week or for a year."

"He married."

209

There had been a harshness in Sulien's voice which surprised her. "At his king's order," she reminded him.

"And given his wife four brats which take precedence over yours."

"No, Sulien, you are wrong. My William is still the Constable's first-born – and always will be."

On the river the air smelled clean, no tainting by ordure such as was always in the roadways and alleys in the town. The eastern branch of the River Cleddau curled away and the settlement on the right bank was a busy place. Early in the morning it might be but farmers must be about their business as soon as day broke. William could see a milk-maid with her bucket going into a byre, a sleepy man rubbing his eyes as he yoked two oxen and led them towards a cart. William guessed it was the farmer's wife who was carrying a huge basket from the house, its doorway almost lost under the deep thatch.

Often, he and Walter had raced up into the market at the east end of Pembroke and at last he could watch one family gather its goods for sale. It would be a long walk into the town and surely the butter and cheese would get there late? Perhaps this was a farm whose foodstuffs were so good the knowing housewife would wait for them to arrive. He had heard his mother and Deris talk of such people.

"Not long now, Master William," Ugo called and William went to join him in the prow of the ship. The foal, rocking unevenly on ungainly legs, was firmly attached to one of its mother's teats and sucking hard. "A good strong lass, she is," Ugo said and stroked the youngling's coat with a wisp of hay. "With God's help she will bring the little Angharad from her far place," he added softly.

Coracle owners were plying their trade across the river ahead of the ship. On the near bank a man almost hidden by bushes called out and the cry was taken up at intervals from there to the solid wood of the quay where the ship was to dock.

Ugo nodded towards the masking bushes. "Your father makes sure his men keep a good watch. After all that has happened, it is good he does."

There had been approval for the Constable in the quiet words and William was glad. So many had condemned his father for escaping from his burning castle and leaving his family to be captured.

"Look! Your brothers and sister await you!" Ugo turned to William, expecting to see delight, but the boy was white and strained. The Fleming cursed himself for a fool. This meeting would raise all the demons which had consumed the boy while in the care of his father's enemy. Almost man size, he was yet a child and one who had lived through terror and flames. Ugo put a strong arm around William's shoulders and felt him shivering.

"Do not forget what you endured to bring all of you back to this," he told William. "You are here – every one of you. Yes, your father lost his castle and all his treasures but there will be many a carver in Pembroke ready to make even more beautiful beds and chairs and stools for the new fort. Then there are the sheep-shearers planning wool for blankets and cushions, potters cleaning their tools to make earthenware for the great hall and the kitchens while iron-smiths will be scouring the countryside for good metal ready to melt and hammer into every kind of device needed in such a palatial home."

William heard the words pouring about his head, the sounds full of hope, of expectation, of happiness. He straightened in Ugo's grasp and at last managed to raise his head and smile his thanks. "You are right. My father never bowed the knee to his enemy. As for me, after today I must do all I can to get my grandfather released. He will be needed to create marvellous ware for my father's table."

With a final pat on the shoulder for the boy, Ugo stooped to the foal, gathering it in his arms as ropes were thrown to men on the quay so the ship might be tied there safely. With the boards in place William waited for Ugo to go first.

"No, lad. They need to see you, feel you, know you really are with them. Go."

There was no second bidding. William ran off the ship and into hugs and thumps from his half-brothers, William and Maurice. There was a tugging at his tunic and he turned to see Angharad's huge eyes gazing up at him. William fell to his knees and gathered the little girl in his arms as he would have done Meleri. With her arms tight around his neck, he felt her cheek against his and a wetness moistening them both.

"You are the best medicine she could have," a warm, gentle voice told him and William looked up to see the Lady Nest smiling at him, tears in her eyes.

"Angharad, let him up!" Maurice insisted and dragged his little sister away with all his six-year-old strength.

His brother had the added wisdom granted by an extra year. "Be patient, Maurice, and leave Angharad alone."

William was allowed to stand at last and he bowed over the hand of their mother, would have knelt to her, but she caught both his hands and raised him, kissing him warmly on both cheeks. "Welcome to Carew, William. I am so grateful to your mother she has spared us this day. Were I her I would be loath to let you out of my sight."

"My mother sends you her regards, my lady, and her prayers. She asked me to tell you it gives her great pleasure to know you are safely back with all your children."

The princess had tears in her eyes at the message but she slipped her hand into the crook of William's elbow and began the walk from the river to the castle. Only then did William notice the myriad pairs of eyes watching them from every corner of the castle, the palisades, the quay, the river, and he was suddenly shy.

There was little time for such an emotion, his father striding from the castle to meet them. Beside him was a man a little shorter than the Constable and not as lean. His face was clean-shaven except for a small moustache and his hair in a longer style than that favoured by William's father. Unlike his host, who wore one of his favourite tunics in green wool with plain banding at neck and sleeves, the stranger's garb was of a lustrous black velvet, simple in cut but adorned with a heavy gold chain carrying a seal of state.

William knelt to his father who blessed him and raised him to his feet. "Sir Walter, my son," the Constable said proudly.

Bowing to the king's justice for Gloucester, William was relieved to stand near and not smell the fustiness he usually associated with black velvet gowns. Pembroke's money lender had worn such clothing and always reeked of dust and decay until he moved to Cardiff and the greater prospects of easing money from other men's pockets.

"I am glad to make your acquaintance at last," Sir Walter said, his voice quiet and light for a man of his size. "Come, we will walk the river bank and you will tell me of life in this shire. You were born in Pembroke, I believe?"

The boy nodded and out of the corner of his eye he saw his father shepherd away the Lady Nest and her children. He knew he must relive for the justice the time Owain had had them all at his mercy. William dreaded the experience but he was the Constable's son and lifted his chin, not seeing Sir Walter's approval of his courage.

The king's man talked of fish he had eaten from such a river as the Cleddau, of hunting in woods such as could be seen on the far bank. Only when William was at his ease did the probing begin and it was very gentle at first. The way the boy felt when he returned home, the moment he knew he was to begin the longed-for journey, the last time he had seen Owain. Justice Walter was skilled in drawing from grown men secrets they did not wish to share so a boy could do little to resist. Gradually, he led William back to the night when he was woken by screaming and by fire, by the sound of clashing swords and the smell of death.

"Something has troubled you since then?"

William stared at a coracle being paddled across the river but Sir Walter was patient. "My father leaving us to Owain. I did not understand – he was always the first into battle, the last to admit defeat."

"And now?"

"The Lady Nest helped me to see what had to be done. Had my father stayed, he would have died at his enemy's hand and his wife been married to Owain."

"You realise you would have followed your father into the next world at the end of Owain's sword?"

The boy nodded. "My brothers and sister too."

"Yet here you are all gathered in such a peaceful spot while Owain rots amongst the ruffians in Ireland. What occurred that terrible night and the decisions forced on your father – you will agree the outcome has been favourable?"

"Oh, yes, sir. My mother says God's hand has held us and brought us home."

"As did her prayers, I have no doubt." Sir Walter studied William's expression. He had used the artfulness of his tongue to unburden the boy of every truth, yet there was something still held from him. "What is it which still concerns you so deeply?"

The law man's words were gentle, but even so it was some time before William could speak. "I never knew his name."

"One of Owain's men?"

William nodded. "He was not of the raiders who took us but he came later from Powys and was welcomed by Owain." Young fingers with bitten nails twisted together in remembered anguish. "I had to sleep in the stable but it was warm there with the horses and no real hardship. One night I woke and he was standing over me, then he kicked me hard in the side, again and again. I had no weapon so I curled like a hedgepig and prayed he would stop. When he did he was breathing hard and cursing all women of my mother's people who slept with Franks and gave them sons. 'Nest earned her punishment with an English king – and his lackey in Pembroke. She, who was born to serve the Wales of Hywel Dda, her ancestor, and give children free of Frankish blood to fight for the freedom of us all. Had I my way, you would be dead already – aye, and your brothers and sister.' There were more kicks. 'Your mother, too, she is paying for her sins against us.'" William looked up at Sir Walter. "I did not know what he meant, sir. When I came home it was to find my grandfather locked away in Pembroke Castle as a thief and my mother unprotected."

The king's man put an arm around the boy's shoulders and began to lead him back to the peace of Carew and his other family. Once inside, William was dragged away to see the new foal.

"Well?" the Constable asked.

"You should be proud of your son. His words bear out everything your wife has already told me, indeed he informed me of beatings the Lady Nest received which she has not mentioned."

Gerald de Windsor was grim-faced as he thought again of all the horrors his kin had endured at the hands of his enemy.

"There is the other matter we have discussed. Since listening to the boy, my instincts tell me it would be unwise to delay a moment longer."

The door was shut fast. William knocked hard on the wood and waited. He heard footsteps in the passageway and then his mother's voice.

"Who is it?"

"Mother, it is William! What is wrong?"

"Nothing, cariad," she reassured him. "Are you alone?"

"My father is with me." He heard the massive key turn in the lock and then the bar being lifted.

Gerald was first across the threshold, taking the bar from Luned. He handed it to William and then grasped the woman by the shoulders, turning her to look at him so he might gaze into her eyes. Whatever he saw there caused him to relax his grip. "Lock up, boy," he ordered William and all three made their way to the warmth and light of the kitchen.

Meleri ran to her father and Walter bowed as courteously as he had been taught. The Constable kissed his daughter, dealt his younger son a familiar blow on the back and then demanded to be told what had occurred since William had left that morning for his visit to Carew. It did not take long.

"Mother, you could have been hurt!" William was clearly upset. "To think someone watched this house to make sure Walter and I were absent with Tegan —"

"Hush, cariad," Luned said. "We were well defended and for the rest of the day we have stayed indoors, Nudd bringing whatever we needed from the market."

"Thank God for Nudd!" the Constable explained. "Has there been any work done in the smithy this day?"

Luned was puzzled by the question. "Of course. After Sulien frightened off the man he —"

"Started on the batch of silver Mother would not allow for the prior's order," Walter finished for her.

Gerald waited for Luned to say more but she was staring at her fingers, folded together on the table, as though they belonged to someone else. "He has completed all the work you set him for the day?"

The French words they had all been using added a formality unusual in the household. It increased the tension in the air.

"Of course. Sulien has worked well and is all my father

216

said of him. Silver for the new pieces will be ready to cast when Father is home and can shape the moulds." Luned spoke carefully.

"That will be soon," the Constable said and rose to leave.

Meleri held his hand as he walked to the main door. William and Walter had followed and saw to the unbarring and unlocking.

"Look to your mother," Gerald told his children before he blessed each of them and bade them, "God and His angels be with you this night."

It was quiet in the kitchen, Deris coming in from the pantry with milk to heat on the fire, bread and wheaten cakes for any still hungry. Meleri and Walter plagued William to tell them about his visit to Carew, and he talked of the river and the men paddling the coracles as well as all the cargo they had carried, human and otherwise. His account of the fat woman screeching as she tried to hold two geese in her arms while she crossed the river had them all laughing but Luned was silent, waiting for the moment William would talk of what was troubling him.

At last the younger ones went to their bedspaces. William took it upon himself to see Tegan had a run in the back yard, after which he became the man of the house and checked every lock on door and shutter. Returning to the kitchen, he found his mother waiting for him.

"Did all go well, cariad?" she asked.

"Yes, Mother. It was not as hard as I feared – most of the time."

"Seeing your other brothers and sister must have given you pleasure?"

William nodded. "Aye, it did. They were well and Angharad much happier now she has the foal." He explained Ugo's mission at his father's behest.

"The Lady Nest?"

"She looks much recovered already, although her smile comes less often than it once did. Mostly, she looked at her children as though she could never see enough of them."

"And the king's justice?" Luned asked and watched blood flow from her son's face.

"He was very quiet, really, although he questioned without cease until I was so drained there were no more words to speak."

"Did that kind of leeching help, cariad?"

The boy gazed at the dying fire, frowning as his eyes followed the sinking flames. "Aye, in a strange way, it did – but it also raised demons, Mother."

She moved to encircle him with her arms and held him until waves of tremors ceased. "It is all over, William. I promise you."

He had been reliving the stable and the man who kicked and threatened. "Is it?" William buried his face in his mother's neck. "I pray to God, day and night, that is so."

Chapter Thirteen

"Mother, look!" William was delighted with his new boots, lifting a foot and turning it this way and that for his family to admire the sturdiness. His last pair had been bought specially for the visit to the new castle at Cenarth Bychan in Emlyn and after the raid were lost to a thieving fist somewhere in Ceredigion.

"And when is it my turn for new boots?" Walter demanded to know, laughing at his brother and using an elbow to poke him in the ribs.

"When you need them, Walter – Meleri too," Luned said with a smile, "but we must not let William cripple about any longer, shod in his grandfather's old boots."

Walter guessed what had happened to William's last boots but still lost no opportunity to tease his brother. It seemed the best way to reassure William he was truly back home with his family.

Old Twm watched with pride as the Constable's son stood tall and strong in leather shaped just as was done for his father. The boy might have suffered but he had lost none of the grace instilled in him by his parents and his grandfather. The old man turned to Walter, understanding what it was like to be a second son. Pointing to the well-worn boots, he gestured to Walter to pass them to him. Puzzled, the lad did as he was bid and watched, fascinated, as Old Twm first cleaned Pembroke's mud from the leather, then took from under the bench a small crock. Reaching for a wide brush he spread the greasy contents of the crock on the leather, letting it dry while he beckoned for Meleri to hand over her boots. William lifted his sister on to a clean section of the bench and all three gazed at Old Twm as he set about improving worn leather.

Manon had watched the activities as she stood at the door of the workshop. "Are you satisfied with Old Twm's workmanship?" she asked Luned.

"Greatly, Mistress Manon. His stitching is so fine not even a raindrop could get through to William's hose, let alone his feet. Now, how much am I in your debt?"

"It was always Gerwyn's wish we should have about us silverware. He loved the shine of it and longed for the day it might sit there on our dresser. If your father would make us a piece – a bowl perhaps – when he is home again, it would be a fair exchange. I have no wish for the finest silver, like the prior expects in his surroundings. Such metal would attract a thief. No, the baser mix with copper would suffice to give us the gleam Gerwyn longed for in his home."

"Of course, Mistress Manon, it shall be as you wish, but my father may be a long time from his smithy." Luned tried to keep sadness from her voice but was surprised by the smile she received.

"And perhaps he may be home sooner than you fear," Manon said gently.

Gerwyn's widow drew Luned into the kitchen, making sure nothing they said could be overheard.

"Home soon? How?" Luned asked.

"There are many who know Ninian is no thief. Too much was happening which made no sense but the wiser among us began to reason together. I know it is still early but today, Mistress Luned, when you go home, send away any not of your family or your household, then lock all your doors and leave them that way until someone you know well wants to enter."

220

Luned could not hide her surprise but Manon laid a finger on her lips. "My father is coming home?" she asked.

Manon took pity on the older woman's hope which lit her from within. "No," she said gently, "he is where he is most safe and must stay there until there is no more danger."

Luned was deeply concerned. "My father safe in the castle where he has become so ill? Are you sure?"

"Indeed, and you are to see your children, as well as Deris and Gwri, stay within doors until summoned."

"But who is arranging all this?"

"Friends," was all Manon would say.

"Friends? Do I know them?"

"Aye, Mistress Luned." Manon's expression softened. "Have you forgotten the last siege?"

"You help me because of that dreadful time, so long ago?"

"Aye, Mistress Luned, and so do others."

Meleri came running in, lifting her skirts to show her mother the shine on her small boots. "Look what Old Twm has done, Mother. We all have new boots – except the ones Walter and I wear are softer and more comfortable."

The improvement in the leather was admired and Luned took her leave of Manon.

"Remember, as soon as you reach your home –" she was warned.

"I will do as you say."

It was pleasant to walk the short stretch of roadway with Meleri beside her chattering of all she had seen in the leather shop, William and Walter striding ahead and looking every inch their father's sons. Luned said nothing, content to be with her children and know her own father would return safely. All she needed to do was think of a reason for sending Sulien away early. He would find it strange, as did Luned, but Manon had been most insistent.

*   *   *

The chair was uncomfortable.

Luned had been impressed by its grandeur as she was led towards it on the dais at the end of the castle's great hall. The carving on the chair's back was of intertwined leaves but when she was seated and tried to sit at ease, edges dug into the soft flesh of her back and she must sit upright, her hands in her lap. Meleri leaned against her shoulder and Luned whispered words of encouragement for the child. Behind them William and Walter stood as if on guard, Tegan at Walter's side in a place which had once been his home.

The noise in the hall was subdued, townsfolk edging along the benches and muttering quietly to each other as they assembled. It was all so strange to Luned and she tried to make sense of all that had happened in the last hour.

It was Gerald who had knocked at the door and waited for the bolt to be drawn, the key to turn. His children had welcomed him gladly and he had responded with wide smiles, a great hug for Meleri, a swift cuff of affection for each son. Tegan, too, was acknowledged and praised for his guardianship.

"All is set in place and I will have all of you dressed in your best this instant. As soon as you are ready, I will escort you. Now, hurry!"

"Gerald, what is happening?"

He held her by the shoulders. "You have suffered so much but I believe that is now in the past and today the cause of your unhappiness will be brought to justice. Your name – and that of your father – was besmirched in the town and it is only right the honour of this family is restored the same way. He will be made to pay for his crimes."

"Who?" she begged to know, but Gerald was already striding away to hurry Deris and Gwri into a semblance of decency.

There was no time for more and Luned must see her

children properly clad before she lifted over her head the green linen tunic, relieved it still hung free of creases. A clean kerchief from her coffer, the embroidered green headband of her mother and she was ready. Not a moment too soon, Gerald bellowing for everyone to march at the double.

"Now, heads up!" he ordered his family, checking Deris carried a large parcel wrapped in old linen and Gwri had a satchel over his shoulder. He held out his hand to Luned and led her from the house. Only then did she realise groups of townspeople were in the roadway, one or two even raising a cheer against the background of murmurs, this time of approval. Two armed men were left on duty at the front of the silversmith's home and workshop as Ninian's kin went towards the castle gate.

"Can I see my father?" Luned asked once they were inside and walking across the outer bailey.

"Not yet." Gerald's brows were drawn in a frown and his mouth was tight, hard.

Luned knew that look. He had a duty to perform and nothing would get in his way until the necessary result had been achieved. All she could understand from the situation was that someone was to be held accountable for the slurs suffered by her father and, through him, by her and her children.

Her thoughts in a whirl, Luned allowed herself to be taken into the great hall and seated on one side of the dais. In the centre was a table and behind that Gerald's great chair. Another, almost as imposing, was beside it with smaller seats empty in the background. Servants had been busy setting out benches and trimming flares which were in every available bracket. Smoke lifted to the high roof and all the doors were open so it was comfortably cool.

Deris and Gwri scurried in and stood to one side of Walter, tucking themselves into a dim corner. Luned looked straight ahead, aware she was the object of whispering and trying not to see who was busy gossiping. Manon she saw and they exchanged smiles. Cynfan the baker was there, leaning against a wall near a door and talking to the big Fleming who had been kind to William on the journey to and from Carew. Others Luned recognised as being part of the market scene when she and Meleri ventured there. One woman seemed familiar, a steward leading her to a space on the front benches which had been reserved for her, a daughter alongside. Both wore black tunics and kerchiefs, even the young daughter, and Luned guessed they were newly bereaved. Whatever was to take place, a canny hand had arranged it and she straightened a neck stiffened by anxiety. Her children were with her and soon her father would join them at home. Gerald had promised and he never gave his word lightly.

Voices in the hall were becoming shrill as their owners tried to make themselves heard until a door opened behind Luned and she felt the wood of the dais shake with the steps of a group of men. Gerald led the way to the chair set out for him and William leaned over her shoulder.

"Mother, the man with Father – it is Sir Walter who questioned me at Carew."

Luned tried to be discreet as she studied the king's justice for Gloucester. He was as her son had described him, smaller than Gerald, yet exuding a quiet power, and appeared to be wearing the same black velvet tunic, the chain and jewel William had seen in place on his breast. She shivered in the heat of the hall. Sir Walter had the look of a man intent on a grim purpose, so how did she and her family fit into his plans?

Gerald ushered his guest to a comfortable chair, pointed two men to stools at the table and waved away Roger fitzHugh to a stool at the back of the dais, well away from all that was important. Luned turned to look for the tanner's widow and saw Manon with a satisfied smile as she watched the shire reeve humbled in the very place he had almost achieved her own death.

There was a hiss of excited whispers and Luned could see the prior walking tall through the crowd to a chair kept for him apart from the ordinary folk at the foot of the dais. When he was seated, Brother Paulinus fussed his way to his own stool at the prior's right hand.

Could there be anyone left in Pembroke town, Luned was beginning to wonder, when Gerald gave a signal to one of his men standing guard at a door. It opened and an armed man led forward a prisoner in chains. From her position on the dais Luned could see the man clearly but she shook her head in disbelief. It was Sulien!

She looked at the crowd, none there showing any signs of surprise. Her gaze returned to Gerald and he saw the shock she endured. He gave a slight nod, and Luned saw his lips were tight with contained anger.

Sulien? Surely not the man who had been anxious to do all he could to help her father and had made it plain he would be content in her bed? Was he the man who had insisted on carrying Margan his supper when the poor lad lay sick in her house?

"Dear God, no!" she said under her breath, longing for forgiveness for letting a killing happen under her very eyes.

She became aware of eyes boring into her and turned her head slightly, meeting the gaze of the king's justice. What he read in her she did not know but it appeared to satisfy him.

Sulien lunged forward against his restraints. "Mistress Luned! What is happening here? You know I have committed no offence against any man – all I have ever done was to be of assistance to you and your family!"

She could feel William's hand on her shoulder, Meleri's small fist curling into the reassuring warmth of her mother's, then Tegan growled, the sound increasing, becoming louder. With teeth bared, the dog Sulien had so despised spoke for the family until Walter leaned forward and soothed the animal.

In the following hush Gerald began his enquiry, speaking in Welsh to the man standing between Fulke and Leon. Loyal to Sir Gerald and, in his absence, ordered to Caeriw by the shire reeve, they had been restored by the Constable to their duties in the castle. Luned barely heard the words exchanged, yet was aware that one of the clerks beside the king's man was whispering to him after each exchange; she realised Sir Walter was having every word translated for him.

"As you consider yourself falsely accused, it is fortunate we have as a witness the very man you thought was near to dying." Gerald informed Sulien and lifted a hand. A slight draught warned Luned of an open door.

Gasps from the crowd in the hall should have prepared her, but only when a familiar hand touched her shoulder and she heard a quiet "Cariad" did she accept that her father was alive and with them once more. He was seated next to her, the children touching their grandfather and receiving his blessings as did Tegan, the massive head resting on the old man's knee.

"You look well, Father."

Her father's smile was as warm as ever, his eyes sparkling with recovered health. "Are you surprised? Mistress Mabli has had the cleansing and feeding of me and the shire reeve has been denied all the best food!" Ninian was with his family again and he could want no more.

Everyone was shushed into silence and Gerald questioned Sulien, demanding to know why he had come to Pembroke.

"To work with one of the great silversmiths," was the defiant answer.

Gerald was patient, leading the man through his disappointment upon discovering there was no place for him in the smithy, Margan doing all that was required. Another gesture and Nudd came forward with a pouch stuffed with scraps of old linen. On the table he arranged them in order, Gwri going forward to help and Sir Walter taking a keen interest in all that was being done.

In silky tones, the Constable explained how the linen had come to be stained. "This group is from bowls from which Margan had supped, carried to him by Gwri – this group from bowls carried to him by you."

Sir Walter was keen to examine the linen and he made his own decision, nodding at the care taken to collect the evidence. Sulien was silenced, staring at Gwri and then at Nudd, two creatures he had regarded as nothing more than idiots, yet they had been quietly making sure he ended in this place.

"Getting Margan to take to his bed must have been achieved elsewhere. How did you do it?" the Constable asked and Luned knew that voice. Gerald's enemies heard it just before a dagger slid into them.

"I did nothing! Nothing!" Sulien protested but a man in the crowd stood and would be heard.

"You poisoned his stew when he ate with you in my inn!"

It took time to quieten the hubbub but the innkeeper protested the quality of food in Pembroke's inns and taverns, the best of meat available from the surrounding fields and the best of bread to sop out the bowls. "Aye, and it was Margan joking about Cynfan's bread I remember. He said the baker was getting strange meal these days, enough grit in it to grind down teeth."

A girl stood, a servant from the inn. "There was no grit in the bread – I ate some myself to show Margan. He said then it must be in the stew but all who fed that night denied any hardness in their share."

"Was it only once that happened?" the Constable asked.

"No, sir. Two, three times at least – only when Margan was there with that man," she said, her not very clean finger pointing at Sulien.

Sir Walter whispered and the Constable translated his question. "The source of the poisonous grit?"

Gwri carried his satchel to Sir Gerald and from it the boy lifted a wooden box with a lid.

Ninian was startled. "That is from the store in my workshop."

After all the exclamations the hall was quietened, every ear poised to hear what Ninian had to say. "It is a sample of silver ore from the mine at St Brynnach in the far north of the shire. I was sold it a long time ago and I keep it well away from idle hands."

"When did you last see it," Ninian was asked.

"I showed it to Sulien the first day he came to see how I work. He asked about local silver mines and I told him of St Brynnach, showed him the ore I had. I also told him it was good silver but very low grade ore, mostly lead coming from the smelting – besides which, the airs given off in the process can cause great harm . . ." he added slowly.

"The ore is poisonous?" Gerald wanted to know.

"Aye, it is."

The Constable reached into the box and lifted a handful of the ore from St Brynnach, rubbing it between his fingers. "It is easily made small, Ninian, small enough to scatter into food."

The old man raised a hand in protest. "Any used to working with silver would have heard of the awful death that would bring about. No man would wish that on his worst enemy."

The two women in black on the first of the benches were sobbing quietly.

"Margan's mother and sister," Ninian whispered to Luned.

"All this to work with Ninian?" Sir Gerald asked. "You must have had good reason to want the place in his workshop."

A standing figure in the hall caught the Constable's attention with frantic waving.

"You have something you wish to say, Brother?"

The prior's attendant was almost hopping with fury. "In the name of holy Mother Church how can you treat a good man so?" he demanded to know of the Constable as all his listeners muttered.

While the friar tried to control his temper and wiped away froth from his lips, Sir Gerald held up a hand for silence in the hall. "Let him speak."

Prepared for a hanging, there were many townsfolk unwilling to hear the voice of authority from the church. Too many knew this brother to be the prior's spokesman.

"At all times, Sulien has only ever wanted the well-being of the silversmith and his family. Why he has done so is a question you must ask Ninian's daughter. She has laid a spell on him and Sulien would have her for a wife, indeed he has said as much to the prior and myself, trying to arrange a speedy marriage to protect such a woman from the violence of a crowd."

"The lady was in danger?" Sir Gerald asked, his tone silky.

"Yes, she was – and is, as you well know, sir. Rejected as your concubine she lives among decent people with three children born out of wedlock. Only Ninian's presence in the home and the respect people have for his skills has kept her safe so far. Now she has bemused Sulien until he swears he loves her beyond reason and –"

"No!" Luned was furious with the stupid Benedictine. She stood tall and proud, her kerchief flying away from her face with the rapidity of her movement. "You smear my children with your words and now you attack me – and

229

would have me bear the guilt for all Sulien has done? Shame on you!"

Brother Paulinus had earned few friends in the town with his pompous and officious ways, using his standing with the prior to allow him many offences against honest folk in Pembroke, so Luned's words earned murmurs of approval right across the crowd.

"First, my children. Everyone here knows their father has loved and supported them since the days of their births – more so than many children neglected under the new laws your pope and your king have decided we must bear." Luned turned and stared at Sulien. "From the first day he entered my father's house, Sulien made it plain to me I was a woman he might desire but Sulien has no love for me."

"How can you be so sure, mistress?" the fat little monk demanded to know.

Luned faced his disgust calmly. "Because of your vocation and your unpleasant manner, Brother Paulinus, you have no idea of earthly love, so I tell you. Even from that first day, I saw in Sulien's eyes the same look my father's customers have when they admire a piece of his silverware. Not love, Brother, merely a means to an end. Something to show he has achieved a status amongst his fellows – much as your altar in the priory church gleams with silver from my father's workshop."

The noise from the crowd became boisterous and the Constable was forced to raise a hand, his men actively quietening the worst offenders with slaps and cuffs. Luned never took her eyes from the discomfited monk.

"There is one more thing which should be told, Brother. The arrangement Sulien made with the prior – that when he took full charge of the silversmith's business, the price of silverware would be reduced."

This time it took longer to restore order but Luned waited.

"As my father's heir, I controlled the workshop in his

absence and found Sulien adding too much copper to the silver, far too much to be to my father's wishes. Because I intervened, the silver you have on your altar is the best available and not the mix weakened by Sulien."

Ninian raised a hand to his daughter. She held it and with the other pointed at Sulien.

"Whatever his reasons, he used Margan, he used my father and he would have used me."

Now the hall erupted. Luned sat with her father, his hand warm in hers. Meleri, proud of the stand her mother had taken, had her arms around her shoulders, while William and Walter stood tall, trying to be as stern as their father. Even Tegan approved, laying his head on Luned's lap.

The questioning of Sulien continued, but it passed almost as a blur for Luned. In succession Anwen came into the hall, ahead of her son, Eynon, who was carried on a litter. He was able to describe the moments before he was stunned into oblivion, remembering the last two people he had seen as Sulien and Brede, the shire reeve's man.

Mistress Mabli stood and spoke of Nudd's efforts which had saved Eynon, and she handed a scrap of linen on which had been drawn with charcoal the shape of the bludgeon nearly causing Eynon's death. Puw came forward with the dreaded club carried by Brede while he lived and there were "oohs" and "aahs" from those nearest the dais when the match was made.

The next entry was more of a shambles, the owner of a house in Pembroke's main street carrying in a huge package. Explaining that his servant girl had found pieces of roofing straw in Sulien's hired bedspace, he described how, with Puw's help, he had ferreted in the thatch. At that point the man opened the package and a massive haul of silver could be seen, no one more surprised than Roger fitzHugh.

"My goblet!" was a scream which could be heard above the shouting. The shire reeve ran forward and reached for it but Sir Gerald smacked his hand away, as would a parent curbing a greedy child.

"Father, look!" Luned exclaimed more quietly. "It is Mother's brooch, the one you made for her when I was born." Even across the dais the gleam of silver, garnets and pearls could be seen.

"Aye, those freshwater pearls and the stones I brought from Scotland, saving them for something special. I did not know the brooch had been stolen."

"You were in the castle by then," Luned said, "and I was sure the shire reeve's men had taken it."

So much was now explained. Luned sat with her father as in a dream. The source of their misery had been exposed and when all the hubbub was over they could return home with the children, shutting the door behind them and excluding the world.

The small part of the world in front of them had not yet finished its surprises. Sir Walter reached into the mass of stolen goods and pulled out something wrapped in oiled cloth. He rolled it open and held up a knife with a curved blade, the steel sharp, clean, as it shone in the light from the flares. The sight of it caused a dreadful silence.

The Constable was the first to break the stillness, beckoning forward the mediciner. She rose from her stool with difficulty, leaning on Nudd's shoulder as she approached the table.

"Tell us, Mistress Mabli, what you saw when you examined the body of the man, Brede," Sir Gerald said and waited, as did everyone in the great hall.

"The worst of the blood had been sluiced away to prepare him for his shroud. The only wound I could discover was across his throat, the cut edges of the big vessels which carried blood for him like huge rings loose and empty. One slice of a very sharp knife was all it took, although the butcher was skilled, I grant you that."

"Did you notice anything else?"

232

"Aye, sir. Tufts of loosened hair in his forelock and a look of surprise on his face. With the help of Nudd and Gwri it can be shown how we think Brede died."

The Constable's large and ringless hand silenced the excited murmurings which arose. Gwri and Nudd stood together on the dais, the younger boy to the left of Nudd. Nudd pointed away from them and Gwri turned his head. In an instant, Nudd had hold of Gwri's hair, forcing his head back, and with an imaginary knife he sliced across the boy's throat. Even as his right hand finished the cut he threw the body of the supposed corpse away from him and Gwri lay as would Brede have done.

"Tell him, Nudd," Mabli urged but had to wait for the excited voices to hush.

"Gwri and I have tried it many times to get it as skilled as we just showed you. Whoever murdered Brede is very used to killing men silently and swiftly."

"Was that why you pushed Gwri to the ground so quickly?"

"Aye, sir. We reasoned blood would spurt and it would be the best way for Brede's slayer to escape the marks of his blood."

The Constable thanked his helpers and was surprised to see Puw pushing his way to the front of the crowd.

"Sir! Sir!" the man cried and the Constable insisted Puw be heard. "What we have just seen, it must be how the little man died – the one we thought dead by the hand of a sailor from the norsemen's ship. When we carried Brede into the castle we remarked how alike were the two wounds."

Sir Gerald was frowning. "What little man is this?" he demanded to know, then was told of the corpse found in an alley, the body of a man no one knew.

"Funny little chap he must have been," Puw said. "I've not seen many so short and with a face full of huge pustules." The memory made him shudder.

Ugo, the Fleming, strode forward. "His legs, were they
. . ." He failed to find a Welsh word and his hands curved
outwards in an almost perfect circle.

"Aye, bow-legged, he was, and must have rocked or
rolled when he walked," Puw added.

"I saw him!" Ugo could not be heard saying more but he
moved nearer the Constable. "It was one morning early
when I was riding in from Manorbier with the horse you
loaned to Sir Odo for covering his mares. This little man
was coming from the silversmith's house – the small door at
the side. I heard someone bar the door after he scuttled
away."

"And I saw him – my girls served him our cheapest beer,"
a tavern keeper said. "Never knew his name but he said he
had come from Cardiff. When I asked him why, I learned he
knew someone in Pembroke who could see him right."

"The same person who slit his throat and then Brede's?"
Sir Gerald wondered aloud. He turned to Sulien and the
man watched him warily. "Any who come close to you or
get in your way appear to die. There is much for you to tell
us, Sulien – if that is your name. Why did you come to
Pembroke and why did you attach yourself like a leech to
Ninian's family?"

Sulien was tall and proud, refusing even to acknowledge
the questions. He had not reckoned with Fulke and Leon,
who stood on either side of him. At a nod from the Constable, Leon held the prisoner steady while Fulke caught
his hands in a tight grip and forced his arms up behind his
back. In a sudden silence, all could hear Sulien's breathing
change as muscles were strained and joints creaked. Still he
did not speak. Fulke increased the pressure and in the heat
of the great hall, what had been droplets of sweat became
rivulets draining down and staining his shirt and tunic.

Luned could not watch the torture, bending her head
towards Meleri who had buried her face in her mother's
shoulder. Ninian sat calm and implacable, seeing the man

who had caused them all such misery finally suffering himself. William and Walter were equally stoic. They were their father's sons and as determined on justice as was he. Tegan, too, was unmoved, his great head on Ninian's lap.

The Constable rose from his chair and went to stand in front of Sulien. "You will answer!" He nodded to Fulke who gave an extra twist to his hold and Sulien bit back a scream of pain. Again, Fulke added pressure to his hold and again. At last Sulien sobbed a reply but it was too indistinct to be heard. Leon leaned across and slapped Sulien's cheek, drawing blood.

"They were your children," those closest to Sulien heard.

All the assembled crowd could see was the Constable fighting to stay calm. "There is to be an uprising against the king?"

"King?" Sulien said and spat his venom at the Constable. "You mean the robber who sits in London and would take all we have? There are good men all the way from Ynys Mon, which you outlanders call Anglesea, down to the marches which border the great River Severn in the south. All will unite to drive you and yours from this land!"

Sir Gerald glanced at the king's justice and they exchanged nods of agreement, then he turned back to the prisoner.

"You came to Pembroke to worm your way into the town and prepare the way for treachery?"

Sulien fought against the men who held him, managing to stand upright. "No. I prepare my own way. Married to Luned and with Ninian dead I would be Pembroke's silversmith. Then I would have control of your children – your children – as their legal father. Through those Frankish brats I would be privy to all you Franks intended."

Sir Gerald did not move, instead he gazed at Sulien, watching every tiny movement of his body and his expression. He waited a long time, until Sulien became filled with unease, this shared with everyone present.

"There is something more," the Constable said at last. "I will have it."

Sulien resisted but Fulke and Leon together used their most persuasive methods until he hung between them.

"What is it?" Sir Gerald demanded of the wreck of a man who finally despaired of all hope.

"The helmet. King Rhys's helmet."

The words were whispered around the great hall, one to another, until it became a shout and all were agog to hear news of the famed helmet worn into battle by their king, Rhys, until he was defeated at the battle of Aberdare. It had become one of the legends of the country and Rhys's people in Pembroke's great hall could all describe it, telling each other the iron shape had been covered in thick silver under a circlet of king's gold from the mines at Dolaucothi.

"Where is it?" the Constable demanded to know, and Sulien's two guards shook him until he stirred enough to answer.

"Ninian has it. Had I married Luned it would have become mine by right."

Chapter Fourteen

As great waves seethe and cream against a cliff, so the voices in the hall rose and shrilled with excitement.

"King Rhys's helmet? Here, in Pembroke?" was the question flung to every ear.

Long before he died, King Rhys's battle armour was well known throughout his kingdom, the most talked about item the helmet which identified him to his men.

When Rhys lost his final battle at Aberdare, it deprived him of his kingdom of Brycheiniog as well as losing him his grown sons. Then, the helmet he had worn with such pride showed his enemies where he rode and Rhys buried it somewhere along the path from the battlefield, towards Aberhonddu, where he died. How the king lost his life as well as his crown, no one knew, neither was the hiding place of his helmet ever revealed.

From that dreadful day during Easter 1093, rumours and wisps of information had flown around the whole of south Wales and beyond. A rich treasure lay buried and every man would be the one to find it. As Franks and their ansels ground into the mire the people of what had been Brycheiniog, the longing for Rhys's helmet to be resurrected grew and grew with every year. In many a heart, the belief was that with the helmet would rise Rhys himself, to free his kingdom from the yoke of the iron men who ruled from their castles and their huge destriers. It had become a symbol of the fight for freedom.

In the hubbub of the great hall, Ninian stood, his unsteadiness a concern until Mistress Mabli waved a steward to him with a staff. Grasping the support and grateful for it, Ninian held himself tall and proud, his eyes never leaving the face of the man who had killed and slandered to desecrate the silversmith's family, his home, his name. The Constable began to move, ready to quieten the shouting, but Sir Walter held his sleeve and Sir Gerald settled back in his chair, noting that the king's justice kept his gaze firmly on the captive held between two determined men.

One by one the voices died away until there was a stillness in Pembroke Castle's great hall.

"You do not answer me!" shouted Sulien to the silversmith.

"Whatever I say, you will call me liar," the old man said quietly, his words heard by everyone in the hushed hall. "Instead, I will ask you, Sulien – if that is indeed who you are – all the time you were free in my home, did you ever find King Rhys's helmet? You wanted to know every part of my workshop to add to your knowledge and your skill, you told me. My home, every corner of it, was yours to search when you were left alone there, trusted by my family. Did you ever find any trace of the helmet?"

Sulien had no answer for the old man who then turned and pointed an accusing finger at Roger fitzHugh.

"And you, sir! When you listened to that man's lies and believed me thief, was there anywhere you did not have your men search for your piddling little goblet? Did you – or they – find the helmet? I grant you, no one would hunt more ruthlessly than you, reeve, yet you did not find the greater treasure that murderer says I possess."

Ninian wiped a shaky hand across his moist forehead and Luned was anxious, whispering to him to rest. He patted her hand to reassure her and then again pointed a finger at Sulien.

"You are not only a killer and evil, you are a stupid, stupid fool. You say you came from Cardiff, yet anyone who has lived in that sprawling town for the shortest time knows that barely a week passes before another newcomer arrives with the tidings he has King Rhys's helmet. Those rogues try first the richest men, then the silversmiths and gold-smiths. Many a time I was offered Rhys's helmet, always from a different spot on the road towards Aberhonddu. Fellow silversmiths who succumbed found the famed item had been 'stripped of its silver, sir, before I acquired it'," Ninian said in a whining tone. "One friend even found he had bought a Frank's dented headgear, the strip of metal to protect the nose still intact."

There was a murmur of laughter in the hall and Ninian waited until it had subsided.

"You came to Pembroke to deceive me, Sulien, but why were you so keen for the helmet? For its worth in silver and in gold?"

The accused man was silent, staring at his feet until Leon jerked him upright and twisted an arm behind his back until he groaned. "You would not understand, you are from the savage north – far away from my people here, in Wales."

It was the king's justice who took an interest when he had been told what the man had said. Whispering in the Con-stable's ear, Sir Walter made plain the question to which he would have an answer.

"Sulien!" Sir Gerald's harshness made many jump. "We will have the truth – and now. Why were you prepared to kill any in your way in order to lay your hands on the helmet? Greed?"

No one had misunderstood the Welsh words Sir Gerald had used but Sulien remained silent, hanging between his

239

two captors while they twisted joints and sinews to persuade an answer. At last it came.

"I wanted to own it, ready for the one who will come and drive you outlanders from our country. When that day was here, I would have been his favoured man and at his right hand because I had such a treasure."

The agony in the man's voice echoed with its truth and Sir Gerald stood, grim-faced.

"Owain ap Cadwgan?" he asked.

Sulien shook his head impatiently, even that small action causing him the greatest pain. "No! Owain is a hot-headed fool and fights on a whim."

"Then who?" the Constable asked softly.

Sulien was encouraged to answer by an extra twist to his wrists. "The rightful king! Rhys's son, Gruffydd!" exploded from him in a violent agony.

Luned was only one of many who were shocked by the revelation. "But Prince Gruffydd is a boy, Father," she murmured to Ninian.

"No, cariad, he is grown. A baby of three years when his father died but that was sixteen years ago. His mother nurtured him well in Ireland and taught him all he needed to know of his inheritance."

She was puzzled. "How do you know these things?"

"I have always found it wise to keep my ears open."

"But if this youngling comes, it will be to fight for the kingdom?"

Ninian nodded, features narrowed by starvation dark and grim. "Aye, cariad. It will mean war."

In the heat of the day Luned was suddenly deathly cold. Her own sons grew fast and would soon be ready for training with sword and bow. They would follow their father and be hacked down by Nest's young brother and his men. Waves of heat began to flood through Luned and the noise of the hall receded and spun around her. Vaguely, she was aware of strong arms, her feet dragging, cool air and there was darkness.

"Come now, Mistress Luned," a voice urged. "It has been a hard day and the heat in that place enough to stun a bull."

Fingers soothed her hair, and Luned realised her head-dress was gone and a wet towel was being wiped gently across her face. She opened her eyes and saw the mediciner, Mabli. Struggling to rise, she was pushed gently back on to her chair.

"Rest, cariad. You have been made to suffer but that evil is over."

"My father?"

"He is out in God's good air with your children."

"I must go," Luned insisted, trying to rise, but Mabli held her still.

"Give them time together. Their own father will join them as soon as he has all in order. By then the crowd will have gone and you can go home in peace."

Luned gazed up at the old woman and saw only the gleam of truth in her smile.

"It is over?"

A nod was sufficient to reassure. "Aye, it is, thanks be to God."

"Sulien is already hanged?"

"Hanged? No. Sir Walter is taking him away. Mind you, the good people of Pembroke would have preferred to see Margan's killer swing from the gatehouse but the king's man wants to question Sulien further. Sir Gerald explained to an angry crowd that Sulien will spend what days he has left longing to be dead and buried in Pembroke, rather than suffer the questioning of Sir Walter's jailers. Suffering? He will do that in plenty, cariad."

Luned lifted her hair free of her neck and allowed a breeze to cool and freshen damp skin. "Why, mistress? What can Sir Walter gain?"

"He is sure the man has more to reveal of his friends. It was something your son said to him of his time with the devil's hound, Owain."

"William?"

"Aye, a good boy and an honest one. Sir Walter was most impressed by him."

"But William knows nothing!"

"Perhaps not – and maybe he sensed or heard something of use to Sir Walter. Either way, Sulien is chained and waiting to go aboard the king's ship after the town is indoors."

"He has left so many to pray for," Luned said softly, "Margan for one."

"Poor soul. It was a dreadful way to die."

"Margan was his mother's rock. How will she manage without him?"

"The Constable has seen to that. All Sulien's treasures which have not been claimed by their owners are to be given to Margan's family, except for a portion for Eynon, in recompense for work lost." Mabli chuckled. "You should have seen the shire reeve. He reached for his goblet and found his wrist seized by Sir Gerald. 'A small way of repaying for your own involvement,' he told young Roger. The shire reeve would have blustered but Sir Walter was watching. It was the justice himself who told the young fool word would go to his mentor, the Bishop of London, that the boy had learned all he could in Pembroke and it would help his ambitions to spend time with his uncle in Palermo."

"Where?"

"I had to ask the Constable. A town on an island called Sicily. Very hot. Very far away from Pembroke – and the court at Westminster – but a very good place for the oil from olives."

"So, all is righted, Mistress Mabli?"

"As it can be, cariad."

"And when Prince Gruffydd comes?"

The old woman was silent, lifting her face to the breeze which came from the river. "He has the fire and ambition of his father, of that I have no doubt, but he will have had the tutoring of his mother. Gruffydd will do nothing to harm Nest and her kin. Remember, it was she, as a child, who stood hostage for his freedom."

"My sons are nearly men. Oh, Mistress Mabli, I fear for my children."

"Then be at rest, cariad. A princess of the blood she may be, but Nest will tend your little ones as the brothers and sisters of her own. They share a father, they share her care."

Luned grasped Mabli's hand, gazing up at the old woman with a yearning for the truth. Whatever was in the mediciner's face comforted her and Luned sighed. "I must go to my father."

"Aye, cariad, he will need a good nurse for a while but to be at home with you and your children, good food in his belly and a clean bed to sleep in, he will soon recover. Nudd will give young Gwri herbs to help."

Luned rose and thanked the mediciner for her assistance.

"Something still troubles you, cariad?"

The younger woman nodded. "I would know why Sulien was so insistent he married me."

"He did say he loved you."

With a shake of the head Luned denied that claim. "No. I have known what love is from a man and there was nothing of that with Sulien, yet he persisted, time and again."

Mabli helped Luned with her headdress. "It is all past now, cariad. Best forgotten." She did not wish to burden Luned further.

The Constable had demanded an answer to that very question and Sulien had been defiant until more sinews stretched and cracked. Sobbing, he confessed that marriage to Luned would keep him near the Constable and his friends, close to their plans and free to find their strengths and weaknesses. Sir Gerald's children would become his and in time would be his hostages. The Constable himself was ready to end Sulien's miserable life in an instant when told Luned's children by him would die as soon as Gruffydd was established. 'All things of the Franks to be wiped from the face of Wales!" was shouted with a final defiance.

"Go home, cariad," Mabli said as soon as she was sure Luned had regained her strength and her composure. "It is ended."

Deris and Gwri had hurried back to the silversmith's home as soon as they could, anxious to get ready for his return. Ninian waited, not wanting the townspeople to see him walk with such difficulty after his time in chains.

"Are you sure the house was secure while you were all here?" he asked his daughter yet again.

"Yes, Father. Two of Gerald's best troopers were to stand guard at the door."

It was a slow cavalcade, Sir Gerald walking with Ninian and ready to lend an arm should the old man stumble. Behind came Luned and her children, Tegan beside them, except when the great hound paced forward to nudge Ninian's free hand, his warm nose the touch of a friend. The inner bailey was soon passed through, the prior a startled face as he came from the chapel by the first gate. The Constable bowed stiffly but Luned and her father had nothing but curt nods for the man who had used Sulien's treachery to aid his own ambitions.

The outer bailey was a longer walk but pleasant in the cool of the evening. Grazing sheep and goats ignored the family but the workers in the castle had gathered to see Ninian pass by and greeted him with shy smiles. At the gatehouse men at arms rattled as they jumped straight and tall in the presence of their Constable. The huge gates were opened wide and Ninian breathed deeply. He was really to be free at last.

Sir Gerald sensed the old man's hesitation and when he saw the size of the crowd outside Ninian's home he offered his arm. So it was that the man dragged into the castle in disgrace walked from it alongside its Constable, the forbidding figures of tall soldiers helmeted and hauberked giving his doorway a mark of respect not lost on the people of Pembroke gathered to see Ninian's return.

Luned saw little. She had spent the last hours where she had once been happy. The castle had not then been a grim and forbidding fortress but the secure home where she lived and loved, her belly swelling with her babes and her arms filled with them. There had been Gerald in her sight and in her bed, filling her days and nights until they spilled over.

It was with a sigh Luned emerged from under the gatehouse and into the hurly burly of Pembroke. Although near couvre feu, there was a mass of men, women, children, in the roadway. As Gerald approached the crowd parted respectfully. The Constable was back in Pembroke and had its welfare in his safe hands.

Rumours had spread from the castle, some of them true. The one travelling with greatest speed was the news of the shire reeve's return to the king's court in London and an unpleasant future. There were smiles along the short walk for Ninian and his family who had suffered so much. Young William was much admired, his height and his proud stature so like his father's. Walter and Meleri were approved and Luned saw hands outstretched to touch her, each one a measure of admiration for her dignity in the face of such dreadful misfortunes – now they were in the past.

After what had seemed like an age, the studded door closed behind them all and the two soldiers stood shoulder to shoulder in front of it, stoically watching the onlookers drift away.

Deris beckoned Luned to the kitchen. "Look, mistress!" Foodstuffs were piled high on the table and a pot simmered on the small fire which glinted cheerfully as evening approached. "The stew is from Mistress Buddyg and here," she held up a cheese in one hand, a crock of honey in the other, "Mistress Manon sent them from the farm by the tannery. Then there is the bread – Cynfan's finest flour. He says to tell you now the shire reeve is off, the first to benefit should be you!"

A great laugh was behind her and Luned closed her eyes, almost unable to believe all was well and Gerald with them. There was no sense of loss now. She knew his life was with Nest, as ordered by the king. The man who had been hers would be faithful to the vows made in front of an altar and she could no longer expect his return to her, but the life they had lived to the full was still theirs and could never be taken from her.

Luned turned and saw the grey in his hair, the lines meshing around his eyes, the weariness in the droop of his lips. When Gerald had been hers he had been a young man, strong in all he did, night as well as day. This was a man who must harbour his strength and use it more sparingly than he was used to do.

The kitchen was full of food and people eating, talking, laughing. Deris and Gwri took themselves off to the out-house and fed well, guzzling the finest produce of the shire.

"Tell me, Ninian, there was a moment back there when I felt you were hiding something from me," Gerald said.

The old man sat at his ease in his own chair. "When was that?"

"You spoke of everywhere being searched – and yet I felt you knew somewhere which had not been touched. Was I right?"

A slow smile was his answer, then, "Do you think

246

I would reveal to the ears of Pembroke where I keep what I have saved for my family all these years?"

"And is your hiding place large enough to hold a helmet? You never did answer Sulien's question."

Ninian looked towards the back door and saw it was closed. "William, Walter, show your father."

Tegan was pushed from his bed in the corner and when it was moved away, Sir Gerald could see the wood of the floor beneath it. With the point of the knife William kept at his belt, he eased up a corner of wood and lifted it clear. Pouch by pouch he emptied the hiding place. Sir Gerald knelt beside his son and felt in the hole, twisting his hand this way and that.

"You have been thrifty, my friend," he told Ninian as he nodded towards the heaped pouches filled with coin, "but there is no way that hiding place could conceal King Rhys's helmet."

"Only if the man had a head the size of a pea," Ninian said with a chuckle.

"A good place of concealment," Sir Gerald admitted as William and Walter stowed away the bags of silver and copper, then replaced Tegan's bed, the dog curling up in it immediately.

"Well, Gerald, I always said I leave Tegan to guard my treasures," Ninian told his guest. "His first duty is to the live ones, but where he sleeps is best left undisturbed."

Ninian sat at peace.

It had taken time and patience, but at last he had persuaded Luned to go to her bed. He had stood at the foot of the stairs to listen to her breathing become deep, even. Meleri had muttered as she did when she was dreaming, while William and Walter thrashed on their pallets, little snorts telling him they were not awake. The fire in the kitchen had a good heart to it, no smoke to reveal its presence to the guards from the castle. The old man smiled.

Tonight might be one of the times he would be excused any wrongdoing.

From the room behind the kitchen, Deris's snores increased, became intrusive, and Ninian stirred. Tegan lifted his great head and when he saw his master move, began to rise.

"Stay, boy. You have earned your rest."

Stiffly at first, Ninian rose and went to his workshop, locking the door so he would not be disturbed. There was little out of place. A carving once used as a mould he stowed away, thinking as he tidied of Deris's ideas for a new line of profit. A good girl, Deris, Ninian decided, and Gwri, surprising everyone as he worked with Nudd to collect the proof of Sulien's murderous intentions. In the morning the boy could begin his proper training in the craft of silver working.

On the bench was a shapeless package wrapped in coarse cloth. Ninian stood in front of it for some time, allowing his thoughts and his feelings full rein. Slowly, he lifted away the cloth and revealed the wreckage and the shards of what had been Tegan's water bowl. The corners of his mouth lifted in a smile as he recalled Deris telling him of Sulien's pain and cursing when he had kicked the bowl out of the way and damaged his own foot. The old man saw most of the painted clay base had gone as had much of the rim, while the body of the bowl was badly cracked, allowing him to pull away most of it.

From the clay store in the corner of the workshop Ninian took what he thought he would need, making sure the bin was covered again with a wet cloth. Clean linen he found in a box as well as sweet oil, and when he had moved a stool so he could sit in comfort he began to repair the bowl. It had taken great presence of mind not to let anyone see how shocked he was when he saw it missing, but Deris had been easily fooled and fetched the remains from under stored wood outside the house.

With increasing care the last of the clay was peeled away, then the oiled cloth around the metal base was cleared. Ninian wiped the foundation of Tegan's drinking vessel with a special mixture of polish and finally upturned the base on a rounded carving. He moved a candle nearer to the object and checked every part of it, at last sitting back and sighing with relief. He had found not even a scratch.

Silver which covered the shaped iron gleamed with the special lustre of candlelight and the gold circlet around it was as bright as it had been on that last day in Aberdare.

"Well, King Rhys. Your helmet is safe. I often wondered if I was right to keep it hidden but now I am sure. Yes, you are right, I kept it known only to me because of greed – though not my own."

Ninian was at ease with the royalty of the helmet, much as with a friend not seen for a long time.

"When Cadwgan laid siege to Pembroke again and again, I knew your armour would add flames to his ambition, so I kept this that was silvered secret and safe. I told myself the worldly cost would feed my daughter and her children if the Franks lost out in their battles against your people. Then Luned had to lose the man she loved so your own daughter could be protected."

The old man covered his face, remembering unending distress.

"Yes, King Rhys, in the end, this helmet became a symbol of my revenge. Is it still, you ask? No." There was a shake of the head and the white hair gleamed fitfully in the light. "The evil one who called himself Sulien wanted it so he could be at your son's elbow when he fought across the whole of south Wales to establish himself king in your place. You may long for that but I do not. My grandsons will perish if your son succeeds and I will do nothing to aid that – do you hear? Too many sons and fathers will die if young Gruffydd wins all his battles. And what of Nest, your daughter? She has been true to you and your blood, a prisoner of the Franks so the baby Gruffydd might grow up in freedom and be your living heir. Are her children to die because their father is a Frank? Is that to be her inheritance from you, her own sire?"

With hands shaking with anger, Ninian soaked clean linen in the sweet oil, wrapping the entire helmet, inside and out until nothing of the metals therein could be seen. That done he took handfuls of clay and covered the helmet until it no longer showed its true shape. The lower edges were formed into a wide foot and the upper edge disguised as a thick rim. Only when he had completed the task he set himself did Ninian stretch aching muscles.

"Once again you and your helmet are silent, King Rhys. Stay that way and let my kin – and yours – live in peace."

Carefully, Ninian carried the repaired water bowl and set it among the warm ashes of the fire, regarding it as though it held the spirit of King Rhys.

"When you have dried out, I will seal and paint you and let Tegan guard you again. Strange a hound can be more faithful than a man. Perhaps you should have learned that in your lifetime, great king."

Exhausted, Ninian blew out the candles in the workshop and kitchen, finding relief in the darkness as he climbed the stairs to blessed oblivion.

Princess Nest

Some facts remain after 900 years.

Easter 1093. King Rhys ap Tewder, Nest's father, loses the battle of Aberdare as well as the southern kingdom of Wales, dying soon after in Aberhonddu. With his grown sons dead or captured, his widow and baby son safe in Ireland, only his daughter, Princess Nest, remains. Little more than a child and speaking only Welsh, she is a hostage at the court of the English king, William II (William Rufus). Terrified she may be, but Nest is very beautiful and a determined survivor, eventually becoming the favoured mistress of the king's brother Henry.

August 1100. King William dies 'accidentally' and Henry claims the throne. He takes a Saxon wife and Nest is married to Gerald, who was born in Windsor, the son of its Constable, Walter, a good friend of William the Conqueror, father of Henry I. The newly-weds return to Pembroke, Nest with gifts of land at nearby Carew and Gerald soon being made Pembroke's Constable.

January 1109. Nest is with Gerald at his new estate in Emlyn, north Pembrokeshire. The castle Gerald built is attacked at night and Nest raped by her cousin, Owain, before being taken captive by him, together with four children, three of them hers. Wales is in uproar at the crimes and, as a most beautiful woman whose abduction has caused war, Nest earns the title, 'Helen of Wales'.

May 1169. To help the king of Ireland free his country from the Danes then ruling from 'within the pale' at Dublin, a fleet sails from Pembroke with an army led by Strongbow de Clare. Of the knights under his command, most are related to Nest by blood or marriage, including two grand-sons with an equal claim to the English throne of the then king, Henry II. After a successful campaign, Nest's descend-ants settle there, giving modern Ireland its first fitzGeralds, fitzStephens and fitzHenrys, through Nest's sons by King Henry and her two husbands.

After a long life it is not known when or where Princess Nest died but in the chancel of Carew Cheriton's church, and honouring remains buried in its wall, is a small effigy of a woman holding a heart in her hands. Nest always loved Carew. Perhaps her heart is still there?

As for King Rhys's helmet, it was famous during his lifetime and he is known to have buried it before he died as he escaped north. Where it was buried remains a mystery, although tales persist that the helmet was later dug up and seen.

Its present whereabouts are a matter of guesswork. Maybe the silver and gold were stripped away to give a poor man a lifetime of ease – or maybe the helmet still lies in the soil of south Wales.